JERRY SNODGRASS

FORGOTTEN HONOR

Outskirts Press, Inc.
Denver, Colorado

This is a work of fiction. The events and characters described herein are imaginary and are not intended to refer to specific places or living persons. The opinions expressed in this manuscript are solely the opinions of the author and do not represent the opinions or thoughts of the publisher.

Forgotten Honor
A story of international suspense, murder, and romance

V2.0R1.0

Outskirts Press, Inc.
http://www.outskirtspress.com

Paperback ISBN: 978-1-4327-1817-6
Hardback ISBN: 978-1-4327-1151-1

PRINTED IN THE UNITED STATES OF AMERICA

DEDICATION

To those brave military men and women who served in Southeast Asia and Korea, and to the memory of those who gave their lives for their country. Let your **HONOR NOT BE FORGOTTEN.**

PROLOGUE

"I hate war as only a soldier
who has lived it can, only as one
who has seen its brutality, its
futility, its stupidity."

—General Dwight D. Eisenhower

September 25, 2004, Atlanta, Georgia

The hot Georgia sun of late September was offering no relief for the mourners gathered at Jeffery Sanders' funeral. *Perfect damn funeral weather, hot as the steamy jungles of Vietnam,* thought the tall man wearing the dark gray suit. If not for the headstones and the funeral, one would strongly believe the green rolling hills of the cemetery were a golf course. Blake Tanner took a deep breath and turned toward the lonely sounds coming from the nearby graveside. He never could get accustomed to the unique sound of Taps and an honor guard firing a twenty-one gun salute at a cemetery. It was especially difficult to say a farewell when the person they were putting in the ground was his best friend. At the solemn sound of the bugler and the honor guard's honorary salute, Blake shook and broke out in a cold sweat; he could no longer hold back the tears that swelled in the corners of his eyes. It just could not be that his good friend Jeff was dead. How could Blake stand at the graveside and reflect back on the memories he had of his friend? He had been so very much alive, so vibrant, so in love with life. He knew that Jeff felt like thousands of other Vietnam and

Korean War veterans. They still had their tattered honor intact, but the American public had long forgotten. Blake knew that Jeff would have stood alongside him, and fought for his family and country when called upon. Honor—was there any honor left? *Damn right,* Blake thought, *there is a lot of honor left in America. Duty, honor, and country are still alive and well. We won the battles, but lost the war.*

Slowly Blake looked over at Jeff's widow, Gloria, and wondered why she was not crying. *She should be saying good-bye to my best friend and her husband with at least a tear*, he thought. His mind then started to drift back in time.

Jeff Sanders and Blake met in Saigon, Vietnam, during the spring of 1969, the first week in April, as he remembered. Blake was a career sergeant first class, and Jeff was a sergeant with a little less than three years in the U.S. Army. The two served together for a year in the jungles of Southeast Asia with the 5th Special Forces. They fought many battles together, and not once did Blake ever hear Jeff complain or show any signs of cowardice. They even laughed when it was the NCOs turn to supervise the disposal of the contents of the latrines with fire. The distinct smell of "diesel fuel burning shitters" would never go away.

After the war, they both returned home alongside thousands of other veterans whose **Honor Was Forgotten** by the American public. The majority of people in the United States looked down their noses at the men and women who had served their country in Southeast Asia. It was a damn shame to come home to a society that had forgotten their military.

On more than one occasion, Jeff had saved Blake's life and that of other members of his combat team. Blake still had memories of that July night in the steamy hot and god-forsaken jungles in 1969, when Jeff pushed him out of the line of fire from a Viet Cong sniper's deadly barrage of AK-47 fire. If it had not been for Jeff's quick thinking and bravery, old Sergeant Tanner would have come home in a body bag. Tanner always felt it didn't matter who was right or wrong in the war efforts. If he could live through the night, the war might end tomorrow. Now thirty-five years later, Jeff was gone to meet his maker at fifty-four years of age. Jeff would often say, "When we die, we will all be just a speck of dust." *Oh, hell, I am sixty years old*, Blake thought, thinking back over his life.

The bugler sounded his last note of Taps, and there was a dead silence that surrounded the mourners, like the world had just stopped. Blake was having deep thoughts about Jeff when he felt a slight touch on his arm. He turned and looked into the stone face of Command Sergeant Major Jon Rider.

"How the hell are you holding up, you old war horse?" the sergeant major said quietly.

There was a brief pause. Each of them looked into the other's eyes; then they shook hands, and the two big rugged men hugged each other. "Damn, Jon, you ain't dead yet?"

The sergeant major was dressed in his blue Army service uniform with ribbons and badges plastered all over both sides of the front of his uniform, and ten stripes on each sleeve indicating he had at least thirty years of military service. He placed a large, gentle hand on Blake's shoulder and spoke in a low, gruff voice. "There is no son of a bitch tough enough to kill me. What's your take on Jeff? You believe he put that pistol to his head?"

Gazing out toward the rolling green hills, his body stiffening, Blake swallowed hard. "I don't know," he responded. "He had no known reason to end his life, none whatsoever, especially in a Hilton Hotel. Jeff never did like the name of Hilton. He always said it reminded him of our POWs who were being held as prisoners at the Hanoi Hilton."

Side by side, Blake and Sergeant Major Rider walked over to where Gloria was sitting with her hands folded in her lap holding a white handkerchief. Gloria looked up at the two close friends of Jeff with a blank look on her pretty face. She did not have tear one, but her eyes were moist and narrow, and her gaze was cold as she turned her head back toward the graveside.

The stillness of the afternoon heat along with the military funeral must have taken its toll on Gloria. She sighed, turned her head back toward the two men, and spoke softly in a low and trembling voice. "Thank you for paying your respects to Jeff. He loved the both of you like brothers, and he talked many times about your experiences in Vietnam. He was so very proud of you two."

Why in the hell Jeff Sanders would put a pistol to his head and blow his brains out? Blake thought it was unbelievable. He was happily married and had a married daughter and two grandchildren. His wife, Gloria, had a successful international antique business, and Jeff was the managing director for an international engineering firm. They had a beautiful home in Atlanta, a large beach house at Savannah, a large yacht and a fishing boat, new automobiles, and no indication of any marital or financial problems.

Jeff attended Georgia Tech after his Army enlistment was finished. He used his GI bill and elected construction engineering, and he ended up with a damn good job. After the Army, they both met again when Blake worked with the U.S. Army at Fort Benning, Georgia. Blake went to night school and after ten years received a bachelor's degree in criminology. After receiving his degree, he graciously accepted the appointment to chief warrant officer. After all the years in the enlisted ranks, he was proud of himself for his successful career advancement.

The families went on vacations together, the men hunted, fished, and told old war stories, and the wives shopped, cooked, and enjoyed each other's company. They were great friends, but they did not see much of each other after Blake retired from active duty with the Army. He and Annie moved to Blake's home state of Colorado, and they rented an apartment in Denver until they could buy or have a house constructed. The Tanners and Sanders both sent the usual Christmas and birthday cards to each other's family, and shared an occasional telephone call just to stay in touch. Both Blake and Jeff had changed since their early days of raising hell and fighting wars. Just trying to put it all behind them was their priority for a good quality of life. Live and forget—there is not a damn thing they could do about it.

Blake tried to focus his thoughts on the soothing words the minister was saying, while the Army Honor Guard was folding the American flag that was draped over Jeff's casket. *You get the American flag to cover up your casket, a military honor guard fires a twenty-one gun salute, and no one really knows the horror a war fighter goes through fighting a war in a faraway land that is unpopular with the American public,* Blake thought. Jeff earned the Purple Heart with one cluster for wounds received on two occasions; he received the Bronze Star and Army Commendation Medal, both of which were for valor and gallantry under fire, and he was awarded the Air Medal with two clusters for air assault missions into Vietnam, Cambodia, and Laos. You had to be there to remember the distinct sound of an UH-1 Huey helicopter. The nauseating smell of the jet fuel vapors filling your nostrils during flight, the roar of the M60 machine guns manned by the door gunners being fired—the unique sounds and smell would never go away. He would never forget the young seventeen-year-old door gunner who gave his life to save the crew and the five-man recon team Blake led during a crash landing on a hot landing zone. The life expectancy of a Huey door gunner was around four months. The young gunner was the real hero to Blake and Jeff. Who really gives a shit besides the men who fought alongside you and shared the unspeakable horrors of war? He still could not believe Jeff was gone. It would be Blake's honor to find out what really happened—if it was the last thing he ever did.

Blake and Sergeant Major Rider bid farewell to each other and vowed to keep in touch. Jon was on his way to Iraq and fight in another war unpopular with the American public.

It seemed like a long flight back to Denver, but the scotch was good, and the first-class seat was comfortable after a long day of watching people bury your best friend. Blake could not get it out of his mind the way Jeff had died, and he felt Gloria was putting on an act. She was a beautiful woman, and looked great for her fifty-two years of age. Her great body, blond hair, and blue eyes had helped her to be very successful with her business ventures. Blake always heard, "Blonde hair is a sign of bad temper, and blue eyes are a sign of evil." *Oh, hell, maybe that was red hair and green eyes,* he thought, and a smile came across his mouth.

What a shitty way to feel about a longtime friend. When most women cry after the recent death of their husband, they usually have red cheeks, and their nose runs. *Not Gloria. Damn, I must be playing James Bond in my mind*, Blake thought. Guess the years of

Army training were taking over his military mind. After forty years in the Army's Criminal Investigation Command as a Special Agent, working on assignments all over the world, everyone seemed suspicious to the old seasoned investigator. He was no Sherlock Holmes, but he was damn good at what he did.

Blake doubted that his suspicious nature would ever change. No wonder Annie got tired of him after he retired from the Army. She knew he still longed for the adventure and the new challenges of visiting exotic locations, and the dangers and excitement that he faced with each assignment.

Gloria and Jeff's daughter, her husband, and two little girls were really taking the sudden death hard.

It had been nearly four years since Annie left Denver and returned to her hometown in North Carolina to visit her close family. Shortly after she arrived, she and her parents were tragically killed in an automobile accident during a heavy thunderstorm. The thought of his wife being gone and the girls living without their mother still hurt him deeply. The two daughters, Karla and Kristy, were very happy; both of them and their husbands lived and worked in Denver. No grandkids yet, but they were working on it, since they all had great jobs and wanted to put away money before having children. Good move on their part. He was not that smart. Annie could not say "no" to a six-foot two-inch tall brown-haired man from Colorado. Her description was not the same as his, Blake remembered. He was still the same height, but his hair was silver, and it matched his mustache and goatee very well; that thirty-two-inch waist had increased a few inches…well, more than a few inches.

Annie had loved him, but she believed he was a bit rough around the edges and could have used a little more tact and diplomacy when dealing with people. She was right, of course, but he was too hardheaded to change. Fighting back tears, he knew that he had lost a damn good woman when she was suddenly taken away from the girls and him. Hell, back in his young days he never thought that he would live to be twenty-five years old, so why save money? He felt that he should have been the one killed, not his sweet Annie. She had so much to live for and so many years of life ahead of her.

If not for his parents actively encouraging him to buy the ranch after Annie was killed, he would be living in an old soldier's home, or in some far-off country, doing mercenary work and getting his ass shot off. Blake Tanner was thankful to have such loving parents, and he was grateful for the encouragement they gave him when he was growing up, and during his military and civil service careers.

Gazing out of the window of the Boeing 757, he could just picture Jeff and him at their deer camp on the Eastern Colorado flatlands. They never shot many deer, but damn, they had a lot of fun trying. Jeff would rather fish than hunt. He just loved to fish, as it was a stimulating challenge to him. Now Jeff was dead, and he had lost a good friend.

Come on, Tanner, put your Army Chief Warrant Officer 5 and GS-14 Criminal Investigator hats on, get your ass on the road, and stop feeling sorry for yourself, he ordered. Jeff would have told him, "Come on, Tanner, get your shit together." Or, as the Vietnamese hookers would say, "Get together your shit."

CHAPTER 1

Castle Rock, Colorado

Blake poured himself a cup of hot black coffee; he then walked to the large and sun-filled family room to check out the news on CNN. The big screen television was in the corner next to the fireplace, and his favorite large brown leather recliner was centered in front of the television and the fireplace. He stood in the middle of the room staring at the pictures on the fireplace mantel. A family portrait of Annie, Blake, and the girls when they were still in college graced the wall above the fireplace. Blake looked at the picture every day and thought about the good times and love the close family had shared together. With the loss of Annie's presence, the room was empty and cold, but the air was filled with her spirit. He liked the big screen TV for sporting events, especially football. He had played a defensive end at Denver East High School, and he had played a few years of military ball. He was a diehard Denver Broncos fan, and he was on the long waiting list for season tickets. *The Denver Broncos and Coors beer; it doesn't get any better than that,* he thought.

As he opened up the first page of the morning newspaper, he heard the pretty television newscaster mention that suicide had taken the life of a wealthy international engineer and former decorated Vietnam veteran. Blake grabbed the TV remote and increased the volume just in time to hear the name, Jeffery Sanders. Damn, old Jeff made the CNN headlines; he would get a big charge out of that. He had a great sense of humor, and he would laugh at anything, Blake remembered. *Brings up the big question again: why would Jeff take his own life?* Blake was devastated. How could he go on not knowing what had happened to his friend? He had every known reason in the world to live. Blake thought about looking into Jeff and Gloria's private life to see what he could dig up. Gloria sure did act peculiar for a woman who had just lost her loving husband of twenty-five years.

After lunch, Blake finished his chores and fed the four riding horses he kept for his daughters and their husbands, as they were all devoted riders. His daughters and their husbands took turns, or both couples came out together to take care of the mini-ranch when Blake was away. Pikes Peak was in plain sight from the large covered front porch, and the scenery was like no other he had ever seen in his world travels. Aspen trees were everywhere you looked, and the air was so crisp and clear you could almost hear it. Blake had spent many evenings sitting on the front porch thinking about his wife and the good times that they had shared together. His wife Annie never saw the mini-ranch as they had lived all over the world, and she just went with the flow. Their daughters and husbands liked the mini-ranch and the large log house that he had built to his specifications. The spacious house was just not the same without his precious Annie around. It was a beautiful log home and Annie would have loved it, but it was empty without her spirit that she always brought to their home wherever it was.

As Blake poured himself another cup of coffee, he cradled the mug in both hands and leaned his head over the rising steam. He was startled momentarily by the ringing of the telephone. He picked up the phone hanging on the kitchen wall. On the other end of the line came a pleasant voice. "Is this Mr. Blake Tanner?"

"Yes, it is, and who wants to know?"

"I hope that I did not disturb you? I can call back later if you like," the man said very politely.

"No, it's okay."

"My name is Donald Higgins. I am the Vice President of Operations for the Mutual of New York Life Insurance Company in

New York City. We are looking into the death of Mr. Jeffery Sanders. We understand that you and he were very good friends?"

"Yes, we were," Blake answered sarcastically, as he wondered why a high-ranking official of Jeff's insurance company was calling him.

"Mr. Tanner," the man from New York continued. "I don't know if you are aware or not, but Mr. Sanders had a five-million-dollar life insurance policy with our company, and the sole beneficiary is his wife, Gloria Sanders. Before we pay out any amount of money to the beneficiary, and due to Mr. Sanders' apparent suicide, we must conduct a thorough investigation. Are you with me so far, Mr. Tanner?"

"Yes, but what does this all have to do with me?"

The company vice president said very clearly, "We know that you and Mr. Sanders go back a long way, all the way back to Vietnam and the Special Forces. You were very close friends, and both of your families were the best of friends. We also know that you are a retired military and civilian criminal investigator with years of international experience. Bottom line, Mr. Tanner, we hope to retain you to conduct the primary investigation into the death of Mr. Sanders."

There was a slight silence from both men, and then Blake, changing his tone of voice, answered very tenderly, "I do have some deep concerns over the allegation and official death report that Jeff committed suicide. I just can't see him taking his own life."

"We have many similar feelings as you do. As the policy and payout are so high, we will make it well worth your time to work with us. We are prepared to pay you one thousand dollars a day, starting from the day you accept our offer until you complete your investigation. Your travel will all be first class, you can stay in the best hotels available, and we will provide you with any other expenses you may encounter. How does that sound to you, Mr. Tanner?"

Blake liked the sound of the money, and the first-class travel he really liked after all the years in the military and government, when he regularly traveled in the rear of the airplane in small, uncomfortable seats, and shitty service. "What's the chance of you flying me to your New York office so we can talk face to face?"

"Consider it done. If you will please remain on the line, my management secretary, Miss Stewart, will talk with you and arrange for your travel to New York. I anxiously look forward to meeting you, and we thank you for considering our offer for employment."

Blake provided the sexy-sounding woman with his travel request. "I always like to depart on a Tuesday and return to my destination on Thursday," he casually told Miss Stewart.

"You sound like a man who has been around the world, Mr. Tanner."

"Yes, and I like professionalism in people, and I can tell that you are a true professional," Blake said, flirting with the secretary.

"I look forward to putting a face with your voice. We will see you at the airport on Tuesday. And, Mr. Tanner, bring your raincoat."

"Thanks," he said, and he hung up the phone. *I believe she will be the one who will meet me at JFK. I hope she likes older sexy men like me,* he thought, and then he grinned.

Blake walked out on the front porch, clutching his freshly filled coffee mug. Looking south, he could see the sun bouncing off the snow-crusted Pikes Peak. Soon the sun's warmth would fill the sunny winter morning, starting a new day. He walked out into the morning sun and looked up at the clear blue sky. His thoughts turned to Annie and Jeff. The hurt would never go away, he thought as he watched two hummingbirds gathering nectar from the feeder hanging on the porch.

CHAPTER 2

It was a beautiful morning for flying at the Denver International Airport. There was a soft, cool breeze coming in from the Rockies, and light clouds had started to fill the blue sky. The sun peaked brightly, ready to start a new day. As Blake boarded the United Airlines flight that would take him to New York's JFK airport, he was greeted by an attractive flight attendant. "Good morning, Mr. Tanner," the flight attendant said as she looked at his boarding pass. "You are seated in 2A this morning. Is that seat your choice?"

"Yes, it is, thank you," and he smiled at the tall dark-haired flight attendant.

Blake traveled light as he had learned from experience that if you don't have what you need when you arrive at your destination, then buy it. That was his motto, and it always seemed to work. He carried one brown leather garment bag and a black leather expandable briefcase that held just what he needed during his trips.

"Would you like a drink, Mr. Tanner?" the flight attendant asked.

"How about a Bloody Mary?" he replied, looking into the dark eyes of the beautiful woman standing in front of him.

Blake always made every attempt to be booked in a window seat while flying on any airline in the States or on a foreign flag airline. The main objectives of his criminal investigation training included the likelihood of a hijacking and terrorist plots to take over the command and blow up aircraft while in flight. Sitting in the window seat permitted him to have his left arm free and hidden from a terrorist walking through the aisle. He often carried a small automatic pistol strapped to his left ankle during his CID missions.

The man sitting next to Blake in seat 2B only nodded and smiled. A frequent flyer, Blake thought, and he knew the rules. Keep your damn mouth shut unless I speak to you. Those are the golden rules of Blake Tanner. *You really are an asshole, Tanner*, Blake thought, and smiled to himself at his usual smart-ass attitude.

The take-off roar of the 757 was pleasant music to Blake's ears. When he was flying, he was making money, or he was going to Las Vegas to lose money, where he usually lost his butt.

The flight attendant gave Blake a little more first-class treatment than the other passengers. She personally made sure his essential needs were attended to. "Are you going to New York for business, Mr. Tanner?"

"Yes. Are you based out of Denver or New York?" he asked her coolly.

"I am based out of New York, born and raised a real New Yorker," and then she smiled at Blake. "Will you be staying long?"

"No, just two nights," and he anxiously waited to see where she would go with the conversation.

"My name is Denise Romo, and I would dearly love to show you my city if you could find the time."

"Maybe I can find some free time." He loved the game he was playing with the young beautiful woman. "I'm staying at the Ritz-Carlton, downtown New York."

"I don't live far from there, as we say in New York." She handed Blake a personal card with her name, address, and telephone number on it. "Call me if you like."

As Blake departed, he passed by Denise at the exit door of the aircraft. "Thank you, Mr. Tanner, and I sincerely hope to hear from you soon." She smiled at Blake. He saw her eyes sparkle, and her left eye gave him a little wink.

"You're welcome, and, yes, I hope to see you soon," and he entered the jet walk.

Blake was dressed in a dark blue single-breasted suit and trousers, without cuffs. He preferred to wear his cowboy boots with all his suits and sport jackets, and he knew that you do not wear boots when the trousers have cuffs. Annie always told him, "You are Mr. Cowboy GQ." *Tanner, you are a conceited bastard,* he thought, *but you are okay for a Colorado boy.*

When Blake walked out of the baggage claim area, he looked around for someone holding a welcome sign with his name on it. He spotted a drop-dead gorgeous redhead near the baggage claim exit who held a welcome sign with his name printed in bright green letters. As he walked over to where the woman was standing, he saw that she had beautiful green eyes that seemed to flash like emeralds.

The woman smiled and spoke first. "Hello, Mr. Tanner, welcome to New York. Do you have all of your bags?" She then glanced at his brown garment bag and a worn briefcase and knew the answer.

"I travel light," Blake, replied. He did manage to take a quick glance at her legs as they walked toward the exit. Nice, very nice, he thought to himself.

"My name is Mary Stewart. I am the personal secretary and management assistant to Mr. Higgins, if you haven't already guessed. Our company limo is just out in front."

The long ride to the insurance company headquarters was typical New York, thousands of cars and people all over the sidewalks and crosswalks, moving in all directions. Blake was able to get a little pertinent information from Miss Mary Stewart during the ride from the airport. He was attracted to her, although she was much younger than he was, which was normal for his taste in women.

"Did anyone ever tell you that you look like the movie star Ann-Margaret?"

"I hear it all the time, and it embarrasses me, as she is so beautiful."

"Don't let 'em fool you, kid. You're beautiful, just as beautiful as Ann-Margaret."

She blushed, but he knew that he was on his way to knowing her better. *Damn, Tanner, you are one smooth talker, for an old guy,* he thought.

Blake was impressed with the insurance company building and the unique architecture. The ceilings were high with tinted windows that were in different shapes, permitting the sunlight to stream in. There is lots of money in this business; they can build what they want. He made a mental outline of the building's interior structure, which he normally did. Just an old habit that was hard to break.

Mary took Blake directly to the executive office of Donald A. Higgins. Before they entered the office, Mary stopped and turned toward Blake. "His office is one to kill for, and an office that most people only dream about working in."

"Mr. Blake Tanner, please meet Mr. Donald Higgins," Mary said with the perfect introduction.

"It is a pleasure to meet you, Mr. Tanner."

Blake sized him up. He looked to be about five feet ten inches tall, around one hundred seventy-five pounds. Maybe a Yale graduate, or possibly a military school.

"Please have a seat. Are you a frequent visitor to New York, Mr. Tanner?"

"No, I'm pretty much of a country and mountain man. Large cities make me nervous."

"Have you thought over the proposition I told you about during our telephone conversation?" Higgins asked, as he put on gold-rimmed reading glasses.

"Yes, I have given a lot of thought to your formal request. I do have a few requests of my own." Blake shifted in his chair to get a better look into the eyes of the man sitting at the large desk in front of him. "First of all I work alone, and if I require assistance, I will select my own people. Second, I do not like to be a puppet and call you every day with a status report that says nothing. I hate that political kind of bullshit. I want a free hand, do as I think is best, and I want to be provided with all the information that you have concerning the case."

Higgins looked down at the notes he was taking while listening to Blake talk. "I don't have a problem with any of your requests. They all are reasonable, and we will honor them. Miss Stewart will provide you with bank accounts, credit cards, and a satellite phone that we have arranged for your needs. You will find an official copy of the death certificate for Mr. Sanders, signed by the medical examiner, in one of the envelopes. The toxicology report will not be available for five to six weeks. Mary will be a main point of contact for you, as I am in so many meetings that I might not be able to speak with you when the need arises. Mary is one of our most trusted and valued employees, and she is just more than a pretty face in the office, she is trusted. I am open for any pertinent questions you might have at any time of the day or night. Mary has arranged for your transportation to the hotel, and she also has a dinner planned for you this evening." Donald then handed Blake a large envelope, stood up from his plush leather chair, and put out his hand. "Welcome aboard, Mr. Tanner."

Standing to face Higgins and looking directly into his eyes, Blake said, "Thanks, I will give you my best professional investigation possible." He shook Donald's hand, turned away, and walked out of the office.

Mary Stewart looked up from her computer screen when Blake stopped in front of her desk. "Is everything all right?" she asked.

"Yes, it's a go, and I am ready for whatever information you have for me."

Mary handed Blake a large package that was sitting on the corner of her desk. "You should have everything that you require. Just sign the credit cards on the back, and familiarize yourself with the satellite phone, which I am sure that you have used before. If you don't mind, I have arranged for us to have dinner together this evening to go over a few more details that Mr. Higgins wants me to personally provide you in private."

Blake began to think about how it would be with an evening with the gorgeous redhead. "That is great. What time and what is the dress code?"

"Around eight o'clock in your hotel lobby, and the dress code is casual." She then smiled at Blake. "The driver of the limo will take you to your hotel. See you this evening," Mary said, waiting for him to leave or say something.

The limo driver was quiet, which Blake liked. Most drivers liked to talk all the time, just chatter and say nothing. He did, however, want to know who was driving him, and his personal background. During many of his past missions, a company limo driver or a taxi driver he had befriended had been beneficial in saving his ass.

Blake glanced out the window of the limo as the driver turned into the hotel guest off-loading zone. His thoughts rushed back to a similar scenario in Amsterdam, in the early 1980s. There is nothing like a five-star hotel to find excitement, and sometimes a person finds danger. It was about this time of year, 1983, around the time the U.S. Army Rangers and 82nd Airborne deployed to Grenada. Blake was assigned a mission to Amsterdam from his office in Germany to investigate the involvement of U.S. Army American Embassy transportation specialists with local drug dealers. The Dutch taxi driver he had contracted to use in his stakeouts was the son of a retired taxi driver. His father was a young boy during World War Two, and he told his son stories about how kind the American soldiers were and how they fed him and his family. He told his son to always respect the American tourists and executives, and do what he could to help them, as they had helped the Dutch in their desperate need years ago. Blake still carried the scar from the cold October evening when Dutch drug dealers ambushed him as he walked out of his luxury hotel. The driver drove his small black taxi through the gunfire coming from the drug dealers and Blake and stopped between Blake and the intense gunfire coming from across the street. Blake jumped in the backseat of the taxi, and the driver sped away to the nearest police station. Blake was then transported to a hospital where he was treated for his wounds. Blake would never forget the brave taxi driver who risked his own life to save his.

"Thanks for the lift," Blake said to the limo driver as he opened the car door for him.

"You are welcome, sir. My name is Teddy. Please let me know if I can be of further assistance to you."

"Sure will, and thanks again, Teddy."

CHAPTER 3

The October air was chilly, but the night was beautiful and full of stars from what he could see between the New York skyscrapers. Blake dressed early, went down to the bar, had a couple of scotch on the rocks, and then walked out in front of the hotel into the cool evening. While he was waiting for Mary, he looked around at the New York skyline. He marveled at the lights of one of the most famous cities in the world. *I wonder what in the hell all these different people do in the evenings? Probably the same as us other folks—watch TV and wish they were somewhere else.*

Blake's thoughts were interrupted as a yellow cab came to an abrupt halt in front of the hotel. One of the hotel attendants opened the rear door of the taxi, and out stepped Mary Stewart. *My goodness*, Blake thought as she walked toward him. She was dressed in tight-fitting blue jeans, a white turtleneck sweater, a waist-length black leather jacket, and black boots, and her jeans were tucked inside them. Her red hair was hanging straight down the middle of her back. What a damn knockout she was. He just about said his thoughts aloud, but caught himself.

"Good evening, Mr. Tanner," Mary said softly as she walked up to Blake and gently put her hand out to him.

Taking her hand in his, he spoke softly to her. "Good evening to you, Miss Stewart, and it's Blake." He was mesmerized by the sparkle of her green eyes, holding her hand and gazing at her for what seemed like minutes.

"It's Mary, please call me Mary," she promptly replied with a sexy smile that displayed beautiful teeth and gorgeous lips. "I sincerely hope you like Italian food."

"I like food, and, yes, I like Italian. As for cholesterol, at my age, who cares? Do we take another taxi, or walk?"

Mary laughed at his remarks. "Oh, the restaurant is only a short walk from here, if you don't mind getting a little physical exercise and smell gasoline-fumed air," she said with a little laugh.

The restaurant was a small out-of-the-way family-owned establishment. "I like it," Blake said. "This is my type of place to dine."

Evidently, Mary knew the owners of the restaurant as they all called her by name and kissed her on both cheeks when they greeted her.

The meal was delicious, as they ate spaghetti vongole with red clam sauce for their main course. Steam rising off the melted parmesan cheese on the sauce made Blake's mouth water. Savoring the flavor of the first bite and swallowing rapidly, he said, "Damn, this is good," as he looked at Mary. The casual conversation was relaxing as Blake and Mary talked freely about any topic that popped into their minds. "Are you married?" Blake asked, as he poured them both another glass of red house wine from the pitcher lined with markings of early Rome.

"No, I'm divorced and have been for nearly twenty years," Mary answered without looking at Blake. "I got married as a naive teenager, and my darling husband decided he wanted to be a movie star. So he left me and a baby girl and headed out to Hollywood."

"Did he ever make it in the movies?"

"Maybe porn, but I have never heard from him, and I hope that I never do," she said, and this time she looked into Blake's eyes. "My daughter, Holly, is a sophomore at Yale, and she is a very nice young lady, if I do say so myself. She has a good head on her shoulders, and she knows right from wrong. I am really proud of her."

Blake looked back into her green eyes, and he thought that he saw sadness and hurt hidden deep inside. "Sounds to me like you have done an excellent job raising your daughter and holding down a good job at the same time. Being a single parent is not a simple task. Life is tough."

"Thanks, we have done well. New York Mutual has been good to me. They paid for my college, and I worked my way up to where I am today. I'm happy and content." Again she looked into Blake's eyes. "I just don't have you figured out, Mr. Tanner, and I'm sure I never will."

Blake told her a little about his life, but he certainly did not tell her more than he thought she should know. He told her that he was a widower, and that he had not remarried, and that seemed to intrigue her. Tanner knew that he should follow her lead, answer her questions, but not talk about himself.

Mary took a sip of wine. "Now, how about a little business talk?" She handed him a white envelope, and then she laid a smaller envelope down in front of him. "The large envelope has a telephone number that you can call from anyplace in the world, and you will reach a special travel agent. The agency will take care of any type of arrangements that you desire, as you can tell when you review the informative brochures. The other envelope contains my personal home and cellular telephone numbers, which you can call at any time you need assistance. You have the phone contacts for the satellite phone to talk with us from anywhere you go. Can I answer any pertinent questions you may have?"

"No. Outstanding. I will memorize the numbers and destroy the hard copies. I look forward to working with you, and hopefully I can see you often."

"You will be seeing me again, you can count on that." She gave Blake a beautiful smile that would knock any man to his knees.

"I'm off to Atlanta tomorrow. I am departing a day early since my work in New York appears to be finished for the time being."

Mary would not take no for an answer as she paid the bill for dinner. "It is company expenses," she said and smiled again at Blake.

Another look at Mary settled it—she was beautiful, just damn beautiful, he thought. *Now, Tanner, get your hand out of your front pockets, get to work, and forget about trying to get this young woman in bed.*

"Do you want me to flag down a taxi for you?"

"No, I will walk with you back to your hotel and catch one. The price is less when a hotel attendant flags down a taxi in New York."

"I will never get used to a big city," Blake told Mary as he guided her across an intersection. "I have lived and worked in big cities all my life, and I have never felt comfortable. It is small towns for me, no big lights or buildings, just a few people, and no excessive noise."

Mary directed her eyes toward Blake. "I love the big city, but that is all I know by growing up here. The small town atmosphere does sound extremely inviting to me."

The two bid each other good-bye over the loud roaring sound of the New York traffic.

A couple of scotches and he was ready for a good night's rest. The quietness usually lulled him to sleep, but not tonight. He tossed and twisted on the bed. He glanced at the clock sitting on the nightstand: one damn o'clock. Blake had too many demons rolling around in his mind, like the death of his friend Jeff, the unanswered questions surrounding his death, and the deep thoughts he had about the investigation.

The sunlight coming through the window felt warm on Blake's face. In his Denver Broncos sleeping shorts and T-shirt, he slipped out of bed and headed for the shower for his morning therapy. After shaving and catching a quick bite of breakfast, he dressed and headed to the airport.

Damn if I would survive in this big ass city, he thought as the taxi came to a complete stop, hung up in the morning traffic.

On the mid-morning flight to Atlanta, on October 20, he was already dreading the trip, as Atlanta would not be the same without Jeff being at the airport to meet him when he arrived. He was always waiting for Blake with a big smile and a friendly hug when he came out of the baggage area. He always asked, "Hey, bud, you want a drink?"

His first business call after checking into the hotel would be to talk with Gloria at her office. He did not intend to let her know that he was investigating Jeff's death, or that he had suspicions about how Jeff died. Just a social call, and hopefully he would detect some crucial information that he could use in his investigation.

The second call would be to the international engineering firm where Jeff was in the management chain. He had arranged the meeting under the assumption that he was putting together a memorial for his longtime friend, and he needed comments from his business partners and colleagues. He hoped that he could obtain information about any wrong or bad feelings that might have been directed toward Jeff.

Gloria met Blake at the door of her office. "Blake, I am so happy to see you." She kissed him on the cheek and gave him a warm hug. "Come in and let's talk. You look great as always."

Blake was thinking as Gloria was talking how damn good she looked. What a knockout she was, especially in her short skirt and a tight-fitting blouse. "You look very good yourself. Are you getting along all right? Or as well as can be expected, I should say."

"I'm coping. Just keep deep in my work and the sadness goes away temporarily. The evenings are the hardest without Jeff at home with me. So, you're putting together a memorial for Jeff and his military service with the Green Berets?"

"It's the least I can do for a damn good soldier who served his country with honor, and was a good American citizen. What do you think about the idea?"

"I think it is a splendid idea. How can I help?"

"Can I have Jeff's shadow box that has all of his military awards, parachute wings, and combat infantry badge that he had mounted for display? I would also like to ask you some personal questions about his life with you after the war. With the personal information, I can put together a tribute in writing that will be placed at his memorial, which by the way will be here in Atlanta at the cemetery where Jeff is buried."

"Good. Will you come over to the house for dinner this evening? We can be alone, you can ask me what you want, and we can gather up his shadow box and whatever other information you want."

"Wonderful, I'll bring the wine."

"Say seven-thirty and chardonnay will do." Gloria rolled the tip of her tongue over her ruby red lips, and her blue eyes seemed to flash, sending out sparks that caused a stir in Blake.

"I'll be on time." He looked at her as she got up from her desk.

While unknown emotions drifted through Blake's mind, he recalled the last time he and Jeff were together. Must have been two years ago last summer, and it was right here in Atlanta. They had played thirty-six holes of golf, and had drunk about the same amount of beers. Gloria had to drive out and pick them up at the country club, as neither one of them could pass a sobriety test. She was pissed; he remembered that poor Ole Jeff just took the tongue-lashing and smiled. Of course, that made Gloria just that much madder. Jeff was a piece of work, that was for sure.

Blake was in deep thought as the taxi stopped in the circle driveway at the Sanders' residence at seven-thirty sharp. *Damn, what a beautiful home,* he thought. *Bet it is worth a lot of money, nearly a million bucks probably.* There were smells of flowers blooming, and Blake detected the distinct aroma of baked cornbread dressing coming from the kitchen. Walking up the stone sidewalk toward the large front double-door entrance, he could not help but think about Jeff not welcoming him at the front door. Gloria answered the door, and she looked stunning, dressed in tight-fitting blue jeans and a light blue blouse that was open at the top, revealing cleavage and well-proportioned breasts.

Hugging Blake and kissing him on his cheek, she grabbed his right hand and guided him into the spacious entryway. "Welcome, come on in. Let us go to the kitchen, and we can talk as I finish dinner. I remember that you like baked pork chops with cornbread dressing and mashed potatoes."

"Yep, I sure do." Remembering that Gloria had asked him to bring the wine, he said, "I just happened to pick up a bottle of chardonnay that will go great with the pork chops. The house looks the same but is different without Jeff's smile and laughter."

"I heard that," Gloria answered. "I have an unopened bottle of Black Label Scotch if you would like a hard drink before dinner." She placed a glass filled with ice in front of Blake. "Jeff liked Black Label," she said with tears coming into her eyes.

"Never turn down a drink of Black Label," he answered in a soothing voice. "Yep, we both drank our share when we were together."

Blake sat on the left side of Gloria, who sat at the head of the large dining room table. From where he was sitting, he could look through the open curtains of the large double doors that led to the patio, and see the surrounding manicured gardens.

Trying to keep ahead of the conversation and ask the right questions, Blake placed his dinner napkin in his lap and looked directly at Gloria. "Are you comfortable talking about Jeff?"

"Yes, as we are old friends. I do not talk with strangers about Jeff's death. It is just none of their damn business. Ask away." Gloria looked at Blake and sat silently, letting out a deep breath.

Blake studied her expression; he saw deep sorrow in her eyes, and felt the hurt in her tone of voice. He did not know why he thought she knew more about Jeff's death than she was letting on, but he did. However, the real content of his thoughts would remain unclear. "Do you have any idea or know of any reasons why Jeff would take his own life?"

She sat quietly just looking at her dinner plate for what seemed like minutes. "No, I really don't know why he would take his own life, or even if he did."

Damn, that certainly got Blake's complete attention. This was the first time she had mentioned any concerns she had about Jeff not committing suicide. "Do you have any reasons to believe that Jeff's death was not a suicide?"

Gloria hesitated again. "I just do not understand why he would even think about taking his own life. We were happy, and our marriage was sound as far as I know. Our demanding work did keep us apart, but we both understood that separation is a big part of what we do."

He watched her as she was talking. Why did she hesitate before talking about their marriage? He concluded it was just the way that she answered his question.

Blake was silent for a moment while his mind changed subjects. "Would you mind if I paid a formal visit to Jeff's office, and talked with a few of his business associates about the planned memorial?"

"I think you have a splendid idea, and, no, I have no problems with you making contact with Jeff's company. He was a very large shareholder, and he was paid a humongous salary as the managing director of the company. As far as I know his replacement has not been named, and his office is just like it was the last day he was at work."

Blake again changed the subject as not to arouse her suspicion about his personal questions. They reminisced about old times when Annie and Jeff were still living. Around nine-thirty Blake bid Gloria good-bye, and he promised to call her from time to time to see how she was doing. He would keep her updated on the progress of the planned memorial for Jeff. She would not know the real reason for his visit to Atlanta.

On the way back to his hotel, Blake could not stop thinking about Gloria's remarks surrounding Jeff's death. He took her to mean she had doubts about his committing suicide. He also thought that he was being critical of her for not showing grief and sorrow at Jeff's funeral. Maybe she just held it all inside of her. After all, that was how he handled the death of his wife and his close friends who were killed in combat. He would need additional time with her after he got further into his investigation. There were unanswered questions that urgently needed to be addressed before he got too deep into the investigation.

Blake made an appointment to speak with the senior management of International Atlanta Engineering, Inc., at two o'clock Wednesday afternoon. When Blake arrived at the firm's office located near the Atlanta International Airport, he was astonished by the architecture of the stand-alone building. He had not seen such a beautiful building in all of his travels. The building was even more lavish than the New York insurance office building. *Why not have an expensive office building?* he thought. *After all, they are engineers, and they have the big bucks.*

Walking into the visitors greeting and information area, Blake was greeted by an attractive receptionist. She welcomed him by name and immediately called the vice president, Mrs. Rhonda Pane. "Mr. Tanner is here to see you," she politely said.

As Blake entered the lavish office of the vice president, a tall and slender blond-haired, blue-eyed woman with the beauty of a movie star took off her gold-rimmed glasses, got up, and walked around her desk to greet Blake. "Hi, Mr. Tanner, I am Rhonda Pane, and we are so happy to meet a good friend of Jeff's. Please let us have a seat on the couch." She pointed to a black leather couch and two matching chairs in the southwest corner of the office. "Would you like a nice cup of coffee?" She poured the coffee into two white cups without waiting for his reply. "I recognized you from a picture of you and Jeff that he kept in his office. You both were much younger then," she said with a smile.

"I am obliged to you for taking the time out to talk with me about Jeff." He glanced at the gorgeous legs of the blond vice president. He thought that she looked so much like Jeff's wife, Gloria. "I'm sure you are aware, Jeff and I go back to the jungles of Vietnam, and we were friends until his untimely death. I am planning a memorial for him that will be placed at his gravesite. I definitely want this to be very special and not just for his time in the war. If I can ask you and other management personnel who knew and worked with Jeff a few personal questions about Jeff's life after the war, I would much appreciate it."

Without hesitation, Rhonda Pane said softly, "Of course, Mr. Tanner. Our president, Robert Jennings, James Connors, our international financial director, and Frank Pane, our director of security, will all be more than happy to talk with you."

"Is Mr. Pane related to you?"

"He is my husband," she answered without any sign of excitement or an explanation.

Seems fishy to me already, Blake thought as Rhonda made a call from the telephone located on the table next to where she sat.

"The others are waiting for us in the conference room. If you would come with me please, we will go meet with them."

When they entered the plush room, there were three men sitting at a large conference table, and an older gray-haired man was positioned in a high-back, plush leather chair at the head of the table. They all stood up to greet Blake. As always, Blake scoped the men out and ran a mind check as he approached them.

The short and overweight gray-haired man introduced himself first. "I am Robert Jennings, this is James Connors, and this is Frank Pane. I'm sure you have made acquaintance with our lovely vice president," he said, pointing to Rhonda Pane.

After the formal introductions were completed, Blake made a mental note about each man. The president evidently was the moneyman, and probably just a front man, or maybe his father left him the company. James Connors looked like the honest one of the group, probably worked himself up the ladder with hard and honest work, and he looked like a yes man. *He was the only one who shook my hand and gave it a firm squeeze. Now for the husband of Rhonda, Frank Pane; he will take some studying. He has a smirk on his face that I don't like. He looks a little bit like Jeff,* Blake thought. *Maybe not quite as tall as Jeff was, but he is a good-looking son of a bitch. He did have a firm handshake, but no prolonged eye contact. Unusual for a senior security guru.*

Robert Jennings spoke first. "We all are so very sad from the death of our dear friend Jeff. His sudden death was so uncalled for and very untimely, and he will be sorely missed. If we can be of any assistance to you in establishing a memorial for Jeff, we will be more than happy to donate whatever amount of money or support you need."

James Connors spoke next. "Jeff was a good friend of mine, and one hell of a golfer, too. He spoke highly of you and your longstanding friendship, Mr. Tanner. I just cannot believe that he is gone, and I do not see how or why he would take his own life. We went on many business trips together. He was a nice guy to be around."

"Jeff was a good man," said the security director, Frank Pane. "He will be missed around the business world, and by all of us in this firm."

"You mentioned seeing a photograph of Jeff and me, Mrs. Pane. I'm sure the contents of Jeff's office are gone, and you have another person to take his position?" asked Blake.

"No, we have not filled Jeff's position, and his office is just as he left it," said James Connors. "In honor of Jeff and his wife we wanted to wait a few months before hiring a replacement for his position."

"Is it possible for me to see Jeff's office? It may bring back a few memories that I can use in the planning of his memorial."

"Of course, I will be happy to show you the office when we have finished here," James Connors said politely.

"I just have a few questions to ask. On the personal and professional side of Jeff, I want to ensure he is credited for his accomplishments in his professional life, besides his bravery in combat and duty to his country."

"Fire away," James Connors replied very quickly.

"Being an international firm I know that Jeff traveled a lot. Could you tell me where he made most of his business trips, and what projects he was working on before he died?"

There were a few scornful looks of confusion, and Blake sensed a tense feeling among the group before James Connors commented. "Jeff loved Europe and especially London, Istanbul, Athens, Italy, and the southern part of Spain. Jeff was fluent in Spanish and Italian, he dearly loved the people and culture, and they loved and respected him. His last project or his project for the last two years was the oversight of building road and railway bridges in Europe, with priorities in Istanbul and London. There were many political problems involved with the international projects, but Jeff had the respect of the people and the vast knowledge necessary to get the job done."

Blake watched the body language and eye contact between Rhonda Pane and her husband during the conversation. There was coldness and a dark cloud that he felt looming over them. With a wife as gorgeous as she, old Frank should be making constant eye contact with Rhonda. Maybe she did not like him, or maybe they were putting on an act due to their executive positions with the company. He would evaluate his mental notes later when he could write down his thoughts and analyze each one of them.

"Any additional questions, Mr. Tanner?" asked the president, Robert Jennings.

"No, not at the moment. You all have been quite helpful. Could I take that look around Jeff's office?"

Jeff's office was located on the corner of the building with a view of the tree-filled outskirts of Atlanta. The decor of the office was all man, and that was what Jeff was, all man. Behind his desk on a glass shelf were pictures of him and Gloria taken at various locations. On the top shelf, he spotted two pictures that were taken in Vietnam. One was of Jeff and Blake taken after a fierce firefight, and the other was a black-and-white picture of the A Team that they both were assigned to. The only problem that Blake could see with the photograph was that he and Sergeant Major Jon Rider were the only members of the team who were still living.

"I'll leave you to yourself so you can look around and think of Jeff," said James. "Please stop by Rhonda's office when you are ready to leave."

Blake looked at the surroundings and thought of Jeff sitting at his desk planning a business trip to Europe. There had to be a clue somewhere if Jeff was contemplating suicide. *Damn if I believe that he took his own life.* He just was not the type; he was a strong warrior, and warriors did not kill themselves under any circumstances. Blake sat down in the chair behind the desk and tried to put himself in Jeff's position. The desk calendar was open and the date was September 2, 2004. There was a telephone number written in green ink just below the day. It was an international number with the country code 44. "That's Great Britain," Blake said to himself. He pulled out his little black book and copied down the number. Jeff must have a daily planner and an appointment book around because he was always good at keeping meetings. The book was no place to be found.

After opening and closing desk drawers, he found a book filled with business cards that were surely points of contact for Jeff when he traveled. Blake took a few of the cards that had comments written on the front or back and placed them in his coat pocket. "Thanks, Jeff," he said. "No one will mind if I borrow your business cards," and then he grinned thinking about his old friend. We always said in the military, "We are not stealing, just relocating government property."

Blake said good-bye to the beautiful Rhonda Pane. She told him to give her a call if he needed anything else.

"You bet I'll be calling you, sweetheart," he murmured to himself. "You can damn sure count on that. She is too damn good-looking to be a corporate vice president. Maybe she is the boss's daughter. Who knows?"

An afternoon drizzle streaked the windows of the taxicab that took Blake back to his hotel. Periodically, he glanced through the window. He thought he saw a familiar face in the crowded sidewalks. He knew that his imagination was running wild on him. He had not been to Atlanta in years, and the people he knew in earlier years were probably living in some far-off location drinking cold beer.

CHAPTER 4

While making notes from memory, and from his little black book, Blake poured himself another scotch and tried to focus on his day with the international engineering firm. James Connors seemed to be an honest person as far as Blake could tell. He might be putting on an act, or he just might be a typical company man. The chubby president, Robert Jennings, was out in left field. He just came to work and went home at the end of each day, and drew a hefty paycheck. The pretty vice president Rhonda Pane and her sneaky-acting husband would take some looking into. Blake went through the business cards he confiscated from Jeff's office, and separated them into geographical locations. There were six cards from London, four from Istanbul, three from Paris, and nine from various cities in Spain. All of the cards had notes written by Jeff on the back. He made another pile with cards from countries in the Pacific that Jeff had done business with, but there were no comments written on the cards. Blake decided he would concentrate on the cards with notes on them first, and then follow up with the others.

The top of his priority list was the phone number that he discovered on Jeff's calendar with a London number, and the six cards of contacts from London. His first stop would be London, and then he would rearrange his priority list after he gathered additional information. He also would make contact with the customers that Gloria had done business with during her trips to Europe. He found no signs of trips that Jeff and Gloria had made together.

Very strange, he thought. *What an opportunity to combine business and pleasure.*

The worst part was not knowing exactly what he was looking for. There were business cards with telephone numbers noted on the back, which is normal in the business world. In his mind, he would find what he was looking for. Good investigators have the seventh sense, so he thought.

Darkness had fallen hours ago across the Atlanta skyline. As the cold, light drizzle coursed the windows of Blake's hotel room, he placed his old black briefcase on the desk located near the balcony door. First, he would make a phone call to his travel agent and request reservations tomorrow evening, departing for London. Now was the time to use the satellite phone that the insurance company had provided and instructed him to use. The numbers were not easily traced, and he had a secure line. He called the special travel agent and provided the representative with his request information.

The woman agent was friendly and polite. "Good evening, Mr. Tanner. How may I help you?"

"I would like reservations from Atlanta to London Heathrow, departing Atlanta tomorrow with an open return. I will need hotel reservations for two nights in the downtown area of London."

"Thank you, Mr. Tanner. We have all your travel requirements and personal information. I will call you back with confirmation. Shall I call the phone number you are using now? Do you want me to use your current profile?"

"Yes, thanks."

Blake had just finished showering and was drying himself off when he heard a knock on his hotel room door. When he opened the door, he saw a slender young man dressed in a dark business suit, smiling and holding a large envelope under his right arm.

"Mr. Tanner, I am Richard from International VIP Travel. I have the travel documents that you requested. I am sure you will find them all in order."

"Thanks," Blake said as he reached in the pocket of his terry cloth robe thinking he had a money clip.

"Oh, no need for a tip, sir. I work for the company. Have a nice evening and a safe journey."

He works for the company. Big damn organization I'm mixed up with here. After carefully opening the package, he found a professional leather document folder with his plane tickets and a scheduled departure for the next afternoon at four-thirty, with assigned seat 2A and hotel reservations for a suite at the Ritz in downtown London. *Now this is what I call first-class service.*

Pouring himself another scotch, he thought about the young dark-haired flight attendant he had met on the flight from Denver to New York. Fumbling for his billfold, he found her business card. She must be all of twenty-eight to thirty years old. *Hell, I have boots older than she is*, he thought. He got the overall impression that she seemed interested in the old guy, so he had better keep in touch with her. A man in his profession could never tell when he might need valuable assistance from a friend. Picking up the hotel room phone from the desk, he dialed her phone number. After three rings, the recorder came on and Blake listened to the short message and the sexy voice of Denise Romo. He left a message and told her he would call her when he was back in New York.

Now since his mind was on women, he thought he would call beautiful Mary Stewart, and tell her that he could not contact Donald Higgins and provide him with travel plans. She was very friendly toward Blake, and he could tell she had some interest in him. In the eyes of Blake Tanner, Mary was one intelligent woman, with a good head on her shoulders and good values.

He did have a fondness for Atlanta; it was a special city to him and Annie. They spent numerous weekends at the Holiday Inn, just to get away from Army life. As he walked through a park, he heard the birds chirping and saw squirrels gathering food for the winter. Life could be so very peaceful, he thought. A man should stop and take time to smell the roses, or he could keel over with a heart attack. *I'm talking about me, damn.* He promised himself that after this investigation he would saddle up and go back to Colorado.

The last time Blake had been to London was the summer of 1997. He stayed overnight before going to South Hampton on a primary official investigation. He liked beer, cold beer, but he could drink a few pints of light and bitter from a British pub. The British are serious about their beer drinking, and they can put pint after pint away without physically feeling any drastic effects. Blake remembered drinking a pint, then peeing two pints. There was something special about pub grub. He thought it tasted like home cooking, right out of the kitchen.

After Vietnam, Tanner had a different outlook on life. He promised himself that he would remember all he could about living, and try to forget the bad memories of war, and the dead. There was no time in Vietnam for tears; lately Blake had shed more tears than he had in the last twenty years. Jeff's sudden death temporarily reversed his outlook on life. How could he forget killing a man who was standing only a few feet away, shooting him in the chest? He recalled shooting other VC soldiers who were trying to kill him. How can a man forget taking the life of another human being?

With women, memories of war, and Jeff still on his mind, he decided to have another drink and put the deep thoughts out of his mind. Later on in the evening, Blake lay his head down on the soft pillow and drifted off to sleep thinking about his loving Annie.

Buttery light streamed through the large double glass patio door, forming dancing flickers of sunlight on Blake. He rose and clamped his hands together behind his neck, not sure if he was ready to face the task ahead of him. He stared at the ceiling, thinking back thirty-five years earlier when he first met Jeff in Vietnam. He was a skinny little bastard, Blake remembered. Always laughing, always smiling. "Sir….?" he would say. "Let's go get a beer." Blake laughed to himself, remembering telling Jeff, "Look, asshole, I am a sergeant first class, do not call me sir." The manner in which Jeff had died was odd. It was just not his nature to kill himself.

CHAPTER 5

London, England

During the long flight to London, Blake had time to put together his plans for a visit with Sinclair Engineering Corporation. He had not made contact with them before departing from Atlanta, as he really did not have a suitable plan in place. The most logical approach would be to pose as a freelance writer gathering information about bridges in Europe. He knew enough about bridges and writing articles to get an appointment with the management of the corporation. He would ask pertinent questions that might give him a lead about Jeff and what he had done while he was in London. The thought even occurred to him that he could use Jeff's name and tell them he was an old friend from Atlanta. Now, finding out who was on the other end of the telephone number that Jeff had written on his calendar would be his next step. *This should be an easy task for an old expert investigator like Tanner,* he thought.

Blake did get some sleep on the plane as it was an overnight flight, and his first-class seat converted into a sleeper. London Heathrow was a very interesting airport. You could see movie and rock stars. He remembered seeing Jesse Jackson one time, just walking through the airport as if he belonged there. Heathrow was not a typical airport, as it was one of the main hubs for air travelers around the world. Great Britain did have strict government regulations, and they expected everyone to comply. The British Customs agents were always polite, nothing like JFK. Blake Tanner loved America, but he was disappointed in the rudeness that he saw in many Americans who worked with the public. He had no tolerance for bad manners, none whatsoever.

After clearing customs and baggage claim, he took a taxi to the London Ritz. The luxurious suite was excellent. The mini-bar was stocked with scotch, and there was an ice machine just down the hall. He had an impressive window view of Piccadilly Circus, with Hyde Park just around the corner. The room's decoration was in the distinctive Ritz style. Although Blake disliked antique furniture, he admitted to himself that he did like the beautifully restored Louis VII furniture.

The long hot shower refreshed Blake. He was now ready to begin his day and have some lunch. He found out many years ago that the only way he could combat jet lag was to stay awake as long as he could, and then work a normal day.

He would call the phone number on the business card that he had taken from Jeff's office. He dialed the local number from the hotel room phone, and a woman's cheerful British voice on the other end said, "Good morning, Spenser International Antiques, how may I help you?"

Blake hesitated for a few seconds. "I would like to visit your shop. May I have your address please?"

The woman gave Blake the address and told him that he would be most welcome. "May I have your name please?"

"Tanner, Blake Tanner, from Colorado."

"Thank you, Mr. Tanner. I hope to see you soon, cheerio."

Blake asked the door attendant where he could get some typical pub grub and a pint of beer for lunch. The directions were simple, and he easily found the small pub down the street from the Ritz.

London sidewalks are always crowded and filled with busy shoppers and people just out for a casual walk. Blake did get a few stares from onlookers, as not many men in London wore cowboy boots. He did like London, and it was on his list of his top ten favorite cities in the world.

The pint of light and bitter went down smooth, and the taste brought back old memories of his past visits to London. Blake preferred his beer ice cold, but he was not back in Colorado drinking Coors. He ordered a plowman's lunch, and drank another pint of beer. He then paid his tab and left the pub for his return trip back to the hotel.

He rode in a distinctive black London taxi to the antique shop. He was amazed at the number of antique shops in London. He could see why Gloria was so fond of her work and travels, but why would Jeff be calling the dealer? There had to be a lot of money in buying and selling antiques.

The black taxi rolled to a smooth stop in front of Spenser International Antiques. As Blake climbed out of the vehicle, he noticed the structure of the building, revealing old, weathered stone. When he opened the door to the shop, an electronic bell rang and he smelled the distinct musk odor of old furniture. An older man wearing thick glasses, a white dress shirt, and a mustard green tie came out from a back room.

"May I be of service to you?" the man said in a strong London accent.

"My name is Tanner. I called earlier and talked with a young woman. I am interested in gathering information about your antiques for a friend of mine back in the States."

"Oh, that was my daughter Julie. She just popped out for lunch. I am Mr. Spenser, the owner, and I will be more than happy to show you our merchandise and answer any questions you might have."

"That's very kind of you," Blake said, trying not to let his rough ways scare off the man. *I must remember to say Jeff was in the antique business,* he thought.

"You mentioned that you have a friend who is in the international antiques business?"

"Yes, Jeffery Sanders. Do you know him?" There was a blank stare on the man's face; he coughed and then muttered, "No, I have never heard his name before, sorry."

Lying bastard, Blake thought. *You know something that I don't know and I intend to find out.*

The front door opened to the shop, and in walked a beautiful young woman. Tanner thought she looked to be about twenty-five years old, about five-eight, one hundred twenty pounds, long black hair, and she looked almost Spanish. She wore expensive-looking clothes—too nice for working around old furniture. Her light blue sweater revealed firm breasts, and her loose-fitting skirt hid a mysterious body. Her perfume was Obsession. Blake loved the smell because his wife had worn it.

"Cheers, my dear," said the shop owner. "I hope you had a nice lunch? This is Mr. Tanner from America. He said that he spoke with you earlier on the phone."

"Oh, yes, hello, Mr. Tanner. Is my father helping you then?"

"He is, thank you."

"Julie, can I talk with you in the back room, please?" her father said.

"Will you please excuse us for a minute, Mr. Tanner?" Julie asked.

While the two were in the back room, Blake tried to figure out what the hell was going on. *The little fat chap knows something, and he knows Jeff. I need to get the daughter by herself, then bring up Jeff's name and see how she reacts,* he thought.

The daughter came out of the back room alone and walked over to where Blake was looking at a wooden wall unit. "This is pretty old?" Blake asked and tried to sound like he knew a little about old crap.

"Very old. Do you know antiques, Mr. Tanner?"

Blake could not stand being such a nice guy and came back with a smart-ass answer. "I know a few." He grinned.

Much to his surprise the young woman smiled at him. "I love your American humor. I think it's very sexy when it comes from a man."

Wow, what the hell is going on here? Blake thought. "Do you know many Americans?"

"Being in the international business I have met quite a few Yanks. I must say you men are most charming, in a crude sort of way."

"Have you ever been to America?"

"No, I have not been, but I am planning on visiting very soon."

"Would you happen to know my friend Jeffery Sanders from Atlanta?"

Just like her father, she tightened up, got jittery, and turned her head away from Blake. "I have met him," she answered sheepishly.

Her comment got Blake's attention instantly. "How do you know him? I mean, he is a good friend of mine, and I have never heard him mention your name."

"We met when he was here in London on a business trip last summer, looking at antiques. I liked his charm and his good looks. He is much older than me, but we are just good friends. You know, dinner, sightseeing, things like that."

"I gather that your father doesn't approve of you seeing Jeff."

Julie hesitated and shuffled her feet around just as she had done during a similar question. "I do not know you, Mr. Tanner, but if you say that you and Jeffery are friends, I will tell you, no, my father does not approve, mainly due to the age difference and him being an American. My mother is dead, and my father strongly believes that I will run away to America and he will never see me again."

Blake did not have the heart to tell the young woman that their friend was dead. Maybe later, he thought, but now was not the time. "When did you last have contact with Jeff?"

"This past July he was in London looking at antiques for export to the U.S. My father caught us together in an Italian restaurant, and he created quite a commotion."

"Did your father threaten Jeff?"

"He did. I do not believe that he meant it, as he is a timid man, but he told Jeffery he would have him run out of England if he ever contacted me again. The Italian manager of the restaurant tried to assist, but Jeffery did not understand what he was saying."

That's peculiar, as Jeff spoke fluent Italian, Blake thought. "Did you contact Jeff after that?"

"Yes, but only on the telephone. Jeffery told me that he would be back over in September, but I haven't heard from him since August."

"Thank you, Miss Spenser. I appreciate your confiding in me and providing me personal information about you and Jeff. I would like to contact you at a later date if that is all right with you."

"That will be fine, thank you very much. Would you tell Jeffery that I am waiting for him, and for him to call me, please? I am so sorry about his losing his wife to cancer."

I'll be damned, that lying, conniving bastard, Blake thought. *Jeff was really trying to get this pretty young thing in the sack, but I can't imagine why, with Gloria waiting at home for him. The asshole even told her that his wife had died, and he did not let on that he could speak Italian. Jeff must have had a good reason to go so far as to tell a lie about Gloria being dead. This is not the Jeff that I knew.* Now the situation was getting more complicated by the minute.

Blake left his satellite phone number with Julie. "Let's keep in contact," Blake told her as he left the shop. "Please call me if you hear from Jeff."

Blake called Sinclair International Engineering Inc., and arranged for an appointment the next morning at ten o'clock with the public relations manager. At least he would get his foot in the door, and then he could make suitable plans on where to go after the meeting.

What a chilly morning, Blake Tanner thought, even for London. It looked like a cold winter, though he was not a weather forecaster. His warped thoughts brought a much-needed smile to his bearded face.

"Good morning, sir," said the plump middle-aged woman sitting at the reception desk at the Sinclair International Engineering building. "How may I help you this morning?"

"I'm Blake Tanner, and I have a ten o'clock appointment with Mr. Street."

"Would you have a seat? He will be with you shortly," the receptionist said tartly. "Would you like a cup of tea?"

Blake could not resist the chance to dig at the love the British had for tea. "Thanks, with sugar, lemon, and lots of ice."

The woman did not crack a smile, and coolly said, "We drink our tea hot in England."

Chock one up for the smartass from Colorado, Blake thought, and then he smiled and almost laughed aloud at his sick humor. Old Bubba would have fun with her if she ever visited Georgia.

Blake was scanning through a business magazine. The woman with no sense of humor got up from her desk and walked over to where Blake was sitting. "If you would please follow me, Mr. Street will see you now."

Sitting at a large desk was a skinny little bald-headed man with black rimmed glasses as thick as a Coke bottle. He wore a bright green necktie and matching socks. He got up from his chair, rounded his cluttered desk, and put out a hand that felt like fish bait when Blake shook it. "I understand that you are writing an informative article on our British auto and train bridges," the man said with a strong London accent.

"That is correct. An international engineering firm in Atlanta highly recommended your company to me. I talked with them back in September, and a man named Jeffery Sanders provided me with your phone number and location." Blake waited to see the expression on the man's face, to see any type of body language that might indicate he knew his dead friend.

Without hesitation the man firmly said, "You must not have heard, but Mr. Sanders is dead. It seems as though he committed suicide the middle part of September. We are all sad, as we liked Mr. Sanders so much. He will be sorrowfully missed by the engineers that he worked with."

Blake did not detect any sign of hidden information that the man might have concerning the death of Jeff. "I'm sorry, I had no idea that Mr. Sanders had passed away. He seemed like such a nice professional man." The hurt inside Blake was strong, and he hated to talk about his dead friend as though he did not personally know him.

"If you would like to speak with some of our engineers who worked with Mr. Sanders, I can arrange a meeting for you."

"That would be great."

The little man picked up the telephone and dialed what looked like two numbers. "Hugh, there is a gentleman from America in my office who is writing an article about British bridges. Could you chat with him, please? He also knows Mr. Sanders. Great. I will then bring him to your office. Cheers," he said and hung up the telephone.

"Mr. Hugh Parsons, our chief engineer, worked with Mr. Sanders on many international projects. Come with me and I will take you to his office."

"Welcome to Sinclair Engineering," the tall blond-headed Hugh Parsons said as he walked around his desk to greet Blake. "Please, have a seat and we will get us a cup of tea, or better yet, we will have American coffee. I understand that you are a free-lance writer, and you are gathering pertinent media information for an article."

"Yes, that is correct. Jeffery Sanders, who worked for Atlanta International Engineering, generously provided me your name. I was profoundly shocked to hear that he had committed suicide."

Hugh said in a low and sincere-sounding voice, "We all were shocked to hear about Jeff, and I personally could not believe that he took his own life. He just was not that type of individual. I knew him as a business associate, and we did drink a few pints together, played a few rounds of golf, and had some nice business lunches and dinners."

Blake could tell that the two men he had spoken with had nothing to do with Jeff's death, nor did they seem to have any secrets that would indicate they knew the cause of Jeff's death. Why would a man talk about drinking beer and playing golf if he had anything to hide?

Blake winged it through questions about bridges; he collected company handouts, and he took notes that basically meant nothing. Hugh introduced Blake to three company mechanical engineers who had worked with Jeff on various projects. They all seemed to like and respect Jeff; he detected no bad feeling or any motive to suspect the men. Blake left Sinclair Engineering with no negative feeling about the personnel he had met. He was chasing the wrong fox in this hunt, he thought, doing his best British impersonation to himself. *You are sick, Tanner, just plain sick.*

The next move would be to call on two international antique dealers who had done business with Gloria and her company. He briefly visited the two dealers the following morning, and he gathered no additional information that would connect Gloria with the death of her husband. All of the people he talked with held Gloria in high regard, and Blake could pick up no negative feelings from any of the contacts. He might have missed a clue, or he may have misread one of the contact's body language during his questioning, but it was doubtful. Blake Tanner was a top-notch investigator, and he missed little during his investigations.

The only bad vibes he had came from Julie Spenser and her father. *My gut feeling is that Jeff was having a romantic affair with the beautiful young woman who was half his damn age,* Blake thought. Besides that, Jeff was using his wife as a means to meet with Julie. He would keep her page open, and would ask Gloria if she had requested Jeff to contact the Spenser antique shop when he was in London.

Looks like London is a closed deal for now, he thought. *Guess I had better head back to the hotel, regroup, and plan my next destination.* Blake called Higgins and provided him with the information that he had so far. "My next destination will be Istanbul. London is still open, and I may need to return at a later date."

"Be safe and good luck. Call when you have any additional information that we can use. Mary sends her best to you."

Blake dined on typical fish and chips at a small shop near his hotel. He grabbed a pint of lager and ate his lunch in the crowded shop. Nothing like fish and chips wrapped in newspaper, he thought as he poured a couple drops of vinegar on his fish.

The day had a slight chill in the air, and it was refreshing after a nice meal. During his brisk walk to the hotel, Blake tried to take his mind off business and concentrate on where he was. London was a special city, and Americans by the millions flocked to enjoy the sights. The weather was usually crappy, but when the sun appeared, there was nothing more beautiful than a sunny day in jolly ole England.

Back at the hotel Blake made his flight and hotel reservations for his trip to Istanbul. The VIP travel agent informed him that his documents would be waiting for him at the Turkish Airlines business-class ticket counter, at London Heathrow. No first-class travel within Europe, only business class, but it would do, especially on Turkish Airlines. They provided individual business-class seats, and the service was always good.

Blake never liked to dine alone. Eating was a precious time to share with close family and friends. He looked at the menu posted on a welcome board outside the various restaurants that were inside the hotel area. The front desk manager informed Blake that the chef was one of the best in Great Britain. He had trained in France, and he and his staff were known for their delicious cuisine. After a few scotches Blake walked to the restaurant, and after looking over the menu he decided on roast beef with Yorkshire pudding, gravy, parsley potatoes, and the typical mixed vegetables. "A glass of burgundy, and keep the dinner rolls coming," he said to the waiter.

His stomach full, his thirst quenched, he was ready for a good night's sleep. He was excited about going back to Istanbul, one of his favorite cities in the world. Blake drifted off to sleep thinking of his last visit to Istanbul with Annie.

CHAPTER 6

Istanbul, Turkey

The Turkish Airline flight from London Heathrow to Istanbul's Ataturk airport was relaxing to Blake. He had worked in Turkey on many occasions, he liked the people, and he enjoyed the executive business-class service on Turkish Air. The seat next to Blake was empty so he had plenty of room to scatter the contents of his black leather briefcase. He had put together a list of the contacts he planned to meet with while in Istanbul. Using his real name was necessary when going to Turkey, as the Customs agents and police did not play games. Just do what is honest and enjoy the stay in Turkey, is what Blake discovered years ago.

He could play the part of a widower from Colorado, looking for a prize antique to ship back to America. The antique act would work for gathering critical information about Gloria, he decided. Now, what about the engineering questions that could connect him with clues about Jeff? He would use the freelance writer act again. It was almost the truth, and he was confident the plan would work.

At the Turkish engineering firm that Jeff visited a few weeks before his death, Blake would use the freelance writer routine about an article on Turkish-built bridges.

Switching his briefcase to his left hand as he walked toward the aircraft exit, Blake stopped in front of the open cockpit door. The aircraft commander was greeting the passengers as they walked by him and the flight attendants. Blake shook the captain's hand, and he thanked the flight crew for a good flight and excellent service. He deplaned and headed for the Customs area where he would purchase a Turkish entry visa. The lines were long going through Customs, passport control, and baggage claim. He decided against looking for a Ritz-Carlton Hotel shuttle, so he took a taxi to one of his favorite hotels in the world. The taxi ride to the hotel was another event that Blake would treasure in his memories. Pedal to the metal, and hand on the horn. Most of the drivers were courteous, permitting other vehicles to make turns and enter traffic. The first thing he noted was that the nauseating smell of coal smoke was gone from the air. Thank goodness, the Turkish government had switched over to natural gas for heating of homes and businesses.

Tanner was always a good tipper, and he was courteous to all people he met when traveling to overseas locations. His philosophy was you could never tell when one of the individuals you met could help you in a time of emergency or danger. The hotel door attendant remembered Blake, mainly because he always wore cowboy boots. The Turkish liked him. They always looked at him and asked, "Are you a commando?"

His room was spacious, and the view was incredible as it overlooked the Bosphorus River and the European side of Istanbul. He would personally visit the contacts for the antique dealers that were on his list, and then he would make appointments to visit the engineering companies. First, though, he would have lunch and a cold beer before heading out toward the Grand Bazaar.

The friendly door attendant flagged a taxi, and Blake could tell by the sound of his voice that he was giving stern instructions to the driver about the safety of his American cowboy friend.

"Where would you like to go, sir?" asked the door attendant.

"The Grand Bazaar, the main entrance."

"The driver's name is Mimmet, and he will stay with you all day. I have instructed him to wait for you while you shop regardless of how long you stay."

"Thanks." Blake put a twenty-dollar bill in the door attendant's hand. "I never did get your name."

"George, please, just call me George."

"Okay, George, see you later." He got in the taxi, and it zoomed away in the snarling and loud traffic of Istanbul.

The Grand Bazaar was a favorite place for Blake. He had memories of Annie and him coming here on their first visit to Istanbul, when they lived in Germany. There were over eight thousand shops located throughout the Bazaar, with some of the shops dating back for hundreds of years. He remembered a few shops from earlier visits and the kind merchants who peddled their goods. The sweet smell of various herbs filled his nostrils. The smells of assorted chocolate, nuts, fruits, vegetables, and the everlasting smell of leather goods were distinct. His memory was correct as the first shop owner he came to offered him hot chai. The first call on any visit, whether it was business or pleasure, was to indulge in a small glass of hot chai. Blake liked the Turkish tea and the small glasses with different designs.

Looking over his notes, he remembered that Gloria has done business with a Turkish rug dealer on many previous occasions. The shop was located toward the middle of the Bazaar. Sarraf Turkish Rug Exports would be his first stop. Gloria told Blake that she did her business on the telephone and that she had never visited Istanbul. Now, finding Sarraf would take some talking with shop owners. That would take time, as they all wanted to sell their goods. They also would tell you that their family or friends could give you a good price. Blake liked to talk with the people, so he made a little game out of it. If he indicated that he had plenty of money to spend, then he would possibly find his contact quickly.

"I'm looking for Sarraf Turkish Rug Exports," Blake told the man working in the first leather goods shop he came to.

"Yes, yes, I know this shop. It is just around the corner. Please come with me."

Sure enough, the shop was just around the corner. *My first stroke of luck*, Blake thought. He thanked the leather goods shop owner for his help and promised to return and look at leather jackets before he departed the Bazaar.

An older Turkish man introduced himself as the manager of the Sarraf shop and asked Blake if he would like some chai.

"Thanks. I like apple flavored, if you please," Blake said softly. His plans were to show interest in buying a few of the shop's most expensive rugs and have them shipped to Atlanta and to the address where Gloria and his friend Jeff lived.

Blake looked at many rugs, but he had to admit that he did not know a damn thing about them. He would just play the dumb part, which was true, and go along with the tourist shopping routine. He still could not figure out what people saw in an old worn-looking rug. Looking at a large rug that was on display, Blake said to the shop manager, "I like this rug. A friend of my wife has one similar to this one, and I saw it when we were at a dinner party at her home in Atlanta."

"Oh, Atlanta. We have a lovely madam that buys our rugs, and she lives in Atlanta. Her name is Miss Gloria. Sanders is her surname. I am a Christian, and we talked about religion and Jesus," he said seriously.

"Well, for the love of Jesus, that is who I am referring to. Gloria said we should buy a rug for ourselves, and she is the one who gave me the name of your shop." *I should get an Academy Award for this acting.*

"Have you seen Miss Gloria lately? We have not seen her since early spring."

Funny, Blake thought. Gloria told him that she had never been to Istanbul. So, why the hell did she lie about her travel to Turkey?

"I have not seen her since this past September. Her husband died, and my wife and I attended his funeral."

The man looked puzzled, and then he said with a frown, "We thought her husband was killed in an airplane crash many years ago."

Oh, shit, Blake thought, *what is going on with Gloria, telling such lies? And Jeff, that asshole, was telling the same story in London.* Blake had to think fast so he would not distract the man and his discussion about Gloria. "This was her second husband. She just married him this April. Guess she is not very lucky when it comes to husbands."

"Would you give her my business card, and ask her to please call me? We have some merchandise that she ordered, and we are still waiting for her Letter of Intent."

"Could I be of assistance and look at the merchandise she ordered? Maybe I could make suitable arrangements with Miss Gloria and pay for the items, and then you could ship them to her."

The man seemed happy with the offer and asked Blake to follow him to the back room. Crates and boxes filled the musty-smelling room. Blake could not help but notice that the majority of the labels had forwarding addresses to various locations in the United States.

He handed Blake an international one-page invoice with only a few items listed. The items were all jewelry, and the total price for the merchandise and shipment was a sum of fifty thousand U.S. dollars.

Damn, this jewelry business is expensive, he thought. *Who the hell is pretending to be Gloria? She lied to me, but why?*

Blake found a way out of paying for the items and shipment to Atlanta. "Sorry, but I don't have this amount of cash with me. I will contact Miss Sanders for you when I return to America."

That seemed to satisfy the man, and he gave Blake his business card. "I will pass on to the company owner and president, Mr. Sarraf, that you will contact Miss Gloria. She is a favorite madam of Mr. Sarraf's."

Bingo, another light lit up in Blake's head. What is going on here, he wondered. I had better try to speak with this Sarraf person.

"Are Mr. Sarraf and Miss Sanders good friends?"

"Oh, yes, they are very good friends as they both lost their spouses," the shop manager replied in a sad voice. "Miss Gloria is such a nice lady. She is so very kind to me."

"Would it be possible for me to talk with Mr. Sarraf about Gloria's second husband's death? Maybe he did not know that she got married again, she lost her husband so suddenly."

"I know that he would most welcome you as he talks about Miss Gloria all the time. I will call him now if you like."

"Yes, I have an open appointment book for this afternoon." Blake attempted to hold back his anger. His upper lip tightened, his stomach became tense, and his heart pounded like a drum.

The man went back to a private office just off the showroom floor, and Blake could see him talking on the telephone. After a few minutes, the man returned. "Mr. Sarraf would like to have dinner with you this evening, if you are free."

"I am free, and I am staying at the Ritz-Carlton."

"Mr. Sarraf will pick you up at your hotel at nine o'clock."

Now to sneak by the leather shop, he thought. No, he remembered the shops where laid out like street blocks. Up a block, then turn right and he would be at the main entrance.

Mimmet, the faithful taxi driver, was waiting for Blake when he came out of the Bazaar entrance. *It is too bad not all people are as dependable as the Turkish people are,* Blake thought. He gave the taxi driver a generous tip, and they drove away, back to the hotel. Mister Mimmet was a very happy taxi driver.

For the evening dinner with his new Turkish contact, Blake elected to wear dark brown slacks, a tan turtleneck sweater, and a light brown sport coat. The dark brown Justin boots would go well, and if not, he didn't care. He grabbed his Burberry trench coat from the closet as he walked out of his hotel room.

Blake waited in the plush hotel lobby near the front entrance for his nine o'clock dinner engagement with Mr. Sarraf. He suspected this man was a lover of Gloria's. He just could not figure those two out, Gloria and Jeff. Both of them were into romantic affairs when Jeff died. Maybe there was no connection at all, but he was sure putting together a list of suspects.

When a distinguished-looking man entered the hotel lobby, Blake knew that he was his contact. The man was tall, looked to be in his mid-fifties, and had thick black hair with gray streaks and the typical Turkish mustache that most men wore. The man looked around and walked over to where Blake was reading a *USA Today* newspaper. He thought by reading a newspaper he would not look like an American crime fighter. Must have been the Justin boots that gave him away, or it could have been the newspaper, he decided.

"Pardon me, sir, are you Mr. Tanner?" the man asked with a British accent.

"I am, and you must be Mr. Sarraf?"

"Welcome to my country," he said, and they shook hands.

When they walked outside Blake saw a black Mercedes-Benz parked directly in front of the hotel entrance. A man dressed in a black suit stood by the rear door of the car. "Please," the man said, and he opened the door for Blake to enter. Mr. Sarraf went around to the opposite door, and the driver arrived just in time to open the door for him.

"Is this your first time in Istanbul?" asked Mr. Sarraf.

"No, I have been here on many occasions, and I will say up-front, Istanbul is one of my favorite cities in the world." Blake was sincere in his statement because he did love Istanbul.

"Thank you for the compliment. Most Americans like Turkey, and we like most Americans. So, you know my friend, Miss Gloria Sanders?"

"She is a friend of my wife. I have only met her on a few occasions." Blake was trying not to let on that he had known Gloria for many years.

The Turk turned in his seat and looked directly at Blake. "We are business partners, and we also are close personal friends. I was sad to hear of her husband's death. She never told me she had remarried."

"As I have said, I don't know her well, and I only saw her second husband when he was lying in a casket at his funeral." Blake tried to keep a straight face, but it was difficult with his warped sense of humor.

"Since you are not a personal friend of Miss Sanders, I will tell you that she promised to marry me, and then she never contacted me after our last meeting during the first part of September. I am so in love with her. She is such a beautiful woman, it is hard not to be with her," the man said with sadness in his eyes.

The dinner went well and, as usual, the Turkish cuisine was excellent. Erhan Sarraf was a Christian, not of the Muslim religion, so the two men drank wine with their dinner, and they drank the typical Turkish *raki* before their main meal arrived at their table, which consisted of a variety of grilled fish and numerous side dishes. Blake could not stop eating the wonderful Turkish bread that the local people ate before the main course, with a marvelous white garlic spread. Later in the evening, Blake's dinner host began to open up more about his relationship with Gloria. By the time the evening had ended, it was apparent that Gloria and the Turkish exporter were lovers. Now, Blake knew that Gloria and Jeff had lived separate lives while they were away from home, but maybe they lived separate lives in Atlanta, also.

Sitting at a table across from Blake and Erhan were three American women celebrating what turned out to be a birthday gift to one of the women. They were having a great time, laughing, singing, and dancing with any man who asked them.

Erhan bought them a bottle of champagne, and he wished them a good stay in Istanbul. "I like American women," he said with a smile. "Your American women always seem so happy, and they all are so beautiful."

Blake took a long, deep breath, and then said to Erhan, "Yes, we do love our women, especially when they are true to the men they love." Blake's remark did not seem to bother his Turkish host; he just continued looking and talking to the women.

"Mr. Tanner, would you take this roll of film with you and give it to Miss Gloria for me? She departed back to America before the film was developed. The photos will give her fond memories of us when we were down in the southern coast resort city of Antalya."

"Sure, I'll be happy to." Blake dropped the film in his side jacket pocket.

Blake and Mr. Sarraf bid each other good-bye. The so-called lover of Gloria thanked Blake for letting him cry on his shoulder. "Please tell Miss Gloria that I love her, and to please call me. I hope she enjoys the pictures."

"I will tell her." He thought, *Yeah, I will tell her all right. She had better level with me, or I will put her ass through the grinder. I might even get the film developed and look at the candid pictures before giving them to Gloria.*

Aware of the time difference between Istanbul and New York, Blake called Higgins from his satellite phone. After four rings, the answering machine came on, and Blake left a short message telling Donald that he was returning to New York day after tomorrow and that he would call Mary Stewart and gives her an update of his progress.

"Hi Mary, this is Blake Tanner. Hope I didn't disturb you."

"No, you did not disturb me. I was just thinking about you and wondering where you were today."

"I am in Istanbul, and will depart day after tomorrow back to New York. The information I have can wait until I meet with Donald."

"Do you have your flight arrangement yet?" asked Mary. If you call me back with your arrival time I will meet you at JFK."

"Will do, and thanks." Blake visualized Mary in his mind as they were talking. *She is a beauty, that's for damn sure*, he thought.

Blake arranged a meeting with Turkish Engineering, Inc., for the following morning. When he arrived at the engineering office at ten o'clock sharp, a slender young man dressed in a gray business suit greeted him. He spoke with a British accent, as did many formally educated Turkish men. "Welcome, Mr. Tanner, I am Engin Mersch, the public relations representative for Turkish Engineering. Please come with me and we will go to my office."

While sipping chai, Blake began with "Thank you for giving me a small part of your precious time. I realize that a large company like yours is very busy. If you please, I would like a little information about bridges being built in Turkey."

"Certainly," said the PR representative. "I will try to answer your questions and provide you with whatever literature you require."

"Your company was recommended to me by an engineer who works for a large firm in Atlanta. Maybe you know him, Jeffery Sanders?"

"We do know Mr. Jeff, and we were so sorry to hear about his sudden death. He was here the first part of September, and we did not notice anything peculiar or different about him. Mr. Jeff was always happy."

"I was not aware that you had heard about his death. I know that he loved visiting your country, and he had the utmost respect for the people of Turkey." Blake knew that his visit was completed, and he must dig up another reason why when Jeff returned to his home from Istanbul he was always depressed.

Blake thanked the PR representative for his precious time and cooperation. He had a funny feeling about the young man. Very well educated, he seemed to be one smart kid. Either his family was rich, or he had an extra job on the side. The suit he wore must have cost three or four hundred dollars, the shoes were Italian, and he had an Oyster Rolex watch on his wrist.

That evening Blake dined alone in the hotel's main restaurant. As he ate grilled bluefish, he thought about his afternoon meeting with the young Turkish executive, but could see no connection between Jeff and the Turk. Blake did have a strong feeling that the young man was gay. It made no difference if he were gay, just that Jeff did not associate with gay men that he knew of.

When he looked back, it all seemed like a nightmare. The death of Jeff, the affairs that Jeff and Gloria were supposedly having, the con of using other people's names, it made no sense to him at all. Blake knew that he would continue playing the jet set and doing his investigation until he completed his mission.

CHAPTER 7

New York City

The long flight to New York provided Blake time to put together his notes and try to make any sense out of why Gloria and Jeff were both having international love affairs. Maybe the affairs had nothing to do with Jeff's death, and again, maybe they did. If Jeff were unhappy in his marriage, then, Blake decided, Jeff would have had the guts to confront Gloria and tell her how he felt. Then again, maybe he did. Now, Gloria's affair with the Turk was a shocker. Blake never believed Gloria would do that to Jeff. As for Jeff, he was a good man, but he always did like the women. Jeff did love Gloria and his job, and Blake thought Gloria loved him. So why cheat? That was the big question. There were secrets that he must dig up if he was going to find out the real reason for Jeff's death. Maybe Jeff had a significant problem between the time he left Istanbul and the time he returned to Atlanta. That page would also remain open.

"Would you like another glass of wine, Mr. Tanner?" the flight attendant asked.

"Sure, thanks. This is a very good wine. What am I drinking?"

The flight attendant smiled and said, "It's French Chardonnay, 1982."

"I wouldn't know if it was Boones Farm 1962, I just like white wine," Blake said with a big smile.

The flight attendant cracked up at Blake's remark. "Me too," she said and moved down the aisle still laughing at his remarks.

Customs at JFK was a goat-roping affair as usual, but Blake finally made it through and walked out of international arrivals with a smile on his face. There was Miss Mary waiting for him, but with no welcome sign this time.

She hugged Blake. "I am happy to see you. How have you been?"

"I'm happy to see you." He hugged Mary back and smelled the sweet fragrance of her perfume and the sweet scent of shampoo in her hair.

"Do you wish to go directly to your hotel, or do you want to get a cup of American coffee?"

"Are you asking to go to my hotel with me?" Before she could come back with a reply Blake answered, "Coffee, oh yes, American coffee. I positively think that is what I miss the most when I travel outside the U.S."

Mary just smiled at his remarks. She had taken a taxi to pick him up at the airport, as it was the best way to get around in New York.

Blake kept looking at Mary as she talked to him about her love for travel. *She sure as hell has more to do than to cater to an old retired globetrotter like me.*

"So, Mary Stewart, where all have you traveled?"

He saw the wild excitement in her eyes when she said, "Italy. I was able to visit Rome and Naples two years ago, and I absolutely loved it. I took Spanish and Italian in high school and college, and I try to keep up with both languages. I was able to visit the Isle of Capri, and it was absolutely stunning."

"Good for you, girl. Go to as many faraway locations as you can. It will stay with you for a lifetime." Blake then started speaking to Mary in Italian, and before she could even answer, Blake started speaking to her in fluent Spanish.

"My Lord, you are amazing. When and how did you learn to speak both languages so fluently?"

"Thanks to the United States Army, I was lucky enough to travel. My wife and I lived in Italy and Spain. My wife was fluent in both languages, and she assisted me with my pigeon talk when I got in trouble trying to make a point after drinking a few glasses of wine or a few dozen beers."

"I have never heard you talk about your wife. I understand that you are a widower?"

"Over five years ago, Annie was killed in an automobile accident. Both of her parents were with her, and they were killed also."

"I am so sorry. I will never talk about it again unless you want to." Mary slightly touched his hand.

They drank cup after cup of coffee, and then Mary dropped Blake off at his hotel. "I will have the company limo pick you up at three o'clock this afternoon for your scheduled meeting with Mr. Higgins."

"Fine. Will I see you there?"

"Of course. I am taking you to dinner this evening." Then she waved at Blake, giving him her natural Hollywood type smile.

Damn, he thought, *I like that woman. If I were a few years younger, I would be camped on her doorstep.*

The four o'clock meeting between Blake and Donald Higgins, vice president of the New York Mutual Life Insurance Company, went very well. Blake provided Donald with what information he had, and with his overall feelings about Jeff's death and the particular circumstances leading up to the day he died.

"What's your deep down gut feeling?" Donald asked.

"Here is what I believe could have happened. I have no firm evidence, but it is a remote possibility that Jeff did take his own life. Again, I say upfront, Jeff Sanders was not the type to put a loaded pistol to his head, but I have looked at the facts as an outsider. It seems as if Jeff was having an affair with a young woman in London. Gloria was having an affair with a millionaire exporter in Istanbul. Jeff could have found out about Gloria and the Turk, and she might have told Jeff about her affair. There are still questions in my mind about Jeff and the young woman in London, and Gloria and the Turkish millionaire. Jeff had a large amount of alcohol in his system at the time of his death. He could have put a gun to his head in a drunken stupor and accidentally pulled the trigger. The big question is what was his reason for reserving a room at the Hilton Atlanta Airport hotel? I do have more investigating to do before I give you my final report, and when we receive an official copy of the toxicology report."

"Fair enough, and thanks for your professional opinions. They sound logical, but we must make certain and have no doubts before we pay out the five million bucks to Mrs. Sanders. You're the man, Blake. Do whatever you feel is right."

After picking Blake up at his hotel, Mary and he took a taxi to a Mexican restaurant near Yankee Stadium. "I hope you like Mexican food and you can sing," Mary said with a laugh.

With a stunned look Blake finally answered, "What does food have to do with singing?"

"It's a karaoke restaurant. Everyone has to sing, or you do not eat."

"You've got to be joking. I can't sing a lick."

"We will just find out, Mr. Cowboy."

Blake had no other choice but to get up and sing. He tried to leave the stage, but no dice, and a great bunch of customers corralled him. "Okay, I will sing, but only if my date for this evening accompanies me."

The crowd went crazy when Blake and Mary decided to sing the George Jones, Tammy Wynette hit, "We're Not the Jet Set." Blake and Mary were laughing so hard that they only had to sing a few lines, and the friendly audience let them off the hook. The applause was loud, and the audience was happy. So were the two karaoke singers.

"This is the most fun that I have had in ages," Mary said with a vibrant glow when the taxi stopped in front of Blake's hotel.

Gleaming with excitement, Blake blurted out, "Me too. Let's do it again sometime. What about when I come back to town on my next visit?"

Mary said in her loving voice, "Great, just great. I do hope it will be soon."

Then Blake went in the hotel and the taxi sped away, taking Mary home.

Blake opened his thoughts on the plane ride back to Denver. His mind was always in motion, as it should be when a big company is paying the big bucks to investigate a suicide. Jeff and Gloria had been longtime friends, and he just could not figure out why they both would be involved in international love affairs. Why in the hell would Jeff kill himself? He could understand depression and mood changes; most all combat veterans dealt with the reality of war. Blake had the same real-life emotions every day. "Damn if I would kill myself," he said to himself.

CHAPTER 8

Castle Rock, Colorado

Blake clearly needed some time to think and put his thoughts together. There was no better place for him to do this than at his little ranch in the Colorado Rockies. He bid so long to Mary, and she made him promise to call her and to return to New York very soon.

Blake had left his beloved 2002 Chevrolet Silverado pickup at a covered long-term parking garage near the Denver International Airport. He liked his truck to be near the airport when he traveled, as he hated to ride in shuttle buses for a long distance, and he did not trust the driving of most taxi drivers.

Wispy clouds in the blue sky cast shadows on the mountain foothills as he drove south down Interstate 25 toward his ranch. He remembered that he had not called either of his daughters to let them know he was coming back home today. Both of his daughters and son-in-laws were good about leaving fresh milk, bread, eggs, and a home-baked pie or cake for him when he arrived home from a business trip. He decided to stop at Wal-Mart, which was located just before he turned on the Ranch Road that went to his mini-ranch. *Let's see,* he thought, *I need bread, eggs, milk, beer—never want to run out of beer—maybe an apple pie, and some fruit, and fresh vegetables.* He remembered that the film the Turk had given him was still in his coat pocket. He dropped off the film in the photo department and asked the woman behind the counter when he could pick up the finished copies. Much to his surprise, she told him they would be finished within thirty minutes. Great, he would just wait for the copies, as it would save him a trip back to town. He grabbed a cup of coffee and a fat pill, his name for a doughnut. He would pass some time in the snack bar while he waited for the film to be developed.

Damn, it certainly feels good to be back home, There is no place like home, Blake thought. *If Annie were here, then it would be perfect.* He put up his groceries, threw the package with the photographs on the kitchen bar, and carried his luggage to his bedroom.

He grabbed a cold Coors from the refrigerator and picked up the pictures that were taken in Turkey. Sitting down in his recliner in the family room, he looked at the pictures. *Damn, that pisses me off that Gloria would cheat on Jeff,* he thought, *and it pisses me off that Jeff would cheat on Gloria.* "Goddamn," Blake said aloud as he looked at the first picture of the Turkish man Sarraf in his bikini bathing suit. Standing next to him, clad in a black skimpy bikini, was the beautiful Mrs. Rhonda Pane. *What the hell is going on?* Blake wondered. Mr. Sarraf was having an affair with Rhonda Pane, the vice president of the engineering firm Jeff had worked for, and Sarraf thought she was Gloria Sanders. Why would Rhonda pass herself off as Gloria? Picture after picture were of Rhonda and the Turk taken during a holiday to the southern coast of Turkey.

It was time to regroup. This was the most peculiar and confusing case he had ever worked on. He would definitely need to go back to Istanbul, confront Mr. Sarraf, and inform him that he was involved with the vice president of an international engineering company and not the real Gloria Sanders. *Maybe Sarraf is an investor in the bridge building project Jeff was working on*, Blake thought. Now, how did the young English woman Julie Spenser fit into the picture? Blake decided to send her a picture of Jeff and get her reaction after she received the picture. Maybe the man she thought was Jeff was not even him. He felt that he was missing something here, but just could not quite put his finger on it. This called for a scotch, maybe two or three to get his mind back on Colorado time.

Blake mailed a short letter via priority mail to Julie in London and included a picture of Jeff. He asked her to call him collect when she received the letter, and he would give her a message from Jeff. Now for Mr. Sarraf. He would need to speak with him in person and ask more questions about his affair with a woman who portrayed herself as Gloria. "Well, I am off again," he said to himself as he went to his briefcase, removed the satellite phone, and hooked it up to its charger.

Before Blake made any travel arrangements, he would wait until he received a phone call from Julie in London. Then he would fly to Atlanta, talk with Gloria, and attempt to gather more crucial information on Rhonda and Frank Pane. Next, he would fly up to New York, brief Donald Higgins, and just maybe spend an evening with Mary Stewart. The personal approach Blake would take toward Mr. Sarraf and his involvement depended on what information he could find out during his visits to Atlanta and New York City.

Blake's daughters and their husbands came out for the weekend, as he was flying out for Atlanta on Monday morning. As always, the close family had a great time eating, drinking wine, reminiscing over their earlier lives, and talking about their mother. Blake's family all knew that business was never discussed when it came down to what Blake was doing, where he was going, or where he had been. Blake felt he loved his family more than anything. Someday he would stop this running around the world and stay at home. Soon, he hoped, very soon.

Packing a suitcase was easy for Tanner. He had prepared for official trips since he was a young man; now, getting old, he was not quite as excited about traveling as he once was. His mind drifted back to the early 1980s, when Annie went with him on a business trip to Italy. It was the same time of year, early December, he remembered. Annie had so many pairs of shoes that it took one large suitcase just for the shoes. She had another larger suitcase that she put the smaller one in, which held the shoes. The empty suitcase was to carry the shoes she would buy in Italy back home. He would always cuss a little. Then Annie would smile at him and tell him that was her job, to take shoes and clothes with her on a trip, especially to Italy.

Annie was the unconditional love of his life. He knew that he would never get over her, and that he would always love her.

He sat on his front porch watching the sun set over the Rockies—it was a beautiful sight to see. He always got sad when his daughters left with their husbands to go back up to their homes in Denver. He kept saying that when he stopped this running around, he was definitely going to get himself a dog. Blake loved dogs, and an outside dog would be most welcome at his house. He knew that having a dog now would be trouble for him as he was away so often. He made himself another promise. *I will get a dog when I finally retire.* His priorities were to buy a dog and then find him a woman. Then he would be living the good life.

Again, Blake felt pain, sadness, and loneliness thinking about Jeff's death. He was angry at him for taking his own life; he was angry at him for taking the easy way out after surviving in the jungles of 'Nam. Jeff had already lived his hell. Why take a chance on going to another hell, if there is such a place?

CHAPTER 9

December 5, Atlanta

Blake called Gloria before he left Colorado and asked if she were free to meet with him on Monday evening. She was delighted that Blake would be in Atlanta, and she again invited him to her home for dinner. "We can be more comfortable and talk freely at my house," she told Blake during their phone conversation. "Seven-thirty, and it will be Italian. You bring the wine and a hearty appetite."

The take-off roar of the Boeing 757 blasted through the cabin as Blake looked out the window from his seat 2A. Two Bloody Marys would set his mind at ease as he prepared for his planned meeting with Gloria. Once the seat belt sign was turned off, he pulled out his battered black briefcase from under the seat in front of him and unzipped the folder compartment. After reviewing his notes, he had a good idea what lay ahead of him in Atlanta.

He rolled over repeatedly in his mind how he would approach Gloria with what he had found out, without jeopardizing his investigation. He felt strongly that Gloria had nothing to do with Jeff's death, but she did have some answers that he would urgently need to get out of her. "Oh, hell," he told himself. "Do it the Tanner way: this is how it is, and this is what I want you to tell me."

Blake removed his light jacket from his garment bag, changed from the winter coat he wore from Denver, and walked briskly toward the taxi stand located just outside the front exit from baggage claim. He did not care for the Atlanta airport. It was nice, but was so damn big you had to ride a damn train to pick up your baggage. No rental car for Tanner. Let the taxi driver fight all the traffic.

"Come in," Gloria said as they gave each other a friendly hug. "I have a bottle of scotch open. We can have a few warm-up drinks before dinner."

They sat down next to each other on a brown leather three-cushion couch in the family room. As it was a chilly evening in Atlanta, Gloria had a nice cozy fire going in the stone fireplace. "So, where have you been, Tanner? Or am I supposed to ask that question?"

"It's all right. I have been in Europe, visited London and Istanbul."

"Two of my favorite cities," said Gloria. "I have done business in both cities but have not been to London in over a year, and I would dearly love to visit Istanbul again."

Blake was ready to make his move. "Do you know a Mr. Erhan Sarraf? He is an exporter of Turkish rugs from Istanbul."

Without hesitation Gloria answered, "Never heard of him. My company does not deal in Turkish rugs, only antique furniture."

"Just wondered as I was in the Grand Bazaar and this Mr. Sarraf told me that he knew you."

Again, Gloria shook her head. "I do not know him. He must have me mixed up with someone else."

"I am going to level with you, Gloria. He told me that he was having an affair with you."

"Why would a perfect stranger tell you something like that? It is so untrue. I would never have cheated on Jeff. I loved him too much for that to happen. I would very much like to face this lying bastard who made these false accusations."

Blake had the impression that Gloria was telling the truth, but he did not know for sure that she did not have anything to do with Jeff's death. "I will deal with him when I visit him later this week in Istanbul. I will let him know that he is lying, and if he continues telling people these lies, then we will file charges against him with the International Police, or I will just kick his ass."

"Good, please do that for me, Blake, please do."

Blake took a drink of scotch and looked into Gloria's blue eyes. "One more question that has been on my mind since our last visit. You mentioned that you had doubts about Jeff's death and his committing suicide. What did you mean by that?"

Gloria sat quietly, folded her hands, and then took a deep breath. "I think Jeff was murdered. I do not know who could have done it, but he did not take his own life. Jeff was drinking more than usual. He seemed to be troubled more and more after he would return from an overseas business trip. His last trip was to Istanbul, and when he returned home and we were eating dinner, he mentioned a few words about a formal contract between his engineering firm and the government of Turkey. Then with drinking scotch and the jet lag, he passed out. That was the first part of September, just a few weeks before his death. I do not understand why he was checked into the Hilton Atlanta Airport hotel. What was he doing?" Gloria now began to cry, and Blake laid her head on his shoulder.

"No more questions. Thanks, you have been a big help to me as I am understanding more about Jeff, his demanding work, and what happens to some of us after our war years are over."

"You are welcome anytime, Blake. You are a dear friend, probably the only one I can really trust. Please come back soon." She then hugged him, and kissed him on his cheek.

Istanbul is on the top of my radar screen, Blake thought as he returned to his hotel in the yellow cab. *Now, if Julie Spenser would just give me a phone call from London so I can get her reaction to her lover, and if he is not really Jeff, I could then make travel plans.* Talk about ESP, his satellite phone rang just as he walked in his hotel room. It was Julie Spenser on the other end.

"I received your letter and the photograph that you enclosed. You have made a terrible mistake. The photograph is not of my Jeffery."

"Silly me," Blake said. "I must have gotten the pictures mixed up at my office. I will send you another picture tomorrow."

"That will be lovely. Things like that do happen. Have you heard from Jeffery?"

"I have, the day after I sent you the picture. He said that he will contact you shortly and that he would like to take you to Spain with him on a business trip. You should have a fun time as Jeff speaks Spanish."

"Please tell Jeffery to contact me so I will know when to plan for the trip. He must be teasing you as he does not speak a single word of Spanish."

"He is a kidder, that's for sure. I will give him your message, and I will send you the picture as Jeff asked me to do." He told her that he would send the photo via the Internet. "Well, good-bye for now."

"Cheerio, Mister Tanner, thank you very much, and I will call you when I receive the photograph of Jeffery. You do have my email address, don't you?"

"I do, and thanks again."

Clearly, I am on to something big, Blake thought. *How do Frank and Rhonda Pane fit into the picture? I know what to do. I will send Julie a picture taken of Jeff and the entire engineering firm management that I took from his office, and maybe she will point out a person who could have been the imposter for Jeff. Tanner, you are so damn smart*. He chuckled.

Blake had copies made of the international engineering firm picture and sent it to Julie via the Internet. When he heard from her, which should be later this evening or early tomorrow morning, he would start his travel arrangements. He made his travel arrangement to New York and informed Donald Higgins and Mary Stewart that he was on his way to JFK, but he would take a taxi to the hotel, as it would be after midnight when he arrived.

The next morning he showered, shaved, put on his New York business suit, and pulled on his Justin boots. His satellite phone rang, and he saw the London area code on the caller ID. "Hello, Julie, did you receive the picture of the group with Jeff in it?"

"Yes, and thank you very much. Jeffery looks great wearing his black leather jacket."

He glanced at the images in the picture. Jeff was not wearing a black leather jacket, but Frank Pane was wearing one. He was standing in the middle of the front row. Jeff was standing in the second row on the left side, wearing a brown sweater. "Yes, that is my old friend Jeff on the front row. Is that what you said?"

"Yes, that is my Jeffery."

The lights began to blink in Blake's mind. *What have we here?* "Jeff said he will contact you soon."

"Cheerio, Mister Tanner, and thank you very much."

Now he definitely had both Rhonda and Frank Pane being in Istanbul and at the same time. Frank was posing as Jeff, and Rhonda was posing as Gloria. The puzzle did not quite want to go together. *There are parts missing*, he thought. In addition, how did Julie Spenser fit into the puzzle?

Blake met with Higgins and briefed him on what he had found out so far and what his next move would be. "This is taking longer than I thought it would," he drawled.

"Do what needs to be done, Mister Tanner. You are in charge, and when you are ready to wrap up the investigation, then you will be finished. When you are in Europe, the flight times between where you urgently need to go can be shortened by chartering a private jet. The options are in your hands."

Mary Stewart and Blake had dinner together that evening. They drank a lot of wine while eating seafood as their main course at one of New York's finest restaurants. There was a small dance floor in the corner of the restaurant, and a three-piece band played slow music. Blake and Mary danced, and each dance they got closer to each other. By the time, they left the restaurant they were making out like teenagers at the high school prom. They kissed and touched each other all over during the taxi ride back to Blake's hotel. "You want to come up to my room?" Blake blurted out as he pulled her out of the taxi by both of her hands.

"I thought you would never ask," Mary said, laughing at Blake and his old-fashioned ways. "Pay the driver, buddy, and let's go."

They made love as if it would be their last time, or they made love as if it were their first time in a long time.

"I'm out of practice, and I just can't get enough of you." He turned over to face Mary and gently kissed her, feeling her soft, warm breath against his face.

"We were great together, and I am also out of practice. I am not easy to get into a man's bed, but you are special, and I really like you." Mary rolled over on top of him, and they started making love again.

"I've got to leave, my dear," Mary said softly as she dressed. "Some of us have a real job, you know." Then she laughed and walked over to the bed and kissed Blake. "Have a safe trip, Mr. Tanner, and call me soon as you can. Bye for now, and don't forget, you are mine." She smiled at him and walked out the door.

I must be crazy, she drives me crazy, maybe we are both crazy, Blake thought. *I am falling for her, and I do believe she likes the old boy.*

Blake had the entire day to himself, as his flight to Istanbul did not depart until that evening. Now would be the time to call the pretty flight attendant, Denise Romo. Maybe she would be free today. His deep thoughts were that he was getting too close to Mary, so if he could secretly see Denise maybe his mind would clear up, and then he would know if Mary was the one he should stick with.

"Hi, Denise, this is Blake Tanner. We met on a flight from Denver to JFK last month."

"Oh yes, Mr. Tanner, from Colorado, seat 2A. How are you? And where are you?"

"I'm in New York on business. I fly out to Istanbul this evening and I was hoping you would be free for that afternoon tour of the city you promised me."

"I would love to meet you and proudly show you my city. Where are you staying at?"

They arranged to meet in the hotel lobby where Blake was staying at one o'clock. Blake was excited about meeting Denise. She was a beauty, and he liked her smile and her body. His thoughts drifted back to Mary and how sweet and sincere she was. He was cheating on her, but they had no official commitments. *Now, Tanner, you are getting cold feet,* he thought. *What if she was meeting a man today with sex on her mind? How would you feel? I cannot go through with this.* His mind changed very quickly when he saw Denise walk in the lobby of the hotel. Every man and even the women turned to look at her as she walked with a sense of *look at me, I am beautiful.* She wore a short blue jacket, tight designer jeans, black boots, and a white turtleneck sweater. Her hair flowed down her back, and she was an absolute knockout. *Oh, shit, how can I turn this woman down?*

She promptly walked right up to where Blake stood, embraced him, and kissed him softly on his lips. "Hi, Mr. Tanner, nice to see you again."

"You too. You sure look beautiful, Miss Romo."

"Denise, please call me Denise. You also look very good," she said, scanning him from his head to the toes of his boots.

"Thanks and it's Blake. Where are we off to?"

She grabbed his hand and said, "How about lunch with a magnificent view of the city?"

They walked out of the hotel lobby, and Denise led Blake to a taxi that she had waiting.

She had picked the spot carefully. They were alone at a table overlooking the New York skyline. They feasted on grilled fish and chardonnay wine. The conversation was mostly about the city of New York, and it was one-sided as Denise did most of the talking.

Nice young woman, Blake thought. *She is way out of my league. Beautiful, but she could be very demanding and selfish.* Looking at her beautiful face and body stirred his desires, but he had this one minor problem. Every time he thought about making a move on her, Mary's beautiful face would pop up in his mind. He now knew that Mary was the one for him, and he would be faithful to her, just as he had been faithful to his Annie.

The afternoon ended with Blake pretending he had a phone call and an emergency meeting. He thanked Denise for the wonderful afternoon and promised to call her during his next visit to New York.

You dumb shit-for-brains, Blake thought. Most men would have taken her to bed, and it would not have bothered them. He was just not that way. He was true to his wife, and he would be true to Mary, unless she proved that she did not care for him, or did not want him.

CHAPTER 10

December 10, 2004, Istanbul

Blake had ten hours of free time during his flight from New York to Istanbul. His thoughts were deep, and he dug back in his mind, attempting to think of a motive that Rhonda and Frank Pane would have for posing as Gloria and Jeff. He put himself and his mind in a think tank. He wrote down anything that came to his mind concerning the people and events that he thought would have any connection with Jeff's death. After scribbling down numerous names of people, events, locations, and suspicious motives associated with Jeff Sanders and his death, he prioritized the list and started evaluating his thoughts and suspicions one at a time.

After hours of using the process of elimination, his final list was considerably short. Rhonda and Frank Pane were his main suspects, followed by Mr. Sarraf. What significant part did he play with his affair with the so-called Gloria Sanders, who was in reality Rhonda Pane? Where did the young English lass come into play? Moreover, why did Frank Pane lie to her and portray himself as Jeff Sanders? Another interest was the young Turkish executive in Istanbul. What did he have to hide?

The first priority, while he was in Istanbul, would be to break down the rug exporter, Mr. Sarraf. He would give him a few of the pictures of him and Rhonda, and then he would tell him that she was not Gloria Sanders. *That should really screw up his mind,*

Blake thought. *He is, after all, a millionaire; he can find another American blond beauty to play with.*

Blake's mind drifted back thirty-five years ago to the small Army Surgical Hospital at Binh Thuy, Vietnam. He was recovering from wounds received in a Viet Cong mortar attack at their compound the previous week. Jeff had just been released from the same hospital in November for wounds he received during a reconnaissance mission. Here came Jeff, half-drunk, drinking hot beer and high on malaria tablets. "Hey, you old sergeant asshole, get out of that bed and bring your ass back to work." Jeff's laughter still rang in Blake's ears. Then Blake remembered Jeff pulling a long length of string from one of his jungle fatigue trouser pockets. He held one end on Blake's head and said, "Hold this." Then he stretched the string down to Blake's toes.

Blake remembered saying, "What the hell are you doing?"

Old Jeff came back with, "What the hell do you think I am doing? I am measuring you for a body bag."

"Get your ass out of here, Sanders," Blake yelled at him. They both began laughing.

"Here, bitch, have a beer," Jeff said with more laughter.

Damn, I miss that crazy guy, Blake thought as he wiped a tear from the corner of his right eye. *He was a real trooper.*

Going through Turkish Customs was no fun, and it took hours to get out of the airport. When Blake arrived at the Ritz-Carlton, his Turkish door attendant friend, George, greeted him. "Welcome. May I be of service to you today, Mr. Tanner?"

"Thanks, George. Later I will need a taxi. I want to go shopping at the Grand Bazaar."

Blake called the office of Mr. Sarraf, which was located in the Rug and Jewelry shop inside the Grand Bazaar. The Turk seemed happy to talk with Blake. He was especially happy when Blake told him that he had seen his lover, Gloria. Mr. Sarraf invited Blake to have lunch with him around two o'clock, and asked if he could come to his shop to meet before going to lunch.

As Blake walked in the main entrance of the Bazaar, the man who owned the leather shop recognized him from his last visit.

"Welcome, sir, I will get us some chai while you look at my leather jackets. You forgot to come back during your last visit."

Shit, now I will have to buy a leather jacket, Blake thought. He could use another jacket, the price was right, and the quality was top of the line. While the shop owner was in the back room, Blake again took in the distinct aroma of various herbs that you can only find in the marketplaces of Istanbul. Looking around at the shops across from the leather shop, he overheard the merchant talking with what sounded like a man and woman from Ireland. "No worry, sir, I will bill your credit card in three different payments. I trust you." Only in Turkey would you hear a businessperson say that.

The shop owner returned from the back room with an armful of leather jackets. "These are especially for you, my friend," he said with pride. Just then a young boy arrived with a carrier filled with small glasses of chai.

"I sure like your chai," Blake complimented him. "How about a dark brown waist-length jacket?"

After the fifth jacket, he found the one that he liked. After short bargaining, a reasonable price was negotiated. Blake looked at his watch as the shop owner was wrapping up the new leather jacket that he had purchased. "Oh, I almost forgot," said the shop owner with excitement in his voice, "I like to take photographs of all the nice people who buy my leather goods. Would you please put your coat on, and I will take a Polaroid picture so I can add it to my photo gallery?"

"Sure, why not. Where is your photo gallery?"

Quickly the man pulled a large photo album out from behind the counter. "This is one of many albums I have. After I take your picture, I will place you with my American friends and customers."

After Blake had his picture taken and the man proudly showed him the finished photograph, he said, "I have the photographs in alphabetical order so I can show my customers pictures of their friends who are wearing my leather goods."

"I'll be damned," Blake said clearly. A thought immediately came to him: maybe Frank Pane was also in Istanbul at the same time as his wife was. "Could I look at your album of people with the name beginning with the letter S?"

He pulled out another large photo album and laid it in front of Blake.

Blake started looking for the name Jeff Sanders. Maybe Frank Pane bought a jacket here, and he was using Jeff's name. After turning page after page, he was shocked when he saw a recent colored picture of Frank Pane wearing the black jacket that he wore for the photo session at Jeff's engineering firm. Below the picture was the name Jeff Sanders, Atlanta, Georgia, USA.

"Do you remember this man?" Blake asked, pointing to the picture.

"Oh, yes, I remember Mr. Sanders very well. His beautiful wife also bought a leather jacket from me." He turned to a page and pointed to a picture of Rhonda Pane. Directly below was the name Gloria Sanders.

"This is so funny," Blake cheerfully said. "Mr. and Mrs. Sanders are good friends of mine. They did not leave a business card, did they?"

"I believe they did. Let me go through my files." After a few minutes, the man emerged from below the counter, and he handed two cards to Blake.

Blake looked at the top card and saw Gloria Sanders' name on it. *Shit,* he thought, *Rhonda had copies of Gloria's business cards.* He then looked at the second card. It had the company logo of "HELLAS INVESTMENTS" imprinted in dark blue at the top of the card. The name on the card was Jeffery Sanders, Director of International Investments. Home office: Athens, Greece.

Picking up the large plastic bag that held his new leather jacket, he walked toward Sarraf's shop. *Now,* he thought, *if this meeting reveals more unexpected surprises, I will have a damn heart attack. This is what causes a man to drink.* A smirk came to his face. *Yeah, right, Tanner, like you need an excuse.*

Sarraf seemed just as happy to see Blake as he had sounded during their telephone conversation. The two men sat down in comfortable dark brown leather chairs, and a young boy immediately served them chai and a dish of shelled pistachio nuts.

"So, how have you been, Mr. Tanner?"

"I am doing great, just great. Thanks for asking. I was able to give your pictures to Gloria. There must have been a mix-up and you gave me the wrong roll of film." Blake waited for the reaction of the Turk.

"Oh no, there was no mix-up. The roll of film was taken while Miss Gloria and I were in Antalya."

"That's real peculiar." He sure did not want the man to go berserk, pull out a sword, and take his anger out on him, but now was the crucial time to tell the man the downright truth. "My friend, you have been betrayed by a woman posing as Gloria Sanders."

Mister Sarraf sat straight up in his chair. "What do you mean by that, Mister Tanner?"

Blake pulled out an envelope with three pictures in it, one of Rhonda Pane and two of Gloria Sanders.

The man looked at the photo of Rhonda, smiled, and licked his lips. "This is my beautiful Gloria."

Blake then handed him the pictures of Gloria Sanders. "What a beautiful woman. Is she Miss Gloria's sister?"

"No, she is not her sister. She is the real Gloria Sanders."

The Turk jumped up from his chair, his jaw tightened, and his eyes flashed anger and hurt. The words of disbelief erupted from his mouth. "How could this be, how could this happen? Why would a woman do this to me, or to any man?"

"Honestly, I am sorry to bring you such bad news, and I sure don't wish to cause you more heartache than you already have, but there has to be a motive why this woman portrayed herself as Gloria Sanders. I have no explanations, but I do have my own gut feelings about why the act, and why she chose you. I would very much like to ask you a few questions, and maybe we will come up with some explanations."

"Please, ask me, and I will seriously attempt to understand why my Miss Gloria used me and lied to me." It was evident that the man was hurt, embarrassed, and stripped of his ego and pride.

"First of all, I will tell you the absolute truth about why I am here." Blake explained who he was, and who he was in a contract with. "The real Gloria was married to one of my best friends, who police claim took his own life this past September. I do not believe he committed suicide, but I have no evidence of my suspicions. Do you have any ideas why this woman would enter into an affair with you? I certainly am not talking about your appearance or your manhood, as I am sure many women are chasing you and wishing to share their life with you. You must be very wealthy, and you must have many outside investments."

The man was quiet for a few seconds or so and then he replied, "Yes, I am extremely wealthy, and yes, I have many off-shore investments. Gloria approached me about a Greek investment company. She told me that investing in bridges that were being built in Great Britain would bring me huge dividends. Gloria, or whoever she really is, introduced me to her brother Jeffery Sanders, who is the director for international investments. Gloria was pushing me to invest with her brother's company, and they were repeatedly asking me to put up five million U.S. dollars."

Blake showed Mr. Sarraf a photograph of Frank Pane. "Is this Jeffrey Sanders?"

After looking at the picture, he said, "He is the brother to Gloria?"

"No, my friend, he is Rhonda Pane's husband, Frank Pane. They both are employed as senior managers for an international engineering company in Atlanta, Georgia. Did you actually meet with the alleged brother, Frank Pane? And did he discuss with you the investment?"

"He did, they both did. Gloria said that I could transfer the five million dollars from my off-shore account in Malta to her brother's investment company headquarters in London. She was very persuasive, and every time I asked a relevant question, she wanted to make love to me. Now I understand sex was a cover up for her to persuade me to transfer the money to her brother and his company. I understood that her brother worked in Athens, but she kept changing the subject when I brought it up." He hung his head and shamefully said, "Most rich men are vulnerable to beautiful women, especially Turkish or Middle East men. We have a weakness for blond, blue-eyed women."

"Thanks for telling me the truth and providing me with much-needed valuable information." Blake sat motionless staring at the pictures hanging on the wall of the office. His eyes stopped at a picture of a family dressed in their native Turkish clothing. With his hand still wrapped around the chai cup, Blake walked over to where the framed picture was hanging. "I can't believe what I am seeing," he said.

"What do you say?"

"Is this your family?"

"Yes, it is my family taken on a holiday in London, just before my wife died last year."

"Who is this young lady?" Blake pointed to a dark-haired beauty. The woman was fair-skinned and looked out of place with the darker-skinned people.

"That is a close friend of my daughter, Julie Spenser, and she attended the same university in London as my daughter. Such a delightful girl. Her father is an international antique dealer, old English furniture, you know. I believe he is quite wealthy."

Blake frowned. "I know her. I met her while I was in London investigating a lead that I found in Atlanta."

"What a small world it is," the Turkish man said with a slight smile.

Blake shrugged, nervously looking at the picture. "I take it that you met Julie's father while you were in London?"

"I did and what a very nice man he is. He was so afraid that his daughter would marry a man who was not British and take her away from London."

"Well, Mr. Sarraf, we have ourselves a delicate situation here. We definitely need to work together to find the underlying cause of the plot to extort five million dollars from you, and involve Miss Spenser in some way."

"I certainly will help in any way possible. Just tell me what you need me to do, and it will be done. You do not know my personal background, Mr. Tanner, but I was an intelligence officer in the Turkish Army before I got into the exporting business. I have many influential friends in the Turkish government."

"Very interesting. Thank you. Now I will give you my personal background." Blake gave a quick overview about his military and federal service career. He explained how he fit into the picture of investigating the death of his friend. "My given name is Blake. Can I call you by your first name?"

"My given name is Erhan, pronounced *Air-hawn.*"

"We need to make suitable plans before I depart," said Blake. "Are you sure that you want to get involved with this mysterious official investigation? It could turn out to be very dangerous."

"Turkish men are warriors. We have been fighting since the beginning of time. The only thing that I am afraid of is a blond-headed woman with blue eyes." He began laughing; then Blake joined in. "Now let's go get rip-roaring drunk and make some plans," said Erhan, and they both started laughing again.

The two newly found friends did get rip-roaring drunk, and they did come up with a good plan. Maybe it was the raki, or maybe it was the Chivas Regal; either way, they had a plan.

Blake departed the next morning for New York with a head that felt like the Astrodome. He thought, *I am too damn old to have a hangover. A man at my age knows better, but sometimes the stupid comes out in a man, especially me.*

Just hours earlier he had been in Istanbul; now just a few hours from landing in New York, Blake Tanner knew he was on to something that was out of his jurisdiction. His job was not to get involved with international extortion, but he sure was deeply involved.

Funny, many men would like to be in my boots right now, he thought. Flying in first class at thirty-eight thousand feet above the Atlantic Ocean, and being paid one thousand dollars a day, plus expenses. Blake was always in deep thought, which in his line of employment was a natural habit.

CHAPTER 11

December 14, New York City

Blake and Erhan put their criminal investigator minds together and came up with a well-constructed plan that would catch the Panes in a criminal act to extort money. It would be Blake's job to dig up everything that he could about the Panes. Erhan would find out what he could about Julie Spenser.

The first line of business for Blake would be to meet with Donald Higgins and update him. He would not tell him everything. He did not trust anyone just now, except Mary Stewart and his Turkish friend, Erhan.

Blake was able to spend a few minutes with Mary before his meeting with Donald Higgins. Somewhere deep down he knew that he loved Mary, and he felt that she really loved him. Despite their age difference and the gray in his hair, he could feel the vibes when he was around her.

"How have you been?" Mary asked, rolling her flashing green eyes. "I think about you every day."

"Doing good, just thinking about you every day." He gently touched Mary's hand. "You keep thinking about me, darlin', and you will never sleep." Then he smiled and winked at her.

"You're right, Mr. Tanner, and I don't go to sleep without thinking of you. Can we meet this evening?"

"You bet. I need some assistance professionally, and I need some help in other ways." He gave her another big Tanner grin.

As Blake approached Donald Higgins' desk, he ran over in his mind again what to tell him about Erhan willingly assisting with the investigation. The initial contract made verbally between him and Higgins provided Blake full control of the investigation, and he could do as he pleased.

"Nice to see you again, Mr. Tanner," said Higgins as the two men shook hands. "Where do we stand on the investigation?"

Blake briefed Donald on the plot to extort money from Erhan and the suspicions he had about Rhonda and Frank Pane. "Somehow all of this is a very important part of how Jeff died, and why he died. I ask you to trust me and have patience."

"I trust you, and you are getting closer to the absolute truth, I can feel it."

"Tomorrow or the next day I hope to finish with my investigation in the States, and then I will go back to Europe and hopefully conclude the investigation. I will probably exceed the travel budget, but you have given me the green light to do as I see fit with travel arrangements."

"Sure, I'll be here if you need me. Do whatever it takes," Donald told Blake as he walked him to the door of his office.

"How about dinner this evening?" Mary asked Blake as he walked up to her desk. Without waiting for his answer, she said, "I'll pick you up in front of the hotel around seven-thirty, and we will go somewhere special. All right with you, Mr. Cowboy Man?"

"How can I say no to a beautiful woman like you?" He smiled and grinned with sheer excitement.

"Yeah, yeah, bullshitter, I bet that's what you say to all the ladies." She smiled back at him and rolled her shoulders.

She was so different from the other women he had met since Annie died. She was truthful and sincere; no bull crap in her life. *There was always that age difference, but this is the new era for dating and marriage*, he thought. *Do what makes you happy is what they say. What the hell is twenty years when it comes to love?*

Wearing starched Wrangler jeans and a blue button-down sport shirt under a black leather jacket, Blake swaggered up to the hotel bar. "Johnnie Walker Black, on the rocks. Make it a double please," he politely said to the bartender.

The evening was cold as Blake stood waiting for Mary. When she arrived in front of his hotel, she was riding in the company limo. "Want a ride, cowboy?" she cheerfully said, leaning up to open the backseat door.

"Damn right I do, and I will shoot the first Indian I see, and rape the first woman who gets in my way." Blake slid in the backseat beside Mary and gave her a passionate, long kiss. "I sure like your vanilla-musk body spray. The scent of it makes me weak in the knees."

"Hot damn, I like this," Mary said. "Oh and, James, take your time," she said to the limo driver. "Well, his name is Teddy, but that's okay." She embraced Blake and kissed him as if she had not seen him in years.

The pleasant aroma of grilled steaks and sautéed vegetables filled the air as they entered the restaurant through stained glass double doors. "Good evening, Miss Stewart, your table is ready," said the tall, thin host at the front door.

"So, Miss Stewart, do you come here often?" Blake asked with a grin.

"Yes, I do, Mr. Tanner, but only with special guests."

They began with a double scotch for Blake and a glass of chardonnay for Mary. As they dined, Blake filled Mary in on what he thought she should know about his investigation.

"Sounds so exciting," said Mary. "I want to go on a vacation to Europe so bad I can taste it. I seriously doubt if I will ever be able to go."

"If you would go with me I would love to take you on a long vacation to an exotic location. You interested?"

Mary leaned across the table and kissed Blake lightly on his lips. "Does that give you my answer, you dear sweet man?"

"Damn sure does. Do you have any problem with our age difference?"

"You must be out of your mind. I find you to be the most handsome, mysterious, as well as the sexiest man I have ever met in my life. You look great, and I am falling in love with you."

"Be careful, my darlin', and thanks." He placed his hand on hers and felt the warm flow of the blood pumping through her veins. "I am not a very good catch. I'm getting old, I have two grown daughters, I am a smart ass, and I have a dirty Army mouth."

"Kiss me, dirty mouth," she said hotly. "Just shut up and kiss me."

She was beautiful lying in her queen-sized bed with the sunlight peeping through the open window blinds. Blake finished drying off after taking a long hot shower; he brushed his teeth and looked around the door at Mary as she shifted in her sleep. Taking a hot shower was good medicine for him; he got a lot thinking done, and he could plan his day. This was the first time Blake had spent the night at Mary's apartment, and it was nice. She really knew how to decorate. *I like her taste*, Blake thought. *I bet she would make one hell of a good wife.*

Blake was dressed and in the kitchen trying to find out how Mary's coffeepot worked.

Mary put her arms around Blake and kissed him. "I'll fix the damn coffee, and you just stand at attention until I come back for you." Mary started the coffee and came back to where Blake was standing. She slid up against him and kissed his waiting lips. "Is it hot in here or is it just me?" Then she laughed, a low, sexy laugh.

"Damn, woman, don't do that to me. You know how I get when I am around you."

"I do know how you get. Now come with me. I have the timer on the coffeepot set for fifteen minutes. Can you handle me in that short of time?"

"Maybe, or maybe only two or three minutes." He followed her to the bedroom.

"Where are you going to next?" Mary asked Blake as they ate breakfast.

He turned his head to look at the beautiful redhead. "Atlanta, going back to Atlanta, and then probably back to Europe for one last time."

"You will call me, won't you?"

"Of course, you know I will."

"Want me to go with you to the airport?" Mary asked as she sprayed her ever-present scent of vanilla musk, her signature fragrance, on her neck.

He put his arm around Mary and softly said, "No thanks, I'll grab a taxi from the hotel. I will ride the metro with you as far as my hotel. How does that sound?"

"Good. I want to spend as much precious time with you as possible. Am I being pushy?" Mary then kissed him.

He could not believe that the check-in process at JFK went so smoothly. *Thank God for small favors*, he thought as he boarded his flight to Atlanta.

Tanner's mind was on Rhonda and Frank Pane. He thought about his plans for a few minutes, then got up from his seat and walked up to the galley. He urgently needed to move around to clear his head and to stretch his legs. After a short conversation with the flight attendants, he took his seat and put his mind in motion. Tanner had worked on plenty of cases in his long history of investigating. *You just cannot solve every case you work*, he thought. This particular case was special, and Jeff Sanders was special. Deep down he knew that the executive couple had something to do with Jeff's death; he could feel it in his bones.

The flight to Atlanta was uneventful, which pleased Blake. He did finalize plans of calling Gloria, attempting a dinner engagement with the Panes, and of calling Erhan in Istanbul. *My ass is getting tired of airplane seats*, he thought. At least he was sitting in front of the plane instead nestled between two fat, talkative software sales representatives from Hackenpuke, USA.

It was drizzling when Blake left the airport for his hotel. *Damn, another hippie taxi driver. Why can't they forget about protesting against the U.S. military?*

The sound of the taxi driver honking his horn as he stopped in front of the hotel brought Blake back to reality. "See, the bastard is so ignorant and rude he honks his horn at the hotel attendant. Get off it, Tanner," he said to himself. Now he was so pissed off that he was talking to himself aloud.

He did give the taxi driver a couple of bucks, just out of respect for all the honest American cab drivers in the U.S.

Tanner had not felt this prejudice since he returned to the States from his last tour in Vietnam. It was March 1973, and the hippie bastards were still camped out at the San Francisco airport, carrying their signs and yelling their anti-war chants. Merle Haggard had it right with his hit song, "The Fightin' Side of Me, If You Don't Love It, Then Leave It."

Maybe if he drank enough scotch, he might be able to forget his earlier days of hate and discontent toward anti-war demonstrators. He knew that was not the answer; one or two drinks would be just fine. He still had not forgiven Jane Fonda, and he would not watch any of her movies. He could still hear the screams of pain and see the death of his fellow soldiers.

Blake remembered Jeff's reaction to an article that appeared in the *Pacific Stars and Stripes* while they were in Vietnam. On the front page was a picture of young American college students protesting at the front gate of Fort Bragg, North Carolina. Jeff was so pissed off and upset that he volunteered to go on a night reconnaissance mission, although he had just returned from a five-day mission that morning. "Goddamn hippie bastards, don't they know that we are over here fighting for their freedom? If they loved America as I do then they would not be protesting against their own brothers and sisters." Jeff just could not understand the logic behind the peaceniks and hippies movements. He vowed that if he got out of Vietnam alive he would try to tell the American public the absolute truth about the war in Southeast Asia. That was Jeff Sanders; he was a genuine American hero.

CHAPTER 12

December 16, Atlanta

"Good morning, International Atlanta Engineering. How may I direct your call?"

"Mrs. Pane, please. This is Blake Tanner."

"Thank you, sir, I will see if she is busy."

"This is Rhonda Pane. Nice to hear your voice, Mister Tanner. How may I help you today?"

"Good morning. Are you and your husband free for dinner this evening? I would certainly like to show my gratitude for your assistance with arranging Jeff's memorial."

"Where can we meet you? And what time is convenient for you?"

"Eight o'clock at The Nava. Will that fit into you and your husband's schedule?"

"That is fine with us. We will see you this evening, and thank you. Nice choice, for The Nava is one of our favorite restaurants," Rhonda said in her mysterious and sexy voice.

What a beautiful creature. Too damn bad she is a criminal, Blake thought.

Blake then called Gloria and asked if he could come by her office tomorrow morning. He was booked on a six o'clock flight tomorrow evening, where he would fly to either London or Istanbul, depending on his meeting with Rhonda and Frank Pane.

"We will have coffee in my office."

Blake gave a lot of thought as to his approach toward getting Rhonda and Frank to make a couple of slips during their conversation. He would try all the tricks of the trade that he had learned over the years.

Blake called his friend Erhan in Istanbul on his satellite phone, as he wanted all the crucial information he could get before his dinner engagement with Mr. and Mrs. Pane. "Erhan, how the hell are you doing, my friend?" Blake said after the familiar voice greeted him. "Have any good news for me today?"

"Hello to you, Blake, Yes, I have very good news. It is shocking news, but I think it will assist you with your investigation. My friends in the Turkish military and the British Embassy found out that there is such a company as Hellas Investments, in Athens, and after contacting them, my friends were informed that no individual by the name of Jeffery Sanders was employed with their company. However, a Jeffery Sanders had visited their office and gathered information about investments. They also informed me that the bank in London that the so-called Gloria told me about is actually associated with Mexcon Engineering Company in Mexico City."

"I'll be damned. Now, that is very interesting. Confusing, but interesting. Would you consider going along with meeting Rhonda Pane? Or, Gloria, as you know her. I could bring up your name this evening at my dinner engagement, and maybe Rhonda will contact you, or you could contact her. I believe it is necessary to contact the investment company in Athens. They may be able to provide me with some valuable information."

"I will assist you. After all, I have nothing to lose but money, and I have everything to gain, having sex again with the beautiful blond-headed creature." Erhan began laughing.

"We can arrange for you to go along with their investment fraud, and you could agree to wire the money to the London account, with one of your friends in London posing as a representative of the bank."

"Good, let's work it. I want to get back to my normal life, but I must admit this does bring back memories and excitement from my old days."

"With the time difference between Atlanta and Istanbul, I will call you after I meet with the Panes. Is that a go, Erhan?"

"I will be waiting for your call, my friend."

Blake drafted an official letter of appreciation addressed to International Atlanta Engineering Inc. (attention: the Panes) thanking them for their generous support with Jeff's memorial. Jeff would get his memorial, but only after Blake found out why he died and if it was indeed suicide or murder.

Blake arrived early at The Nava restaurant to scope out the surroundings and request a table that was secluded so he could talk freely with Rhonda and Frank. During Blake's assignment at Fort Benning, he and his wife Annie and friends came to The Nava on many occasions. One of the waiters remembered Blake, as he was always a good tipper and was very kind and friendly to the waiters and restaurant staff.

"Welcome back, sir. I have not seen you in here for a long time."

"I live in Colorado now, and I only get back to Atlanta occasionally." Looking at the name tag the waiter had pinned on his jacket, Blake said, "Thanks, Larry, for remembering me. I have two special guests who will dine with me at seven-thirty. Can you seat us over in the corner so we can talk business in private?"

"Consider it done. Will you want to pre-order? Or should I wait for you to order after your guests arrive?"

"We will probably order your house special, Kobe flank steak, and a few bottles of cabernet. Right now I need a scotch on the rocks."

Blake slid a fifty-dollar bill in Larry's hand as he walked by.

"Thank you, sir." He was smiling from ear to ear as he walked toward the bar.

Blake was sitting at the end of the bar when Rhonda and Frank Pane walked in the main entrance of the restaurant. *Holy shit*, Blake thought as he looked at Rhonda. She was dressed in a light blue dress that showed off most of her gorgeous legs. She must have been in her mid-forties, but she could pass for a woman in her twenties. *Good for Erhan. He will have fun trying to send her to jail.* Frank Pane looked the same, nice-looking, but Blake knew he was no good, and he looked like a sneaky prick who probably could not be trusted.

Larry, the waiter, met the Panes and escorted them over to where Blake was standing at the bar. Blake held out his hand to Rhonda. "Nice to see you both," he said and then shook Frank's hand. "Shall we go to our table and have a drink?"

The waiter showed them to their table, which was located next to a window overlooking the Atlanta skylights. "I hope this table is all right," Blake said as the two sat down across from him.

"What have you been doing, Mr. Tanner?" Rhonda asked in her soft, sexy voice.

"Oh, just catching up on my traveling. I have been visiting locations that I have never been before, such as London and Istanbul." He watched the two of them for any body language that would alert him that they were not comfortable with his answer. They both did a little shifting in their chairs, and Rhonda took a drink of water. "Have you two ever been to either of those locations?"

Frank answered, "I have never been to Istanbul, and I hear it is a great place to visit. I have been to London on business a couple of times, and I liked England. I went one time with Jeff Sanders, back in June or July of last year."

"How about you, Mrs. Pane? Have you had the opportunity to visit outside the United States?"

Rhonda hesitated as the waiter took their drink orders. "The company does not like for their vice president to travel outside the U.S. I have been to Paris and Frankfurt on holidays, but that is about it."

Many diverse thoughts were coming to Blake. Now they were both telling a deliberate lie. Hell, they would have entrance and exit stamps in their passports. This spoiled the plan with the possibility of Rhonda calling Erhan. Erhan would just have to call her. "While we are waiting for our drinks, I wanted to present you with this letter of appreciation and a personal thank you to the two of you for supporting the memorial that I am arranging for Jeff. The memorial would not have been completed if it had not been for both of you generously providing support."

"We are happy that we could help out with such an honorable contribution to our friend," Rhonda replied.

"It's the least we could do for Jeff," Frank said quickly.

During the evening, Blake tried to ask a few questions without alerting the two that he was on to their game. The Panes started to get a little jittery, so Blake changed the subject so as not to alert them of his devious intentions. For a security guru, Frank was not very swift. A seasoned veteran would have caught on to Blake's game.

"We really hate to call it an evening," said Rhonda. "My mother is a house guest, and we do not want to leave her alone as she is not feeling well."

Lying bitch, Blake thought. "I understand, and I appreciate you taking the time to have dinner with me. Again, thanks for your support with the memorial. I do hope your mother feels better. Oh, one more thing. Is Jeff's old office still vacant?"

"Sorry, we had all of his personal effects packed and delivered to his residence," answered Rhonda.

The three of them bid each other good-bye. Blake watched them get in their BMW 750 parked in front of the restaurant. They drove away seeming to be in a big rush. *Probably to break away from me*, he thought.

After entering his hotel room Blake immediately called Erhan. "Our plans have changed, my friend. Rhonda Pane told me that she had never been to Istanbul, so there was no way I could tell her that I knew you. Can you call her and coax her to come to Istanbul? I suggest that you tell her that you have decided to go along with her and invest the five million. The plan should work as they are after your money."

"I can do that. Matter of fact I will make the invitation when we hang up."

"Damn good move. If I fly to London, could you have your friends in the British Embassy meet with me? I have a proposal that I know will work. It will take some air miles and coordination, but it can be done."

"Of course. How did my Gloria look this evening?" Erhan asked.

Blake answered quickly, "As we say in America, she looked hot. We will have our plan in effect before you arrange to transfer the five million. We sure as hell do not want you to lose the money."

"And as they say in our military and yours, 'Roger that,'" Erhan said, and he was still laughing when the two completed their conversation.

Blake gave Mary a quick call from his hotel room. He told her that if she saw Donald to please tell him everything was going as planned and on schedule.

"I miss you, Tanner. Please be careful."

The fried eggs, bacon, and grits hit the spot for breakfast. After another cup of coffee, Tanner was ready to begin his day. Sounds of the morning traffic and the nauseating smell of motor vehicle exhaust fumes reminded him why he did not live in a large city. The only sounds of traffic he ever heard at his mini-ranch were an Army helicopter from Fort Carson flying over. His motto was *Don't drive up my driveway unless you are invited.*

CHAPTER 13

December 17, Atlanta

Blake met with Gloria at her office at nine-thirty for coffee and a fat-free doughnut, which tasted like a piece of cardboard. "Great to see you again. You look more beautiful every time I see you."

"I bet you say that to all the widows you meet. What's on your mind today, Blake?"

"Just wanted you to know that I will be gone for a week or so, and I wanted to wish you a Merry Christmas, if I have not returned to the States by then. Would it be possible to go through Jeff's personal effects that he had in his office? I need a few more facts about his work before I finish with his memorial."

"Sure. I will tell you where the spare key is hidden and provide you the code to the alarm system. I would very much like to go with you, but I have a sales meeting that will last most of the day."

"Thanks, Gloria. You know I will not disturb anything. Well, maybe get a glass of water and use your bathroom, and I will remember to put the toilet seat back down when I finish."

That brought a laugh to Gloria. She leaned over and kissed Blake on the cheek. "You are my dearest friend, and being around you brings back memories of Annie, and all of us when we would get together. Jeff was such a happy man until about a month before his death. I just wish someone would find out the real truth."

"Maybe someone will." He hugged Gloria, kissed her on her cheek, and left her with her sorrow and broken heart.

The hidden key was exactly where Gloria told him it was. *Hell, anyone could find it,* Blake thought. He turned off the security alarm and went to the home office where Gloria told him the boxes of Jeff's personal effects from his office were stacked. *I really would like to find Jeff's daily planner. That would give me more information on his meetings in London,* he thought. As Blake went through Jeff's personal effects, he came across many items that brought back memories of his old friend. *What is this?* Blake wondered, and he opened the cover to a small black book that was lodged between two pages of a novel written by Stephen King. When Blake opened up the first page, he found entries dating back to April 2003. The last entry, dated September 18, 2004, was just three days before Jeff died. The entry was in Jeff's handwriting. Blake had seen his penmanship on many occasions, and it was definitely his. "El Chino Restaurant, 7 p.m., Come alone." *Wonder what that was about,* he thought. Maybe ole Jeff was actually screwing around on Gloria.

Blake took a seat in front of the desk and started reading the entries in the book, starting from the first page. Some of the entries made no sense whatsoever, and other remarks he understood. As he glanced at the dates where Jeff had made entries, he suddenly saw a name that struck a bell. "March 11, 2004, Meet Frank at the Airport Hilton bar, 7 p.m. Bring telephone number of Istanbul contact." He must be referring to Frank Pane, and the Hilton Atlanta Airport, and maybe Erhan was the contact. Why would Jeff have the telephone number and address of Erhan? Blake continued looking through the book and stopped at an entry made on April 16, 2004. "Meet Gloria at her office, 6:30 this evening, dress formal, International Antique Show, Hilton Airport." Jeff had accompanied Gloria to an antique show, and since it was international, there would be dealers and buyers attending from all over the world. *There does not seem to be anything wrong with attending a business trade show. Seems normal,* he thought.

He continued reviewing the pages of the little black book and when he got to May 23, 2004, Blake's heart seemed to stop. He looked away for a second and then returned his eyes to the entry in the book, just to make sure that his eyes were not deceiving him. "Transfer $50,000 from mutual funds account to account number 48594939, Barclays Bank, London." *Brother Jeff, what the hell were you doing?* Blake continued looking at the book entries, and they continued to make sense. The entry for June 15, 2004, read, "Get new passports for Gloria and me. Tell Gloria I misplaced both of our passports." Oh crap, ole Jeff was in trouble.

Tanner continued with his review of Jeff's little black book, and he was now beginning to see what had been going on between Jeff, Rhonda, and Frank Pane. The next entry really did it. "August 19, 2004, Rhonda met me in my office today. She demanded another $50,000, and of course, I rejected her demands. She told me that she would have Frank talk to me. I told her that if Frank came near Gloria or me I would waste him." Blake knew that he had discovered very important information, and he knew that most of it should be turned over to the FBI. Apparently, Jeff lost his daily planner or someone stole it, and then he started his secret entries in his book. It looked like Jeff was being blackmailed, and Gloria knew nothing about it. But why? That was the big question.

He then spotted another box sitting in the corner of the office. Since it had Jeff's name on it, he carefully opened it to see what he could find. As he went through the contents, he came across a bundle of what looked like brochures from international antique shows. He removed the large rubber band that was holding the contents and began to go through the stack of brochures. What would Jeff be doing with antique brochures? As he opened a brochure dated June 15, 2004, Blake noticed a note and numbers written on the inside edge of the first page: "Large dealer in Istanbul, Erhan Sarraf, Turkish rugs, jewelry, and gold. Gloria does not know him but he is on the millionaire list. Business telephone number, Istanbul. 90-212-461-9400, Ext 223."

Blake sat down in the chair and again put his mind in high gear. *Okay*, he thought, *Gloria does not know Erhan.* Jeff must have provided the information on Erhan to another person so he or she could contact him. *It has to be that son of a bitch Frank Pane and his bitch wife, Rhonda.* They were blackmailing Jeff, and it had something to do with Gloria's antique business. *Where in the hell do I go from here?* He now needed to dig up the reason for the blackmail, or find out if the Panes were even blackmailing Jeff. One last box and he would be out of there. "Bingo," he said as he dug through the last box and picked up a roll of undeveloped 35mm film. Blake put the film in his jacket pocket, and then he placed the boxes back in order. He left Gloria a note of thanks.

Blake asked the taxi driver to stop at a quick print photo shop. He asked the young man behind the counter if he could develop the film while he waited. After thirty minutes, the photo clerk handed Blake the envelope with pictures developed from the roll of film. He paid the clerk and quickly walked outside the shop. Anxiously he opened the film envelope. "Holy shit," he said aloud. The picture was of Jeff with a young and beautiful woman sitting next to him with her arm around his neck. Blake found more pictures of Jeff and the woman taken during the summer, as some of the pictures showed them both in bathing suits. The background restaurant signs in two of the pictures were in Spanish, and the surroundings looked like Mexico or Spain. He looked at the pictures again, and this time he examined every detail on the photographs. *Spain, these pictures were taken in Spain*, he thought. *What a beautiful young woman.* Ole Jeff was indeed having an affair, but it was in Spain and not in London. Blake must be correct; the Panes were blackmailing Jeff over his affair. *I just cannot figure where Erhan comes into play.* Why the Panes were using Jeff and Gloria's identity was a big mystery. *Looks like my next trip will be to Southern Spain. It's a tough job, but someone has to do it.* He smiled.

Talking with Mary gave Blake a warm feeling. She was now a big part of his life, and he could not get her off his mind. He still clung to the precious memories of Annie, but she would want him to move on with his life. Blake thought that she would approve of Mary. They always told each other that if one of them died first, the other was to meet a nice person to be with. Mary did make Blake Tanner happy.

CHAPTER 14

Blake knew that an expert would be required to review the photos and identify exactly where the pictures were taken. It did not take him long to find the telephone number of the professional expert. He made the phone call and contacted a retired Army civilian friend of his who lived in Atlanta. Glenn Webster was an intelligence expert who had worked with the Army CID for over thirty years. Glenn could look at a photograph and identify the exact location, and after a few scotches he could tell you the time of year and probably the time of day.

"Hey Glenn, you old warhorse. Blake Tanner, here. How the hell are you doing?"

"Great, where the hell are you?"

Blake met his friend at the nearest bar from Glenn's house. "What can I do for you, my friend?" Glenn said as he took a drink of his scotch on the rocks.

"Do you remember me talking about my old friend from Vietnam, Jeff Sanders?"

"Yes, I remember you telling me some wild tales about you two. How is Jeff?"

"He's dead, Glenn. The police report is recorded as a suicide, but I have my doubts. Will you look at these pictures and give me your professional opinion where and when they were taken?"

Glenn put on a thick pair of glasses and carefully studied the pictures one at a time. "Barcelona, Spain, in July."

Blake sighed and looked at the pictures lying in front of Glenn. "Damn, are you positive?"

"Does a grizzly bear shit in the woods?" he replied with a laugh.

"You're great. Thanks, bud. If you could tell me the young woman's name, it would make my job a lot easier." He laughed as if he had just cracked a joke.

"Her name is Casilda."

"You're shittin' me."

"No, no, I'm not. Take a look on the woman's right wrist and you will see a bracelet with her name engraved on it." Glenn handed Blake the thick glasses he had used for scanning the pictures.

Putting on the glasses, Blake looked at two of the pictures, and then he looked a second time. "I'll be damned, her name is Casilda, or she is wearing another person's bracelet. There are probably thousands of women in Spain with the same first name."

"You are absolutely wrong, my friend. The name Casilda is rare, and it comes with royalty. The name is taken from Saint Casilda, and you do have a very good picture that many people will remember such a beauty. You know the geographical location, and you can use a computer Internet, so get with it, Tanner." He took another drink of scotch and laughed softly at the expression on Blake's face.

"Thanks, Glenn, for your help. Next time we meet I will tell you how this all turns out."

By the time Blake returned to the hotel he was starting to put the puzzle together with some very valuable links. Pouring a double scotch into his glass filled with ice, he began writing down his thoughts as to how he would approach this confusing situation. His top priority was to find out how Rhonda and Frank fit into the picture surrounding Jeff's death. Now he would ask Erhan to arrange a business meeting with Rhonda, under the assumption that he had no doubts that she was Gloria Sanders. With the assistance of Erhan's friends in London, he would find out how Julie Spenser was involved, and why Frank Pane had an affair with her under the name of Jeff Sanders. He urgently wanted to find out about Jeff and his relationship with the beautiful young woman in Spain. With the help of Erhan, he would catch Rhonda and Frank with their plan of extortion and possibly espionage.

Blake grabbed his satellite phone and hit the instant dial key that would connect him with Erhan in Istanbul.

"How are you doing, my friend? Are you ready to do some espionage work, with some good tangible benefits?"

"If it involves the lovely blonde who calls herself Gloria, I am ready." Erhan laughed with excitement.

"You got it, brother. Can you persuade Rhonda to visit you in Istanbul? She can bring her sleazy husband along, you know, the one who says he is her brother. Then if you can convince them that you are ready to invest the five million, we will be on our way."

"I will do that, and after she accepts my offer, and I know that she will, I will contact my friends in London, and we will arrange for the transfer of the funds. My friends have already arranged a bogus account that cannot be detected or traced by anyone except us."

"Great. Please let me know when you have all of your plans in place. And, Erhan, be careful, my friend."

"I am always very careful, and where are you off to next?"

"Southern Spain. It's a crappy job, but someone has to do it. Talk to you later."

"Hello, Blake," Mary Stewart answered the telephone cheerfully.

"Hey, darlin', how are you doing? Is your passport up to date?"

"Did you say is my passport up to date?" Mary answered with a touch of confusion in her voice.

"That's what I said. How would you like to visit sunny southern Spain with me?"

"Are you joking with me, Tanner?" she said with delight in her voice.

"I would not joke with you about an opportunity for you to visit Spain with me. I will clear it with your boss if you are interested."

"Am I interested? My bags are halfway packed, and I am waiting for you. When do we leave?"

"I will return to New York tomorrow, and we depart for Spain this coming Saturday."

"Oh, Blake, that is wonderful. Should I pick you up at the airport?"

"No, thanks. I will just go on to the hotel and meet you at your office later in the afternoon. I will brief Donald, and then we can spend some time together."

"I miss you, and I will be happy to see you. You are starting to get under my skin, Mister Tanner."

"That's me, the get under your skin guy." He chuckled. "See you tomorrow, sweetheart."

Another boring flight from Atlanta to JFK, and then the circle jerk at the baggage claim area. *Why the airlines cannot make it easy for a person to travel is beyond me*, he thought. *Half of the workforce at the JFK airport needs to be fired and replaced with individuals who want to work, and people who have a decent personality. Half of them don't even speak English. You are on a roll again, Tanner.*

Blake got out of the Yellow Cab in front of the New York Mutual Insurance Company office just after two o'clock. As he walked toward the security screening area, the sound of his cowboy boots making a hollow noise on the marble floor alerted the security guards. They knew that this man was no local New Yorker. One of the two guards recognized Blake from earlier visits as he got closer to the entrance of the security area.

"Welcome, Mr. Tanner, nice to see you again," said the older of the two guards. "Are you here to see Miss Stewart?"

"Yes, I am, and thanks for remembering me."

Mary looked up just as Blake casually walked up to her desk with a big smile on his face.

Mary's eyes beamed as she greeted him and asked him how his flight was.

Blake hesitated for a few seconds, just gazing at Mary. "Good morning, back to you, and the flight was okay. You're looking lovely this morning, as usual."

Mary laughed as Blake handed her a single red rose. "Thank you, how thoughtful. You cowboys amaze me—tough on the outside, but a big heart on the inside."

A grin spread across Tanner's mouth, and his eyes flashed with mischief. "Is Higgins free?"

She glanced at him again. "He is expecting you. Go on in, the door is not locked."

"Mr. Tanner," Donald joyfully said as he stood up from his desk and greeted Blake with a hearty handshake. "You must have some news, as Mary gave me a short briefing about you needing her assistance in Spain."

"I do," answered Blake as he followed Donald to the chairs facing the large windows that overlooked the city. "She is the only one we can trust, and what a nice travel companion she will be." Leaning back in his chair Blake began briefing Donald on what he had discovered up to this point. "By you permitting Mary to accompany me to Spain for a few days, I believe that we can come up with concrete evidence that will lead me to the conspirators involved with Jeffery Sanders and to additional circumstances surrounding his death."

"Whatever you need, Mr. Tanner." From the table next to where Donald was sitting he picked up a long white envelope and handed it to Blake. "I don't want to be out of line, but I thought you might need a portion of your contact salary."

Without looking at the contents, Blake put the envelope in his jacket pocket. "Thank you, sir. I will add it to my retirement account, if I live long enough to take the time to enjoy it."

The overcast and cold afternoon was about gone when the insurance company limo stopped in front of the hotel. Teddy, the limo driver, was out and grabbed Blake's bags off the bellman's luggage cart before Blake got out the front door. Mary was in the backseat and smiling from ear to ear. Her eyes could beam airplanes through fog. She was one happy woman, and Mary Stewart was a woman who seemed to especially love Blake Tanner.

Blake slid in beside her, and she put her arms around him and kissed him before he hardly got his long legs inside.

"I hope this is going to be a great trip for us," Blake said cheerfully. "Checklist time. Do you have your passport?"

"Yes, well, I had better look again, Yep, I have it, and my international driver's permit, camera, traveler's checks, and my burning desire to be with you. How's that?"

"You got it all, girlfriend, especially the last item."

The check-in at Iberia Airways went very quickly. Blake's VIP travel agent had all the documents neatly arranged, and she had sent a special VIP letter to the business-class check-in supervisor. It read, "Special Customers, please treat with care."

After going through security, they went to the Iberia VIP lounge. Mary looked pretty in her light brown slacks and white sweater. "You're a beauty, my dear," Blake told her as he set a cup of cappuccino in front of her. "Maybe this will calm your nerves a little. You are as nervous as a cat shittin' peach seeds."

"Tanner, where do you come up with all those corny sayings? I never understand them, and why would a cat be eating peach seeds?"

"Never be like the other men. Keep the women guessing, that is the Tanner way. See, you are laughing. You forgot about being nervous."

"No," she said, taking in a deep breath. "I am still nervous, but a happy nervous if you know what I mean."

"Yes, my dear, I know what you mean." He could not help but laugh aloud at her remarks.

Blake excused himself, slowly walked to the communications area, and gave Erhan a call from his satellite phone. He told Erhan that he would call him after they arrived at their hotel in Barcelona.

CHAPTER 15

December 22, Barcelona, Spain

Mary was so excited about finally fulfilling her dreams of visiting Spain that she just looked around the business plus cabin of Iberia Airways Flight 1149, and then hugged Blake before she broke out in a big smile. She was sending out sparks like a brush fire.

"Are you all right?" Blake asked with a laugh of happiness for Mary.

"Thanks for bringing me. Oh, I am so excited that I have forgotten how to speak Spanish."

"It will come back to you. Just speak Spanish to the flight attendant when she comes around," he said, and he watched Mary break out in another big smile. Blake turned and gazed out the window at the black sky and stars that seemed to be moving at the same speed as the Airbus 343. *I hope to hell we can find the mysterious and beautiful woman friend of Jeff's*, he thought. *Casilda, what a beautiful and catchy name. Now to find out her last name. That is the big million-dollar question.*

"Have you ever stayed at the hotel we are booked in? Is it on the beach? Can we walk to the city center of Barcelona from there? Oh, hell, too many questions, I'm sorry," Mary said.

"All the answers are yes, and, no, you are not asking too many questions." Blake smiled again at Mary's excitement. "Just remember, we are married, so act like a nag, and bitch at me all the time."

Mary hit Blake on the arm. "You know that I would not do that to you. I love you and respect you too much for bitching. Now, order me another glass of wine or I will nag and bitch at you." She leaned over and kissed Blake on the cheek. "All right, cowboy?"

After a change of aircraft at Madrid, they would fly to Barcelona. They cleared customs at Madrid. Spanish customs was a blast. Mary soon found out that the Spanish people have a great sense of humor, and they have an unconditional love for life. Blake had exchanged currency at JFK before they departed, so he and Mary walked from customs directly to their departing gate.

The Hotel Gran Rey Don Jaime had a five-star rating, and it was beautiful. Again, Mary looked around and just stared at the magnificent décor of the hotel. "My God, this is so beautiful. Thanks, Blake, for bringing me."

"For the twentieth time, you are so very welcome, my dear." He then gently took hold of Mary's arm as they followed the porter toward the elevator.

The luxurious suite had one bedroom with a living and a dining area. Adjoining the living area was a walkout balcony that overlooked the ocean and the white sands of the shoreline. Mary stood erect with her face in the swirling wind, smelling the soft, cold sea breeze and catching the wonderful aroma of cooking olive oil. Mary loved the smell of olive oil. She had fond memories of growing up in an Italian neighborhood where the everyday use of olive oil for cooking was a normal way of life. The sun spiraled lazily, marking the beginning of a beautiful day.

After a long hot shower together, they had breakfast served in their suite. "Are you ready for some work?" Blake asked as he poured more coffee from the porcelain pot into their half-empty matching cups.

"What do we do first?" asked Mary, her eyes lighting up like fireworks on the Fourth of July.

"We will explore the area where the pictures were supposedly taken of Jeff and the mystery woman. I think when we find the exact location, that then our gut feelings will take over." Blake took the last bite of his cheese omelet.

His satellite phone rang and the caller ID indicated the call was Erhan. Pushing the speaker mode button Blake answered, "Good morning, my friend, how are you doing?"

"Great," the familiar voice of Erhan greeted Blake. "I hope that I am not disturbing you. I have some very important information. I contacted Gloria, I mean Rhonda, and she will arrive in Istanbul the day after tomorrow. She said her brother Jeff, or really her husband Frank, is coming with her. I have willingly agreed to invest the five million with them. She really sounded excited. I am ready to put our plan in motion. Do you agree with me that we should make our move?"

"Yes, indeed. The timing is just right as Mary and I are in Barcelona, and we can fly to London from here so we can monitor the transfer of the funds. With help from your friends at the Turkish Embassy, our plans should work. By the way, I have you on the speakerphone.

"That is wonderful, just wonderful. I will keep you updated on the progress of our meeting, except the bedroom scenes, of course." Erhan began to laugh. "I could not help myself from making that remark. After we make the bogus transfer of funds to London, I will be on the first plane from Istanbul to London. I will meet you there."

"I will be happy to see you, and you can meet my friend Mary Stewart." Blake smiled at Mary, who sat across from him cradling her cup and sipping coffee. "She is not very pretty, and she is cross-eyed and a bleached-out redhead, but damn, what a body." Blake had to dodge the kick that Mary threw at him. She then slowly reached over and put her outstretched hand on his leg, and begin to rub it softly.

"She is beautiful. I know she is," said Erhan. "I will talk to you later, my friend, and regards to you, Miss Stewart."

"Adios, amigo," Blake told his Turkish friend, hoping that he understood a few words of Spanish.

The day was sunny and clear, and the blue sky was silent as Blake and Mary took a taxi to the beachfront area of Saint Sebastia. Glenn had identified the surrounding area from the pictures of Jeff and the pretty mystery woman named Casilda. Upon Blake's request, the taxi driver stopped in front of a restaurant that was in the middle of all the restaurants. The location where they stood was perfect, as they could see along the beach in two directions.

Raising her arms and taking in deep breaths of fresh ocean air, Mary blurted, "This is so beautiful. I believe that I could live here, I just love it, how wonderful."

"It is beautiful and refreshing here. I have always had a fondness in my heart for Spain." Blake looked to the west and then to the east at the rows of restaurants. "We had better split up or we will never find the right restaurant." Blake handed Mary copies of the pictures of Jeff and the woman named Casilda. "Let's meet back here in, say, an hour," he said, looking at his wristwatch. "We will then discuss what we have found. Are you going to be all right, my dear?"

"*Si*, I will be just fine, and my Spanish has come back to me." She turned and started walking quickly toward the row of restaurants going east. Turning around she waved at Blake and blew him a kiss; then she laughed and continued walking at a fast pace.

After about an hour, Blake walked back toward where he was to meet Mary. He'd had no luck at all, but he did have a strong feeling that they were in the same area where Jeff had been. He looked up and saw Mary waving her arms and walking at a fast pace toward him.

"I found it, I found the restaurant," she said with excitement in her voice. When she reached Blake, she put her arms around his neck and kissed him. "I found where the pictures were taken, and the owners know Casilda, and they remember your friend Jeff. The name of the restaurant is Casa Maria, and it is family owned. They have known Casilda since she was a little girl, and they know her family."

"You done good, girl. Let's go back and you can introduce me to them."

"They are waiting for us, and they are preparing a special seafood lunch in our honor. I don't believe they are aware of Jeff's death. They also told me that they could call Casilda and have her meet us for lunch, if we wanted."

Blake was silent and his mind was working like a clock as they walked toward the restaurant. "Let me talk with the family first, and then I can decide what will be the best plan of action. We still do not know who this woman really is, and she might not want to even talk with us, and she may not know that Jeff is dead."

The Casa Maria was a typical family-owned restaurant; small with inside and outside dining, and open the year round. Blake looked around at the surroundings of the outside dining area. It definitely looked like the same location that was in the pictures.

"Welcome, señor, to our restaurant. We have met your beautiful señora. Please come in. I am Carlos, and you will meet my wife Maria in a few minutes. We are preparing a special seafood lunch for the both of you. The señora tells me you would like to meet with our friend Casilda?"

"I am not sure she would want to meet with us, as we are friends with this man," Blake said and he showed the photograph of Jeff and Casilda.

The man broke out in a wide grin, "Oh, Mr. Jeff, we all love him so much. He is our good friend, and he is very good friends with Casilda and her family."

Now we are getting somewhere, Blake thought. "Have you seen Jeff lately?"

"July. It was in this past July when he was here with the Baccara family." Señor Carlos continued to look at the photograph, smiling and showing happiness in his eyes.

"The Baccara family?" said Blake. "So the woman in the photograph is Casilda Baccara?"

"*Si*, she is the oldest daughter of Dr. Jorge Baccara, and her mother is Señora Rosario Baccara. Mister Jeff is good friends with Dr. Jorge and Casilda. She is a respected doctor in his family practice."

What he heard took his breath away. "Did I hear you correctly, señor? The woman in the photograph is Dr. Casilda Baccara?" Blake asked without trying to sound overly inquisitive.

"*Si*, she is a doctor, just like her father. Mr. Jeff was sick with the cancer, and they were treating him, but I'm sure you already knew that."

Blake was caught by complete surprise, and it had been many years since he had been stumped for words. *What the hell*, he thought. He looked at Mary; then Mary looked back at Blake. "No, we did not know he had cancer. He probably did not want anyone to know. That was the way, and I mean that is the way he is. Come to think of it, Señor Carlos, it would be a splendid idea to invite Casilda to lunch, and her father also if he is free. You could tell them that we are very good friends of Jeff Sanders."

"Consider it done," said Carlos in perfect English. "Now, let us meet my Maria."

As Blake and Mary sat at a large table next to the window in the inside dining area, Carlos escorted an attractive older plump woman to their table. He introduced them to his wife, Maria, whom the restaurant was named after.

"I am so happy to meet friends of Mr. Jeff. You are so welcome to visit us," said Maria in broken English. With a flick of her wrist, she motioned at two young boy waiters who came to the table carrying the famed Spanish tapas and a pitcher of Peleon wine, which is natured in oak barrels. "That special process is what gives it its distinct taste and flavor," Maria explained.

"Oh, I have heard about real Spanish tapas ever since I was a little girl," said Mary. "Let's see, olives, nuts, cold cuts, cheeses, fried calamari, raw calamari, and small fried whitefish. I love this. It is wonderful, *gracias*."

"How about saving a little for me?" Blake laughed. "I do love to see you happy. You are not going to get sad on me when the truth comes out about Jeff, are you?"

"I will try and not let it bother me. I feel like I know Jeff, but, no, I will be all right. My father and mother used to take me to a little Spanish restaurant near our house when I was a little girl. I will never forget the tapas, the music, and the generous hospitality of the Spanish people. I have that same feeling right now. It is wonderful," said Mary, her eyes dancing.

The front door opened to the restaurant and in walked a trim, athletic-looking raven-haired beauty who appeared to be in her late twenties. "It's Casilda," Mary said softly to Blake. A tanned, silver-haired man followed her. "That must be her father, Dr. Jorge Baccara."

"You must be right, my dear. What a nice-looking father and daughter."

Carlos led the two guests toward the table where Blake and Mary sat. After introductions were made by Carlos, they all four sat down at the table that by now was covered with all sorts of food and wine. Blake looked at their guests and began the conversation by thanking them for meeting with Mary and him.

Casilda was the first to speak. "My father and I are very pleased to meet you both, and we are so happy to meet friends of our dear friend Jeffery. Have you seen him lately?"

Blake hesitated for a few seconds before answering. "I have bad news for you. Jeff is dead. He died in September of a gunshot wound to the head. The coroner and police report indicate that it was suicide."

"Why would he do that? His cancer was in remission," said the father, his voice cracking. Blake then looked over at the daughter; her eyes were filled with tears, and she begin to sob, holding both hands to her head.

Unusual for a doctor to cry, Blake thought. "We do not think that it was suicide. Jeff was not the type," Blake answered with a break in his voice. "Can you tell us more about Jeff and the medical treatment that you were giving him?"

"Yes, we both were providing care for him at our clinic and hospital. He was being treated with a new medicine that was discovered in Sweden, and this medication is not available for use in America," said the father. "His cancer was in remission, which is unheard of for patients who have contracted cancer caused by the deadly chemical Agent Orange, used by your government in Southeast Asia."

Blake gazed out the window at the open sea with tears filling his eyes. He felt so very bad for the loyal friends of Jeff, and he did not like the way they discovered Jeff's death. "This is a bad day, and we sincerely apologize for bringing you the bad news."

Casilda sat motionless and then her voice filled with emotion as she said, "Jeffery was a very special man, and we both got very attached to him."

"She looked at him as a big brother," the father said, "and I looked at him as a strong warrior who was fighting his battle for life. Our goal was to prolong his life for as long as possible, and the medication was working. He did have minor depression, which was caused by the medication, but other than the periods of depression, he was progressing just fine."

"In your medical opinions do you feel that Jeff was depressed enough that he would take his life?"

"Absolutely not," Casilda cried out. "Jeffery was in sound mind, and his pleasant attitude and outlook on life were very good for a man who knew that his lifetime would not be a long one."

Dr. Baccara was the expert on treating cancer patients. He had actively researched the deadly disease and its drastic effect on the human body. His research results were known in Europe and America. He sat quietly for a few minutes before he spoke. "You must be told that Jeffery had other problems besides his cancer. He did not say much, but I could tell in his voice, and I could see in his eyes that he was troubled. On one occasion during one of his medical treatments, he did drop a hint, or it was a slip of the tongue. Seemed as though he was talking about transferring large quantities of money to a private bank in Mexico, and then he mentioned London."

"That is very interesting. So maybe he had grief that was beyond the cancer and the extreme worry of dying before he was ready," Blake said, still fighting back his emotions.

Blake's satellite phone rang, and he jumped. He pulled out the phone and looked at the name on the screen. It was Erhan; he excused himself and went out on the patio to take the call in private.

Erhan's voice was calm and clear. "I am in London, all the plans are in place, and we are ready for you to arrive and provide us with further instructions."

"We are finishing up here. We will be there by tomorrow morning. Due to the holidays, all commercial airlines are booked. We will charter a jet at the Barcelona airport and fly to London as soon as possible. The key to this current situation is to move fast. Do you agree with me, my friend?"

"I do," Erhan answered, "and this part of the plan will be taken care of. Call me when you have a firm arrival schedule and a destination airport."

"Roger that. See you soon."

Blake and Mary said good-bye to the two doctors, and they thanked them for the valuable information surrounding Jeff's illness. They thanked the wonderful people at the restaurant and wished them all a Merry Christmas and a Happy New Year.

Since they would not depart for London until after midnight, they decided to spend Christmas Eve Spanish style. Blake was familiar with the Spanish customs as he and his family had spent a holiday season in Spain when his daughters were small. He explained to Mary that Christmas Eve was the first of three joyful celebrations during the holiday season. The hotel manager told Blake that they were having a Christmas Eve celebration and all of the hotel guests were invited at the expense of the hotel.

Mary wore a beautiful Spanish-style dress with a silver belt and knee-high black boots. Blake was more comfortable wearing slacks, a turtleneck sweater, and sport coat. Of course, he wore his brown Justin cowboy boots.

The Christmas Eve (Nochebuena) Blake and Mary both remembered the Spanish celebration started at the homes of the townspeople. They then flocked into the hotels, restaurants, and discos. Before long, they both were invited by friends of the hotel manager to join them at their table. The Spanish people were delighted when they found out Blake and Mary could clearly speak their language. Sparkling wine flowed like a river, and tables were covered with platters of seafood and cold meat cuts. The waiters brought out hot soup, which tasted like minestrone. After the soup followed a roast leg of lamb and suckling pig, with the typical apple stuck in the mouth of the pig.

"Spain is known for its desserts," Blake told Mary. "Have you eaten any Spanish desserts?"

"Yes, my parents would take me to a Spanish bakery when I was little. I believe the two most popular desserts are turrón and marzipan."

"Brilliant. You are correct, my dear. I do hope you are having fun."

"I am. Thank you, sweetheart. I am truly grateful to have you in my life." Mary kissed Blake, and he responded to her very passionately.

At the end of the evening, or early morning celebration, they bid good-bye to their gracious Spanish hosts and told them that they were scheduled to depart within a few hours.

"I will never forget this evening as long as I live," Mary told Blake. "Thank you again for making my life so wonderful. Do we have time to make love before going to the airport?"

"There is always time for lovemaking, my dear, always time," Blake said, taking hold of Mary's hand.

CHAPTER 16

Christmas Morning, London Heathrow Airport

Blake chartered a Citation business jet from an air charter company at the Barcelona airport. The early morning was dark and overcast, it was cold outside, and there was a light drizzle falling as he woke Mary from her fully reclined, light blue leather seat. "Let's go, sunshine. It's time to play the loving husband and wife again."

"Where are we?" Mary asked as she wiped her face off with a hot washcloth that the private flight attendant handed her. She stood up, straightened her dark blue sweater, and looked at her gray slacks to see if they were wrinkled; then she pulled her compact from her overnight bag and began to apply her makeup.

Blake stood up, banging his head on the low ceiling of the aircraft interior. "We are on the backside of London Heathrow, at a private charter company aircraft parking ramp. Erhan should be waiting for us."

Mary could not believe how luxurious it was to fly in a private jet and how quickly they had traveled from Barcelona to London. "Now I see why all the movie stars and rich people travel this way."

"Come on, Miss Movie Star, shake your pretty butt and let's get moving," Blake told her as he walked down the narrow stairs from the plane.

"Are we having fun yet?" A familiar voice came from the cold darkness. It was Erhan using his best James Bond impersonation.

"You do a ridiculous James Bond," Blake said. "Have you ever tried to impersonate a Turkish private investigator?"

"Only once, and I got shot. How was your flight?"

"Good, real pleasant. Just be careful when the New York beauty comes out. She is a bear when she doesn't get her beauty sleep."

"I heard that, Blake Tanner," Mary said as she walked gracefully up to where he and Erhan were standing. "Hello, Erhan. I am Mary Stewart, and regardless what Tanner has told you, I am a nice person."

"Yes, you are, and you are a beautiful person. Even standing in the dark with cold rain pouring down, you are stunning," Erhan told Mary.

"Thank you, sir," Mary said and put out her hand to Erhan.

"What did he say?" asked Blake.

"He said you were an arrogant American asshole," Mary said, and then she started laughing.

The three of them hugged each other on the tarmac, and they could have cared less about the cold rain.

Blake glanced quickly up into the dark and rainy London sky, and then focused his attention back to Mary and Erhan. He moved toward the VIP lounge, walking on the dark, wet tarmac with Mary and Erhan close beside him.

The warm, dry lounge felt good to the tired travelers. Blake suggested they go to the hotel where Erhan had made reservations earlier in the day, and get a few hours of sleep before going over their plans and strategies.

Erhan told Blake that he must fly back to Istanbul later in the afternoon as the Panes would arrive from New York on Thursday morning, and he had many urgent tasks to complete prior to their arrival. "The brother or husband—whoever that thief is—will stay at the Swiss Hotel, and his beautiful wife or whoever she is will stay with me at my apartment in Istanbul. That part of the plan is taken care of."

On the way to the hotel, Blake could not figure out why Jeff had chosen medical treatment in Spain instead of in the States. He was clear on the special medication that Jeff was receiving from the Barracas. *Gloria did not know that he had cancer, or she knew and did not want to tell me. The Panes were involved with extorting money from Erhan, blackmailing Jeff, and they sure as hell were suspects in Jeff's death. The easiest way would be to eliminate Rhonda and Frank Pane. It would be easy to wipe them out,* he thought.

Blake and Erhan met for an early Christmas morning breakfast at the London Ritz hotel, in the main dining room. They elected the buffet as the selection permitted them to order what they wanted, and eat all they wanted, too. The fruit was fresh, and the eggs were prepared the way the customer wanted them.

With a cup of steaming hot coffee in his hand, Blake laid down a gray folder on the table and began thumping his pen on the folder. He had been going over a plan of action for the last two weeks, and maybe, just maybe, he had the right scenario that would surprise Rhonda and Frank Pane. Blake had insisted that Mary stay in bed and catch up on her rest. He sure did not want her to get sick, as she was a very important link in their plans.

"Looks like we can talk while we eat. There are only a few people out for breakfast this Christmas morning," Erhan said as he poured coffee for him and Blake.

"You're right. It should be safe where we are sitting. Now, my friend, let me present to you what I have for our master plan, which should cause the Panes to make a grave mistake that will incriminate them. Please provide your input at any time. You are one of the main spokes in the wheel."

"Spokes in a wheel. Now that is real cowboy." Erhan laughed. "Not a problem, but I have been giving considerable thought to our involvement without the respective police authorities being involved. What would happen if one of them pulls a gun on us? Or, on the other hand, if one of us wounds or, god forbid, kills one of them? We do have our own lives and future to think about."

Blake opened the folder and pulled out a handwritten letter. "We're lucky that the law is on our side, and it sure helps that we both know law enforcement officials in Turkey and Great Britain. This letter is from the director of Interpol, and they will have international police agents from both countries in position to apprehend the Panes, if our plan works."

"Of course." Erhan laughed. "Why should I have not known that you had all the quacks in a row, or is it ducks in a row, as you Americans say?"

"It's ducks, and you and I are on the same wavelength." Then Blake began to laugh. "Now, Mister Turkish Intelligence Agent, or whoremonger, are you ready for the plan?"

"Fire away, Mister International American Cowboy." Erhan broke out in a laugh, which started Blake laughing again.

"The best way to present the plan so we can follow each step is to list a sequence of events that we can follow." Blake arranged a typed document on the table so they both could follow, and in the event that someone walked by the table, that individual could not see what was printed on the handout.

"CONFIDENTIAL"

January 28 Istanbul
You invite the Panes to your apartment for dinner. Agree, and allegedly make plans to invest $5,000,000 with their fraudulent company. Make plans to wire to the bogus account in London. Have fun with your mistress when you can. Beware of Frank, as he could be dangerous. Interpol agents will be alerted.
January 28-29 London
Blake will be in London with your Turkish Embassy friends. We will intercept the transfer along with the Interpol agents.
If the plan works then the Panes will be apprehended and extradited to the United States on extortion charges. Then we can openly find out about them blackmailing Jeff.

"How does the plan look?" Blake asked Erhan.

"It will work. You have a good plan. Of course, I will be the one who will benefit, as I will sleep with the beautiful blond-haired, blue-eyed woman with the great body. No sex, no money. How does that sound?"

"You're one hell of a man, my friend. Good luck, and protect your worm from the bird."

Erhan laughed. "See you in Disneyland, baby."

The majority of the day Blake and Mary got caught up on some well-deserved sleep and lovemaking. "How about some sightseeing today?" Blake asked Mary after they had taken a long hot shower together. "Most of the shops and stores should be open until around six o'clock this evening. What if we ride the typical British red double-decked bus and just look at the sights in London? We can go out to Windsor Castle and have some lunch at a little Italian restaurant I know. What do you think?"

"I say, hell, yes, buddy. I have always wanted to do the London tour and see where the queen lives. Does she really have her doll collection on display at Windsor?"

"Yes, and you will love it. Get your pretty butt moving. We got things to see."

"I thought you were going to say, people to meet and fish to fry."

"You're catching on, woman. You might make a good redneck yet."

The corners of Mary's lips turned upward in a smile full of sexual desire. "What do you have planned for Christmas Eve?"

Blake leaned down and kissed Mary gently on her lips. "I'll make love to you until the sun comes up Christmas morning."

When the kiss ended, Mary looked into his eyes. "I want to spend the rest of my life with you, not just one night."

CHAPTER 17

Blake and Mary spent a quiet Christmas evening together in downtown London. The hotel staff made reservations for them at a small family-owned restaurant near Marble Arch. The walking tour from the underground to the restaurant was delightful, and Blake and Mary loved the brisk London evening air. The shops and restaurants were closed except for a few of the older established restaurants, as they should be. Christmas is a time for family and friends to be together.

"Blake," Mary said in a low voice, and then took hold of his hand. "Do you love me?"

"I am sure that I do. Yes, I love you, Mary."

"Oh, Blake, I am so in love with you that it feels like my heart is going to burst."

"Well, damn, woman, don't let that happen. What would I tell your boss?"

"You shithead, can't you ever be serious?"

"I really do love you, Mary. Remember what you are getting into if you get involved with an older man. I will love, honor, and cherish you, and I am as faithful as an old hound dog, but I may fall asleep in my recliner at times."

"You can fall asleep, and you are not a hound dog. I don't get that joke."

They found the restaurant and were immediately led to their reserved table located in a corner near the back window. Mary loved the décor, the old tablecloth, silverware, china plates, cups, and saucers. "This is real crystal. It's great. Thank you, my darling man, for bringing me with you." A plump middle-aged waitress cheerfully greeted them and asked if they would like to order their special Christmas Dinner. Her sweet and English accent sang out the menu. "We have roasted turkey, bread sauce, roasted red potatoes, Brussels sprouts, gravy, hot bread, mince pie, pudding, and chardonnay wine, if you prefer. You will also get a British cracker."

Blake looked at Mary, and she smiled. "Yes, that will be fine with us, thank you.

"I don't understand what a cracker is," Mary said after the waitress left.

Blake took her hands in his and told her softly, "A cracker comes in a small cardboard box. It is a tube that we each put a finger in, and then we pull and it pops. It is supposed to bring good luck. You know, kind of Chinese."

"I never heard of anything like that. Of course, we New York girls don't visit international hot spots like you big-time investigators do."

Blake's gaze wandered from his empty wineglass to the woman sitting across from him. "Got a good idea. You interested?"

"Depends on what you have in mind, Tanner."

"Do you ice skate?" he asked with a big grin.

"Matter of fact I am an excellent ice skater. Why do you ask?"

"Remembering when my wife and I would visit London in the eighties and we ran across an indoor ice skating rink called Hampton Court Palace. We can do some fancy skating after all the sherry and wine we will drink."

Their Christmas meal was wonderful. During the casual walk from the restaurant to the ice skating rink, they held hands, bumped shoulders, and said very little to each other. Their eyes and smiles to each other were their conversation. Love filled their hearts and the air around them. They were very much in love with each other, and the glow on their faces lit up the London skyline.

"Can you ice skate?" Mary asked Blake as they put on their skates.

"You bet, backwards. I can only skate backwards. Skating forward hurts my ankles, even when I was young and my ankles were strong."

"Well, come on then. Let's go skating, Mr. Skate Only Backwards Guy."

Blake recalled memories of Christmas day in Vietnam 1969. He, Jeff, and all members of his A-Team were in their compound after a Christmas Eve recon mission. Jeff and a couple of the men had found an old cassette with Christmas music from the 1940s. *We sat on a bunker, drank hot beer, and dreamed of home. The distinct sounds of a Huey helicopter landing at the landing zone were sweet sounds to our ears. Our chopper crews were on the ground, so we knew that our Christmas dinner was on the incoming chopper. Walking toward the LZ, we could not believe our eyes. Jumping down from the chopper door were two round-eyed Red Cross Donut Dollies. Life cannot be all bad in Vietnam—hot turkey and all the traditional trimmings, and sweet American women to share our Christmas day.*

"Blake, Blake, are you okay?" Mary asked.

Cold, dark eyes stared back at Mary. "Sorry, babe, thoughts from years ago in a faraway land."

"Oh, darling, can I ever help heal your bad memories?"

Blake stared, then blinked his eyes and swallowed hard. "Just try and understand me. That is all I ask of you. Love me for the way I am."

"I will love you forever, and I am here for you when you need me." She then hooked her arm in his, and they skated away in step with the music playing over the rink speakers.

CHAPTER 18

Blake was restless, and a hotel room was not his favorite place to be. He was so thankful that Mary was with him, and the lovemaking certainly was worth the wait for Erhan to call him and pass on good news. He remembered 1995, when he was working a criminal case in Bosnia and Hungary. The Hilton in Budapest overlooked the Danube and was opposite the Fisherman's Bastion. Regardless of where he was, after a few days, the hotel life sucked, and he was ready for some action. He found out the best way to beat boredom was to go for a long walk. Walking along the Danube was depressing, not because of where he was, but the overall idea of being away from his family in a strange country always made him feel sad and empty inside. Tanner got used to the loneliness and being away from loved ones, but he never could deal with the boredom. Keep busy, that was the Tanner way. Just keep busy.

They both jumped when the satellite phone rang. Blake, who sat next to the window, laughed at their surprised reaction, and he answered the phone. "Hello, Erhan. We are doing just fine, getting a little cabin fever, but all is well in London town."

"We heard from the Interpol agent here in Istanbul, and the news is not good. Seems as though our associates, the Panes, must have got cold feet or our plans had a leak in the system. They were not on the scheduled flight from New York this morning. What is our next move?"

"Damn, all of the time and money and all the effort just went down the tubes. I will give Donald Higgins a phone call. Maybe he can shed some light on what happened to them. He has been talking to the Atlanta and New York police departments and the FBI about Rhonda and Frank Pane. I will get back with you as soon as we have any further information. Sorry, old friend, I know you were looking forward to having an orgy with the blond bombshell."

Erhan was still laughing when he hung up his telephone.

The satellite phone rang again just as Blake laid it down on the desk. Looking at the caller ID screen he saw a strange name and telephone number.

"Mr. Tanner, you're a difficult person to get hold of," a strange voice greeted him. "I am Special Agent Norman Gregory of the Atlanta FBI field office. Mr. Donald Higgins gave me your satellite telephone number. Our agency is aware that you have been working a case where Rhonda and Frank Pane were being investigated for alleged blackmail and extortion. Is that correct, sir?"

"That's correct. So why did you contact me?"

"Mr. and Mrs. Pane were found dead in their estate outside of Atlanta last evening. We have classified the case as a murder and a robbery, as their home had been ransacked as though the felons were looking for something specific. We know your involvement. Can you provide us with any additional information that might be helpful to the case?"

Blake hesitated for a few seconds before answering. "I will provide you with a full report upon my return to New York, which will be within the next two days. I will ask Interpol to send you relevant information on how they have been involved with our case."

"That will be just fine, sir. Sorry to have ruined your plans and add more confusion to your case. Upon your return to Atlanta, please come into our office. Maybe we can share information and assist you."

Blake disconnected the call and threw the phone down on the desk. "I'll be a son of a bitch. Now what the hell else will go wrong?"

Mary heard most of the conversation, as the volume was turned up on Blake's satellite phone. "The Panes have been murdered. Is that what I heard?"

"Yep, ain't that a pisser?" Now he would call Erhan and give him the news. His life would be better without those two trying to steal his money, but there went all the leads they had that surrounded Jeff's death. It was back to the drawing board. "Pack your things, sweetheart. We will attempt to fly back to New York tomorrow morning."

"Erhan, got some news that is good, yet it is bad."

"Don't tell me that my beautiful blonde and her husband have chickened out on us?"

"Well, they chickened out all right, but not by their choosing. They were murdered yesterday in their home in Atlanta. The FBI called me. They want an investigative report about our involvement, which will not be a problem."

There was dead silence on the other end of Blake's phone. Erhan came back on the line. "That is quite a sudden shock. Even though they were thieves, they would have been better off in prison than dead. Any ideas on who killed them, or why?"

Blake shifted the phone to his other ear. "None, none whatsoever. Do you have any ideas?"

Erhan said, "No, but I believe your clues, or what clues you have remaining on your list, will be found back in the U.S."

"You're so right, Erhan. I'll keep you abreast on the happenings. So long for now, my friend."

Blake had not reached the bathroom before his satellite phone rang again. "This place is like a damn police station." The caller ID screen showed an Atlanta number. "Tanner here," he yelled into the mouthpiece.

"Blake, is that you? This is Gloria."

"Yes, it is I, the world-renowned traveler. How are you doing, my dear?"

"Not too bad." Then she was silent for a few seconds. "The Atlanta police just told me that Frank and Rhonda Pane were murdered at their house."

"Yes, I just received a phone call from the Atlanta FBI informing me of their deaths. Do you know anything about it?"

"Well, no," she uttered. "What would I know about them? I am scared, Blake. I just have a strong feeling that the situation and circumstances are somehow linked to Jeff's death, and I am afraid."

"I am flying back to New York tomorrow. I will call you as soon as I get an opportunity.

"Thanks, Blake." Gloria hung up.

"Sounds to me like you will be going to Atlanta," Mary said as she started pulling her clothes out of the closet. "You do not have a thing for Gloria, do you?"

Blake answered bluntly, "No, of course not. She is just an old friend, a very pretty one, but we are just friends. Are you jealous, my dear?"

"You bet your ass I am. You are mine, cowboy, and do not forget it." She then walked to Blake and put her arms around him. "I love you, and, yes, I am extremely jealous."

"Don't worry, baby, I am true as an old…"

Mary stopped him from finishing his quote by putting her hand over his mouth. "I know, an old hound dog. You are silly, but I love your old-fashioned, redneck quotes."

At any unexpected time, Blake would think of Jeff. He still thought Jeff had been murdered. Who would murder him? And why? He did not know, but he felt that Jeff had not taken his own life. He thought back on all the times he had heard Jeff laugh at the simple things in life. Jeff loved life, and he cared for the people who loved him. *It all is a damn nightmare.*

CHAPTER 19

Blake was in deep thought during the six-hour flight back to JFK. Mary would give him a broad smile, put her hand on his, and lean on his shoulder occasionally, and he knew she was there if he needed her.

The thump of the plane's tires hitting the runway woke Blake up from a much-needed catnap. Sweet Mary was looking out the window, admiring the spacious hangars and buildings of the various airlines and freight companies.

"Are you happy to be back home, darlin'?"

"Yes, but I am so happy that you and I have been together. And thank you for taking me with you." She kissed Blake on the lips. "I love you."

"You're welcome, and I love you, too," Blake said, responding to her kiss.

Going through customs and then fighting the crowd at the baggage claim was a circle jerk as usual. "Let's just stay home, baby. I'm getting tired of this traveling shit," Blake said over the intense noise of the crowded airport.

"I'll take care of you, my dear man. You will feel better when I get through with you. Will you stay with me at my apartment?"

"You bet. Only if you promise not to wear me out and make me do bad things, like write bad checks and say naughty words to you."

"No promises, cowboy."

That evening Blake called Higgins and provided him a fully detailed report. The instruction he got from Donald: "Do whatever it takes to find out how Jeffery Sanders died."

Blake returned to Atlanta two days later. With the information he had gathered from Jeff's personal office effects, he did have a few clues to go on. Going to visit Gloria would be his first stop.

Gloria was waiting for him at the Sports Bar at the Atlanta airport. She sat at the end of the bar, sophisticated-looking, with blond hair, blue eyes, and a body that any man would want to hold. *I hope to hell she had nothing to do with Jeff's death or the Pane murders,* he thought.

She softly said, "Hi, handsome. Can I buy a cowboy a drink?"

He walked up to where Gloria was sitting, put his garment bag and briefcase down, and stood next to her.

"Oh, Blake, I am so happy to see you." She stood up and put her arms around his neck, and then she kissed him on the lips for the first time. "Yes, I will buy you a drink, and as many as you want."

The affection Gloria showed sent an instant hot flash through his body. *Get hold of yourself, Tanner*, he thought. *Don't let your pecker lead you astray. She is just happy to see you, that's all. Nothing else.*

Blake took a seat next to her at the bar. "Are you feeling more secure? Or are you still feeling threatened?"

"It is instinct only. I cannot prove anything, but there are people everywhere watching me. I've observed two men parked in front of the house, and the same two men have followed me home from the office on more than one occasion."

"Maybe it is the Atlanta police, even the FBI," Blake said without trying to alarm her. "Frank and Rhonda Pane did work for the same company that Jeff did. First, I am going to level with you and put my career on the line. New York Mutual Life Insurance Company hired me to investigate Jeff's death. You are fully aware that Jeff had a five-million-dollar life insurance policy, and you are the sole beneficiary. Have you ever wondered why you have not received a settlement from Jeff's insurance policy?"

"The insurance company has contacted me on two occasions. They informed me that when death of a policyholder is by suicide there is an in-depth investigation conducted before the beneficiary can collect the money."

Blake watched Gloria as she was speaking, and he listened very carefully to her choice of words. She was telling the truth. He felt it in his gut. "You just did not know that I was the investigator, did you?"

"No, no, I did not, but I am pleased that it is you and not some stranger. Who else would be better qualified than you are? After all, you were Jeff's best friend, and you knew him well. I believe you also believe that he did not take his own life."

"Is there anything that you have not told me? Any little clue that might help me uncover what really happened? The Panes took most of their secrets to their graves. You were aware that they were blackmailing Jeff, weren't you?"

Gloria stirred her drink with the pink straw and turned her head to look at Blake. "Yes, but after Jeff died. I went through his boxes from the office just as you did, and I found our mutual fund account records. Those bastards, they deserved to die." Then she started to cry.

"Have you contacted the police or FBI?"

"Yes, and they were already aware of the blackmail situation. Jeff notified them just days before his death."

Okay, Blake thought, *now I know why the FBI knew where to contact me and notify me of the murders.* "Did the police or FBI contact you and inquire about me?"

"Yes, but the only thing that I told them was you were Jeff's longtime friend and war brother, but nothing else. They seemed to know who you were."

Blake walked Gloria to her car at the short-term parking lot. "Thanks for the information, the cocktails, and your pleasant company. Call me anytime you want as I will be around Atlanta for a while."

"Please come over to the house and have dinner with me. I will fix you something special."

He told her that he had a dinner date. "I will call you very soon." *Damn, maybe he should just take her to bed*, he thought. *No, keep it professional, Tanner.*

By following his plan of action, he felt that he could somehow link the killings of Rhonda and Frank to Jeff's death. They were blackmailing Jeff and attempting to extort money from Erhan. He thought that it was all tied together some way or the other, but how? Why would they want to involve Jeff?

It was almost ten o'clock on a cold, rainy January evening when Blake walked in the front door of the El Chino Restaurant, on the west side of Atlanta. Jeff had met a mystery person or persons at the restaurant only three days before he died. The bar was only half-full, so Blake took a stool toward the center of the bar, next to the area where the waitresses picked up drink orders for the restaurant customers. *What in the hell are you doing here, Tanner? This case is for the police or FBI.* The smell of smoke, booze, and Mexican food filled his nostrils and brought back old memories of Cancun and his good friend Jeff. Ole Jeff boy loved the nightlife in Cancun, and always ordered the same thing to eat. Three beef tacos, a burrito supreme, refried beans, fried rice, and a margarita on the rocks. He did like the Mexican food, drink, and the raven-haired women. Being fluent in Spanish, he had a great time talking his trash. At times, he forgot that Blake also was fluent in Spanish and understood what he was saying to the señoritas.

He heard a man's voice coming from a table directly behind where he was sitting at the bar. The accent was pure Mexican, deep tones and broken English. Blake had a full view of the man by looking into the large mirror that stretched the entire length of the bar. His hair was long and tied back in a ponytail. He had a thin mustache and wore jeans, a dress shirt that was buttoned down, and scarred-up cowboy boots with a pointed toe and a silver cap on the end. *Drugstore Mexican cowboy*, Blake thought. He probably was just another Mexican trying to make a living in Atlanta.

The bartender looked to be around fifty-five to sixty years old. His gray hair was cut in a fifties flattop, and he was burly and tough-looking. He had an airborne tattoo on his left forearm and an

Army eagle on his right forearm. "What will you have, partner?" the bartender asked Blake in a deep Southern accent.

"How about a Johnnie Walker Black on the rocks. Make it a double, will you?"

"You bet." The man eyeballed Blake as he poured the scotch in a tall glass over the ice. "I can tell in your eyes that you were air-borne. Or it may be the flat forehead." He then laughed and placed the drink in front of Blake.

"All paratroopers have a flat forehead, that's for damn sure. I'm Blake Tanner, former member of the Fifth Special Forces, with three tours in 'Nam."

The burly bartender proudly said, "Ray Bennet, 173rd Airborne, Third Brigade, Lo Ke, Vietnam, 1965 to 1966."

"I guess we ate some dust and sweated some blood together during that time." They shook hands, and Blake felt the strength of a fellow trooper who had gone to war and come back home to a bunch of unforgiving sons of bitches. The memories just would not go away. Blake could tell that Ray Bennet had also had his honor forgotten by the American public.

"Been working here long, Ray?"

"Yeah, seven years come April. I retired from the post office and got bored, or let me say, my wife got bored with me being home and in her way all the time. The money is good, and there are many fringe benefits when you are a handsome bartender like me." The burly ex-paratrooper let out a hearty laugh that filled the air throughout the restaurant.

Blake thought he might be on to something. Maybe he was even working when Jeff made his contact in September. "I had a good friend who was with me in the Fifth. He told me that he came in here occasionally. As you see so many different people, don't suppose you would know him if I showed you his picture?"

"I like people, and especially military vets. Let me take a look."

Blake pulled the picture of him and Jeff out of his wallet and handed it to Ray. The man studied the picture for a long time, tilted it toward the lights behind the bar, and then looked at it again. "You know, brother, I am not one hundred percent sure, but I think that I have seen him on a couple of occasions. The last time was, oh, I would say September. He met two men at the bar, and then they went to a table in the back corner of the restaurant. Spoke real good Spanish, if I remember right."

"That's him all right. Jeffery Sanders was his name."

"Was his name? You say was his name?"

"Yeah, he died in September. Just a few days after he visited here, looks like to me. You couldn't describe the men he met, could you?"

The former paratrooper-turned-bartender thought for a long time. He closed his eyes, rolled his head from side to side, and then all of a sudden, "Yep, I do remember what they looked like, and I believe I can find out where they were from. They were Mexican, that's for damn sure, not Mexican-Americans but the ones who come from down around Mexico City. Stand by. I will be right back."

When Blake looked up, Ray was standing in front of him with a huge smile on his face. He handed Blake a business card with the logo MEXCON ENGINEERING COMPANY printed across the top. In the middle of the card was the name Hector Franco, Director of International Operations, Mexico City printed in bold green lettering.

"Holy shit," Blake said. "Can I borrow this card? I will return it to you within a few days. My company is looking to do business with this firm, and we have been unable to make a connection with them." Blake thought to himself. *Do not reveal yourself yet. Wait until you make some more contacts. Have the FBI check out the bartender named Ray before you go any further with him. Just be-*cause he is a Vietnam combat vet does not mean he is honest, but I sure hope he is.

"Keep it. He left it with me along with a large tip. He seemed to have plenty of American greenbacks in his pockets."

"Thanks, Ray. I'll see you around, brother."

"You too, and welcome home, brother," Ray said as Blake turned and walked toward the front door and into the brisk, cool Georgia air.

The soothing words of "welcome home, brother" sent a chill up Blake's spine. Only the American public did not welcome the Vietnam and Korean war veterans home. The words of honor came from those who served their country with dignity and pride.

Now I am very confused, Blake thought as he gazed out the window of the fast-moving taxicab. What in the hell was Jeff mixed up in? Company contracts could not be the motive for him to get involved with Mexican engineers; his company did not have formal contracts with Mexcon Engineering. At least, that is what James Connors had told him.

Blake stopped by the hotel bar to indulge in a scotch before going up to his room. He cursed himself for drinking too much, and then he ordered one more before leaving. Something about being alone was the only excuse he had for drinking. *What the hell,* he thought, *I never drink while I am working, and I have never missed work because of drinking too much booze. Annie always told me, "When you drink the hard stuff, drink only single shots. The doubles will screw your mind up." She was right, God love her.*

CHAPTER 20

January 30, Atlanta

In his hotel room, Blake Tanner leaned back in the desk chair and clamped his hands behind his neck, not sure if his plans would work. He had developed a suitable plan that he hoped would provide him with suspects who could shed some light on Jeff's death. He began to make a final list of what he would need to know before going to the FBI with his theory. He did know that pursuing additional information about Frank and Rhonda Pane would be a losing battle. He would stop by the international engineering company and pay his respects to the senior management about the murders of their top executives. There still might be a vital clue at the engineering company that he had overlooked.

The worst part was he did not have a clue as to how deeply Jeff was involved with the Panes, and what he was doing to free himself from the situation and circumstances. Blake thought about Jeff as he was anxiously waiting in the engineering company's VIP room of the international operations director, James Connors. Why would a man go to a war and then come home and kill himself? Jeff was just not that type of a man. Blake recalled an incident in Vietnam during the fall of 1969. Jeff was on a five-man reconnaissance team that Blake was leading in the Que Son Valley. The team came across a wounded Viet Cong soldier who apparently had been left for dead by his comrades. The man begged someone to murder him and put him out of his misery. Jeff tended to him for over an hour, talking with him, wiping the blood and sweat from his eyes. Although the enemy soldier did not know what Jeff was saying to him, you could see in his eyes the fear he had of dying. The Vietnamese ranger on the team told Jeff that the soldier wanted a pistol so he could kill himself. Jeff would not permit that to happen. "A soldier has honor. He does not commit suicide." Blake never forgot the words that Jeff said to the dying enemy soldier through the translator.

James Connors was just as confused as everyone else was about the brutal murders of Frank and Rhonda Pane. "First it was Jeff, now Frank and Rhonda. We just don't know what to make of it."

Without wanting to tip him off, Blake chose his words carefully. "Have you heard if the police have any leads on the murders?"

"They don't seem to know anything, although they will not tell us what they have discovered, as we are not family. We all believe robbery was a motive for the killings. They were very wealthy, you know."

Blake left the engineering building with no leads at all. He did have suspicions about James Connors. He seemed a little nervous; he just might be hiding something. *Looks like ole Tanner is in the boat all alone, and with only one paddle*, he thought as he left the engineering building.

Special Agent Norman Gregory parked his black Dodge Intrepid in the parking lot at the Atlanta Ritz-Carlton Hotel, located in the heart of the city. A light, cold drizzle was filling the air as he got out of his car and walked toward the hotel lobby. Norman Gregory was an Annapolis graduate who served with the 7th Marines in the Gulf War and who was a distinguished graduate at the FBI Academy. He was not a large man, he wore contacts, and he was losing his hair. Other than that, he was a tough little bastard, persistent, and he would never give up on a case.

"Nice to meet you," Blake said as he shook hands with the agent. "What brings you to my humble home away from home?"

The special agent thanked Blake for the package he had sent to the FBI office with pertinent information on the Panes. "It is too bad they are not alive to spend time in our prison system. They could provide us with the missing links we need. I will be up front with you, Mister Tanner. We have your classified military file, and we know how you operated during your years with the Army CID. You are aware that all information is classified. The Panes were deeply involved with international drug trafficking. Their main activity was in Spain, the United Kingdom, Turkey, and with the big boys in Naples and Sicily. They had approximately fifteen million U.S. dollars in offshore banking accounts, which we have frozen. We do not know your plans, Mister Tanner, but we suspect that you are going after suspects who were connected with the death of Mr. Jeffery Sanders and the Panes."

"Pretty good for a Marine," Blake answered with a smile. "So you have doubts about the death of my friend Jeff Sanders?"

"We do, and we have a closed lid on the case. No one, and I mean no one, knows the status or progress of the case but my office. Our agency would like to solicit your services and have you work with the FBI and the Interpol in Europe. Are you interested?"

"I'm sure you know that I am on contract with the New York Mutual Life Insurance Company."

"Yes, and we have no problems with you working with them and us concurrently. We cannot pay you what they do, but the contract salary is quite good. I think five hundred a day, plus per diem."

"Count me in, as this will be the only way I will be able to finish my investigation and get back to Colorado and my normal life as a free-living retiree."

"One other thing. Forget about Mexico and Mexican suspects. They are only small-time dealers, and they use phony credentials to attract customers. The suspected killers are in Europe, probably Naples or Sicily."

Blake caught the early bird flight from Atlanta to JFK at seven-thirty the next morning. He called Mary before he boarded and told her to get ready because big daddy Tanner was coming to see her.

"Bring your handsome body on up here, cowboy. I will fix us a special dinner tonight at home. You want me to pick you up at the airport?"

Blake told her he would take a taxi. "You just stay in where it is warm and dry. Remember, it's New Year's Eve in New York City tomorrow night."

They were like lovers who had not seen each other for years. Mary told Tanner she had fallen deeply in love with him on any occasion she could find. Tanner told Mary he loved her as no man could ever love a woman.

He did like Mary's apartment and especially her queen-size bed.

"Damn, woman. If you don't give me a breather and let me rest, I will not be able to make my flight to Rome. Staying up all night New Year's will likely take its toll on this old warhorse's body."

"Come here, you old warhorse, I will make you feel better. You want on top or do you want me to do all the work?" She laughed as Blake rolled over on his back just like a puppy dog.

"Be gentle, darling. I will still love you in the morning."

Mary glanced over at Blake as he was drinking his morning coffee and reading the early morning edition of *The New York Times*. "There is still a mystery about you, Tanner, that I cannot figure out. Will you ever tell me what is hidden inside your mind?" She had told him months ago that he was her life, along with her daughter and her family. No questions asked, just love each other, and move on with their lives.

His hands were warm as he graciously reached over and placed them on her hands. "I love you, woman. You hear me? You are my woman."

"Yes, Blake, I hear you, and I love you more than I can ever tell you."

Somewhere deep down, he suddenly let out a deep breath. "Thanks for your love, Miss Mary, thanks for understanding me and giving me the opportunity to love you." The old retired soldier was a tough bastard on the outside, but he had a heart as big as Pikes Peak. Blake Tanner knew that he would be a good husband for Mary if she would marry him. The question was would she marry him? Moreover, why would she want to marry an older man? He thought he knew all the answers to what a woman was thinking. Come down to it, he did not really know a damn thing about what Mary was thinking.

He neatly arranged each item in his garment bag, which was lying on the bed, just as if he were getting ready for an Army full-field inspection. Everything in order, he closed the bag, grabbed his briefcase, and headed off for another far-off country. Of course, going to Naples, Italy, was not a bad place to go. He did dread the long flight, but he could catch catnaps during the flight. The VIP travel agent told Blake that the new Boeing 777 had comfortable first-class seats that converted into sleepers. He was booked for a single seat on the port side of the aircraft; no one would bother him unless he wanted them to.

CHAPTER 21

January 2005, Naples, Italy

It all started on the 4th of January, a Wednesday. After the long flight from New York to Rome, then a plane change to Naples, Blake was bushed. The Ramada was located within walking distance to the town center of Naples, which was ideal for conducting business and enjoying the Italian atmosphere and cuisine. Naples has a flare and mystery about it that brings out the excitement in a person. The distinct smell of pizza baking in special ovens, the odors coming from spices, fruit, and fresh vegetables fill the air twenty-four hours a day. His favorite time of the year was in the spring, when all the fruit trees began budding after being dormant during the cold season. Then the constant smell of motor vehicle and motorcycle fumes makes up the other part of being in Naples. You can frequently see an entire family, maybe four or five, all riding on one motor scooter. They had loaves of freshly baked bread tucked under their arms; a large jug of wine would be balanced on top of a woman's head, a jug of olive oil, fresh vegetables, fruit in a wicker basket, and whatever else they wished to carry with them. There is no other city like Naples, and there are no other people like the Neapolitans. They will invite you to their home to eat, even if they do not know you.

The distinct ringing of Blake's satellite phone startled him, as he was not expecting a phone call until tomorrow. Blake found the phone in his briefcase and looked at the caller ID screen. He did not have a clue as to who was calling him.

"Mr. Blake, my name is Marco Russo. I am the director of Interpol for Southern Europe," the man said in his Italian accent. "Welcome to Napoli. I hope your flight from New York was comfortable."

"Good to hear your voice, Mister Russo. I have been told good things about you and your organization. I do look forward to working with you."

"Thank you. Can we meet this evening for dinner?"

"Of course," Blake answered. "It has been many years since I had the pleasure of eating the wonderful foods of Naples. What time should I be ready?"

"Nine o'clock. Is that too late for you?"

"I will be waiting for you in the hotel lobby."

Blake finished unpacking and then took a long hot shower. The hot water splattering on his neck and shoulders always relaxed him and cleared his head. "Shower logic" is what he called it, when he would put together a plan and then go over his next plan of action. He lay down on the king-size bed and caught a few hours of sleep before getting dressed.

At eight-thirty that evening, Blake went to the hotel bar and ordered a double Chivas Regal on the rocks, his drink when in Italy. Drinking Chivas was like driving a luxury car. It was first class to the Italian natives. From a dark corner of the hotel, an older man dressed in a tuxedo was playing soft music on a piano. *That guy is good,* Blake thought. *Wish the hell I could play an instrument. Mom was right when she told me, "You need to play more piano and less baseball."* Now all he could play was the radio.

Blake had just finished his second scotch when he noticed an older man entering the hotel lobby through the revolving door. *Cop is written all over him*, Blake thought. Once a cop, always a cop, you just cannot hide it. He casually walked over to the man. "Mr. Russo?"

"Yes, and I can tell from your looks and accent that you are Mr. Tanner."

"Please call me Blake."

"Please call me Marco. Shall we proceed to our dinner engagement? Please, my car is waiting in front."

Indeed, he did have a car. It was a black four-door BMW 750, and Blake could tell it was armor-plated. Two men were standing by the rear passenger door. The smaller of the two men, who Blake guessed was the chauffer, graciously opened the door and held his arm forward. *"Prego."* He slid in and Marco entered the other side. The larger of the two men climbed in the front passenger seat. *He is the bodyguard*, Blake thought. *Big bastard, bet he would kill his grandmother if it were for the cause.*

"Have you been to Naples before, Blake?" asked Marco.

"Yes, on many occasions. When I was in the Army and stationed at Vicenza, my wife and I dearly loved to come to Naples every opportunity we got. The Isle of Capri is my favorite spot in the whole wide world."

"If you don't mind we will need to talk business during the evening. We have many things we need to discuss before we start working our case tomorrow morning. I do not know your entire background, but our intelligence agents informed us that you are one of the best in what you do. Over forty years of experience in international criminal investigations, I have been informed. In addition, we know that you are familiar with drug trafficking and money laundering."

"You have a good snapshot of my experience. This will be my second experience working with the International Police. I've seen my share of what drugs do to people, especially when foreign countries are involved."

The glaring lights of Naples and the bumper-to-bumper traffic and car horns would drive most Americans crazy, as the Italians have no discipline when it comes to driving a car, Blake thought. The chauffer moved the large BMW in and out of the hectic traffic as if he were driving a small Alfa Romero. The car came to a sudden stop in front of a crowded street that was too small for the BMW to enter.

"We will walk a few meters to our restaurant. Hope you do not mind walking."

"Fine with me. I can use the exercise," Blake answered as the large bodyguard opened the car door for him.

The décor of the restaurant retained history of its past. Ancient pictures of Naples and Mount Vesuvius, and naked male statues lined the entry of the narrow hallway leading to the main dining room. The smell of cooking meats and pastas filled Blake's nostrils, and it sent signals to his stomach that he had not had anything to eat since breakfast.

There was a greenery-lined outdoor patio, complete with a retractable roof, but due to the cold evening, Blake and Marco decided to dine inside near an open fireplace. The chauffer and the bodyguard sat at a small table with two other men about halfway between the front entrance and where Blake and Marco sat. "I hope you like seafood," Marco said as he glanced around the dining area. "Do you speak Italian?"

Blake answered him in fluent Italian. It surprised Marco, and brought a big Italian smile. "We will get along just fine," Marco spoke back in his native Italian.

Marco commenced by telling Blake about the drug trafficking problems that they had in Naples. The local police pulled bodies from the bay every day. "We just cannot seem to control the movement of drugs and stolen supplies. The FBI asked if we would authorize you to work with us on a temporary basis. Seems as though the De Luca family has mafia all over the world. If we can get the godfather, Franco De Luca, to flee Italy, then your American FBI can get involved. The De Luca families are suspected of murdering numerous people in Atlanta. I am sure that you are familiar with the murders of Mr. and Mrs. Pane?"

Blake was amazed by how much Marco knew about the Atlanta crime activity. "The FBI has just told me enough to get me interested. I knew Rhonda and Frank Pane, who were upper management in an international engineering company in Atlanta. I was tracking them and trying to get evidence on them for blackmail and extortion, but they were killed before we had firm evidence on them. My good friend Jeffery Sanders died last September in what the Atlanta police called a suicide. I strongly believe he was murdered, and he was involved with the Panes in some way."

Marco took a drink of his wine, topped off Blake's glass, and said, "We do receive a lot of information through Interpol links concerning American crimes, especially if the suspects have ties with Italy. I reviewed an investigative report about your friend. There was not much information since the autopsy revealed death by suicide. There was some indication that foul play was involved. Sorry, I do not have any additional information."

"You've told me more than what the Atlanta police and FBI have given me. So, am I to understand that I cannot assist you, only if any of the drug traffickers attempt to leave or actually leave Italy?"

"As you say in your country, 'That's it in an eggshell,' or something like that."

"If you don't catch me, then I can conduct my own investigation? Is that correct?"

Marco sat quietly for a few seconds before he spoke. "We cannot stop you, but interfering with our investigations could land you in hot water, and you could get yourself killed during the process. If by some chance you were able to persuade Mr. De Luca to leave Italy with you, we would be extremely grateful. Your American justice system gives out stricter prison sentences than ours. We have many family members in our judicial system, which has a tendency to be lenient toward the bad guys."

The two men feasted on grilled swordfish, scampi, and baked pasta. The vino de casa was excellent, and they finished their meal with a cup of espresso and a shot of cognac.

Blake called Mary, told her about his wonderful dinner, and explained what he ate. He asked her to pass on to Donald Higgins that he was on schedule and making progress. "If you could just be here with me, my visit would be complete. We will come back here someday, and you can visit Naples and the Isle of Capri again. Italy has not changed since you were here years ago. The Italian people just go with the flow, and they love life."

"I wish…I wish. I love you, Blake. Please stay safe, and come back to me soon."

A stilling sadness came over him again. Damn, he wanted to complete this investigation and get back to the mountains. Lying his head on the large pillow, he drifted off to sleep thinking about the peace and quiet of his country home.

It was midmorning when Blake walked out of his hotel and toward the Bay of Naples. Walking always helped him think out his plans, and actually being at the location, and in the same environment where his plan would take place, started the adrenaline flowing. The distinct smell of the fishy water and a soft, cold breeze blowing in from the dirty bay brought back old memories. How many times had he started his investigations from the shore of a large body of water? Car horns honked, and motor bikes and scooters whizzed by making god-awful sounds, as they usually had no baffles in their mufflers. *The drivers in Naples are just plain crazy*, he thought. *They are great people until they get behind the wheel of a car or sit on the seat of a motorcycle or bike.*

Blake knew that catching the crime boss alone would be virtually impossible as heavily armed bodyguards always surrounded him. He really had no conclusive evidence that Franco De Luca had anything to do with Jeff's death or the murders of Frank and Rhonda Pane. Why should he even be concerned with Frank and Rhonda Pane? His interest was only with the death of Jeff, so he thought. *Marco is right. A man could get his ass shot for even asking questions.* He wanted to make damn sure that he was on the right track before continuing his investigation.

The day was a complete flop for Blake. He was getting nowhere, and he was starting to believe that locating De Luca or even attempting to talk with him was a losing battle. His satellite phone rang, and as he removed it from his coat pocket, a black BMW pulled up along the curb next to him and stopped. Marco Russo rolled down the window from the backseat and smiled at Blake. He held a mobile phone to his ear. Marco had been calling Blake when the driver spotted him walking along the crowded street. "Sorry about that, Blake. Sometimes these mobile telephones are too quick for us Italian boys."

Blake started laughing. "Yes, and they are fast for a Colorado cowboy. What's up?"

"We just received a confidential email from Norman Gregory of the Atlanta FBI. He asked me to pass on to you that they have new clues pertaining to the murders of Frank and Rhonda Pane, and additional information about the circumstances of your friend Jeffery Sanders' death." Marco handed Blake a large sealed white envelope taped on both sides with "CONFIDENTIAL" marked in red. "Why don't you get in the car and we will take you back to my office? You will have privacy, and you can use our confidential email Internet if you like."

"Great. Thanks for your help." Blake got in the backseat of the BMW.

Blake went silent as he read the classified message from FBI Special Agent Norman Gregory. The message was not long, but Norman got right to the details.

FBI Headquarters, Atlanta Field Office

"CONFIDENTIAL"

Mr. Blake Tanner,

I apologize for the way you receive this message. It was the only secure method to send you the following classified and sensitive information. We decided against calling you on your secure satellite phone for fear that you would be in a location where you would have been unable to talk. Details are as follows:

Franco De Luca is not our man. Please disregard any plans that involve him or his organization.

The United Kingdom Interpol has discovered an international drug trafficking organization in London. Their leads indicate ties to Spain, Turkey, and the United States.

The New York City FBI has detained two suspected drug runners. There is one female carrying a Great Britain passport, and a Turkish male carrying a Turkish passport.

Our Atlanta office has found evidence connecting a Mexican hit man to the murders of Frank and Rhonda Pane. We also suspect he was involved with money laundering, extortion, and blackmail. He may have critical information concerning the death of Jeffery Sanders.

Suggest you return to Atlanta, via New York ASAP.

We also suggest you involve your Turkish contact, Mr. Erhan Sarraf, to assist you with the London and Turkey investigation.

The London Interpol will be heavily involved along with the Turkish police.

The FBI cannot get involved outside the United States on this international situation. Request your continued assistance with our office.

We will meet you upon your arrival in Atlanta. We understand that you must brief the New York Mutual Insurance Company vice president prior to departing for Atlanta.

God Speed,
Norman Gregory
Special Agent in Charge
Atlanta, FBI

Blake shot a short email back to Norman with confirmation on receiving thc mcssage. "Norman, I am making a one-day and overnight trip to Athens. Clues I have received may lead to information toward the extortion case. I will keep you informed of my arrival at JFK."

Catching an Alitalia flight from Naples to Athens that afternoon worked out wonderfully for Blake. He had his travel agent contact a limo and a driver to meet him when he arrived at the Athens Sparta Airport. Blake requested that his hotel be booked at the Divani Apollon Palace Hotel and Spa in Vouliagmeni. He was familiar with the area as he and Annie had taken numerous vacations to Greece, and they had established a warm friendship with people in the area. He especially looked forward to visiting his two old friends Johnny and Christos, who owned a restaurant on the strip near the Vouliagmeni beach area.

After checking into the hotel and freshening up, he caught a taxi from the hotel to his friends' restaurant. They were two brothers who had fought in the Korean War with the Greek army. They loved Americans, and many catered to their restaurant when the American Air Base was active. Their specialty was lamb and pork. Blake always ate pork chops and everything else they put on the table. The menu offered pork chops of various sizes, and he always ordered the "Jerry Pork Chop." It was so large that it hid the dinner plate, and it was always juicy and tender. The fascinating story goes that a Department of Defense civilian, his family, and friends were favorite customers of Johnny and Christos. The man named Jerry asked for a big pork chop one evening, so the chef, Christos, handed him the meat cleaver, and Jerry cut off a huge pork chop. Therefore, the name "Jerry Pork Chop" was born.

Blake had difficulty getting away from his friends at the restaurant. They called in all the family and proudly showed him pictures that had been taken of Annie and him back in the early 1980s.

After a good night's sleep and an American breakfast in the hotel restaurant, Blake caught a taxi to the Hellas Investment office. The office was located in downtown Athens near the Acropolis and Parthenon. The owner of the company, Mr. Hellas, was cooperative and told Blake that a Mr. Sanders from Atlanta, Georgia, visited their office in the summer.

"He was polite and interested in making a large investment with us," Mr. Hellas explained. "My secretary gave him brochures and handouts, and he told us that he would be contacting us soon."

Blake handed Mr. Hellas a picture of Frank Pane. "Is this Mr. Sanders?"

"That is him."

Not wanting to get the company involved with his investigation, Blake thanked Mr. Hellas for his precious time and information.

"Is there anything wrong?" asked Mr. Hellas.

"No, I am just running a credit inquiry on Mr. Sanders for a large corporation."

The rest of the afternoon and evening belonged to Blake. He walked to the downtown area of Glyfadia, and visited the various shops. Blake ate lunch at a beach restaurant, eating his favorite Greek salad, fried calamari, fresh bread, and retsina wine. Life was good in Athens. The Aegean ocean water was always a greenish blue color, and the musical sound of the water washing up on the rocks was sweet music to Blake's ears.

CHAPTER 22

The flight from Athens to JFK was a long haul. The change of aircraft in Paris was smooth, and he was able to do a little shopping in the duty-free shops. Thanks to Blake's contract package with the insurance company, his sitting in first class prevented him from being completely drained when he arrived in New York. The familiar sound of the tires of the Airbus touching down on the runway at JFK reminded Blake that he had been away more than a week. He missed Mary, and he hoped she had received his voice mail asking her to meet him upon arrival. *One night with my sweet Mary*, he thought. *She will take care of me. She always does.*

He shifted the heavy garment bag to his right shoulder and stopped at the Custom Officials desk before exiting into the terminal passenger meeting area.

He needed to call Erhan in Istanbul before he departed from the customs area. By calling now, he would have more time with Mary. Blake found a quiet location near the men's restroom and called Erhan.

"Hello, you old Turkish warhorse. How the hell are you doing?"

"Very good, my old cowboy friend. Where are you?"

"I'm back in New York. I've been on a wild goose chase. I need your help. Are you available for some more adventure?"

"Yes, but only if there are beautiful blondes involved. You know that I will help you. What do you want me to do?"

"The leads all come back to London. The FBI and Interpol have given me the green light to pursue suspected drug kingpins and other low-life mafia-linked figures. Can you contact your Turkish Embassy friends and meet me in London, say, within three days?"

"Consider it done. There are individuals at my dinner table as we speak who can assist us. Please send me your flight itinerary, and I will meet you. Anything else I can do in the meantime?"

"No, thanks, Erhan."

Back in Istanbul, Erhan turned to his trusted friends, and in their native Turkish language, he updated the military intelligence officers about the situation that he and Blake were investigating. He knew that the trust he had in his friends would be beneficial to him and Blake.

After carefully listening to Erhan explain what they were up against, the men raised their glasses filled with raki, known to Turks as *The Milk of the Lion.* "Insallah, God willing," they cheered.

Mary ran to Blake and wrapped her arms around him as if she had not seen him in fifty years. "I have missed you so very much," she told him as she kissed him repeatedly. "There is no denying it. I love you, Blake."

"You know what? I love you, too. Just don't get used to the idea that you can boss me around and take advantage of my youthful body." He laughed, and then again kissed her sweet, moist lips.

Happily, she said, "To the office or my place?"

"Take me to your love nest, and make it quick as I have work that has to be done, and I have no time for a New York, over sexed woman."

"Ha, the hell you say," Mary said hotly as she flagged a taxi and grabbed Blake's hand.

He gently put his arm around her and guided her into the backseat of the taxi.

Their time together was priceless, as always. They loved each other, ate what they desired to eat, and drank fine upstate New York wine. Mary had arranged a late morning meeting with Donald Higgins. She said she wanted Blake to rest and that she wanted more time to be alone with him.

The morning was beautiful. Behind the tall buildings, the sun peeked brightly, ready to shine on the people in New York City. There was a soft, cold breeze blowing through the trees in the parks, and the view was breathtaking.

Blake met with Higgins at eleven-thirty. Donald was fully aware that the FBI had detained two suspected drug dealers from Great Britain and Turkey. The only questions Donald had were, "When can you complete the investigation? And do you need any additional funds? Just be careful, Mister Tanner. You are fully aware of the dangers dealing with drug trafficking."

"I hope to wrap this up in a couple of weeks. I will talk with the detainees, then fly down to Atlanta and work with the local FBI. Our plans will include going back to London and meeting with Erhan and his embassy friends, and of course with the British Interpol."

"Whatever it takes, do it." Donald bid Blake good-bye with a smile and a friendly handshake.

Blake met with New York City FBI Special Agent in Charge George Holden at the international detainee area. "They are a couple of green dealers," said George. "The woman is about as weak as I have ever seen." George handed their files with photographs to Blake for review prior to talking with them.

When Blake opened the file folder of the woman, he almost dropped the folder to the floor. "I will be a son of a bitch. This is Julie Spenser from Spenser International Antiques in London. I thought she was just a little naive girl with hot pants for an American adventurer. What a waste. She is a beauty. That's for sure."

"So you have met her?" George asked with a blank look.

"Yes, she will have valuable information that we can use, if we can get her to talk."

Opening the folder of the Turkish man, Blake stared at the photograph. He blurted out, "Well, I will be go kiss my ass. I know this man, also. We met in Istanbul. He works for a Turkish engineering company. Guess I am getting old and out of practice, because this man gave me no suspicions that he had any role in my friend's death or in any wrongdoings. I did find out through Erhan's Turkish friends that the man is gay. Can I have a few minutes alone with the woman?"

"Sure, take whatever time you need. You are very heavily involved with this case whether you know it or not," said the FBI agent.

Julie Spenser looked like she had swallowed a sour pickle when she looked up and saw Blake walking into the interrogation room. Suddenly she began to panic, and fear showed all over her face. "Oh, no," she said.

"Surprised are you, Julie? Just to let you know up front, I will not play games with you, and I do not have to. I am not a federal agent, and I can pull your teeth out one by one and stick them up your privates. Do not play your dumb druggie games with me. I am not amused, and I sure as hell am not scared of you or any of your so-called mafia friends. Are you ready to talk?"

She commenced crying. "I want a lawyer, and I want my father. Please don't hurt me, and remember, I am in love with your friend Jeffery."

"Shut the hell up. The real Jeff is dead, and so is your Jeffery, who has been murdered. Does that tell you anything about your friends?"

"Oh, no. My Jeffery is dead? How could it be? He was to meet me here tomorrow evening."

"When did you talk with him last?"

"It was just two weeks ago this Friday. He sent me a plane ticket and told me to meet Engin Mersch." She continued to cry and shake as if she were having a convulsion.

"Where were you to meet your contact who called himself Jeffery?"

"At the Hilton, the JFK Airport Hilton," she cried.

"What time? What time were you to meet him?" Blake leaned over the front of the table and looked into the tear-soaked eyes of Julie Spenser. "You are actually crying. I'll be damned, I thought you were acting."

Wiping her eyes and blowing her nose with a Kleenex taken from a box that was sitting on the interrogation table, she moaned,

"I have never done anything like this before, Mister Tanner. Please believe me."

"You know, I do believe you, but I will still recommend to the FBI that you be deported back to the UK, and the British Interpol will send you to prison for a long time. If you tell us everything, and I mean everything, it will go easier on you. You must agree to cooperate with the FBI. Do you understand?"

With tears rolling down her face she answered, "I understand. Please don't let them hurt me."

"The FBI will not hurt you. Just feel lucky they picked you up, or you would probably have been in the harbor with cement tied around your feet," Blake snarled.

Along with the FBI agents, Blake continued to interrogate Julie. After gathering all the information they thought she could provide, they sent her back to her holding cell.

"What about the Turk? Do you think he will talk?" asked the FBI agent.

"He will probably be a tough nut to crack," answered Blake. "Don't you think it would be best if he just saw me in the room, and you do the interrogation?" Blake had found out years ago that if a suspect knows someone is watching their every move, and listening to every word they say during an interrogation, they get very nervous.

"I do. That is a good plan, and we can tell you have done this many times before, Mister Tanner."

The young Turk Engin Mersch did not break, but he continued to glance over at Blake during the interrogation. George Holden stood up, looked at Blake, and winked; he then leaned over the desk and got into the Turk's face. "We are finished with you. I will turn you over to Mr. Tanner, and he is not associated with the American FBI or law enforcement. May God, or whoever your God is, have mercy on your soul. The last person he interrogated was buried three weeks ago. All yours, killer." George could barely keep from laughing as he walked out of the room.

The FBI agents were behind the two-way mirror, and they had recorded the entire interrogation. "This man is shit hot," said one of the FBI agents to his partner. "He is one tough interrogator."

"I want a lawyer," cried the young Turkish man. "You cannot kill me. That is against the American law."

"Want to bet? I am not the American law. I am a Wild West bounty hunter, and I will hang your ass from the nearest tree if you don't talk to me. Better yet, I will just take you back to Colorado with me and let the mountain lions eat you alive. No, I will just send your ass back to Turkey. Your officials know what to do with people like you. Before you leave this room, I will stick a cattle prod up your ass, known on the streets as a joystick." Blake made a gesture with his hand and finger, simulating the joystick going up the Turk's rectum.

The Turk grimaced. "Please do not do anything like that. Please don't," he pleaded.

Blake walked out of the interrogation room with a smile on his face. "He's all yours, boys. You might work on him some more. He is scared to death about going to a Turkish prison. It doesn't help him any that he is gay. Just remind him of the joystick."

"I can't believe you told him you would stick a cattle prod up his ass," said the agent running the video equipment. "And the way you explained to him what a cattle prod was." The agents all laughed at Blake's remarks during the interrogation.

The company limo carrying Mary and Blake stopped at the passenger check-in at the JFK airport. After a few kisses, and "I love you. Be careful, and I will miss you so much," Blake disappeared in the busy terminal entrance. Tanner did not care for goodbyes, and he did not want Mary to go into the airport with him. That was the Tanner way.

CHAPTER 23

Atlanta, Georgia

When Blake walked from the Atlanta airport's baggage claim, he spotted FBI Special Agent Norman Gregory standing behind the people congregated at the arrival gate. "Have a nice flight?" Norman put out his hand to Blake.

"It was good, thanks. How have you been doing? Anything new and exciting since I left New York?"

"Plenty. We have a good list of suspects thanks to your tough interrogation tactics. George Holden told me on the phone that there was a job open for you in New York if you wanted." Norman smiled and proceeded to update Blake on the report.

After the briefing, Blake and Norman met with a special agent from the International Drug Trafficking Division. The special agent told them that they were dealing with the worst kind of drug dealers, hardcore, who were involved worldwide. They had millions of dollars, they had international connections, and they had no problems with whom they hurt or murdered. All official reports indicated the names of the drug warlords, and the ones who probably murdered Frank and Rhonda Pane, and possibly were connected with the blackmailing of Jeffery Sanders, and had ties to his alleged suicide.

"That is very interesting. Thanks for the excellent briefing," said Blake. "How can I help?"

Greg Norman asked Blake if he would like to go back to London, work with the British Interpol, and request his Turkish ex-military intelligence officer friend Erhan to work with him. "Can you do that?"

"Of course," Blake answered quickly. "Just give me a chance to review all the reports you have before I depart."

"Whatever you need," Norman replied. "We are at your disposal since we cannot work in the U.K. We sure as hell do not want the CIA involved any more than what they are already."

While Blake gathered important information in Atlanta, Erhan was doing the same in London. Blake felt the two seemed to know what each other was doing, what their next move would be, and how they would react to dangerous situations.

Blake gave a quick call to Gloria Sanders. He told her that he could not visit her during this brief trip to Atlanta and promised that he would see her soon. "We should have some good news within a few weeks concerning Jeff's life insurance policy. You will be able to put away the five million dollars that old friend Jeff left you. In addition, I hope to have an answer as to how he actually died."

She seemed happy to hear the news, but she also sounded a little frightened to Blake. *Damn, I hope she is not involved with any of the wrongdoings* he thought.

Blake made one phone call to Donald Higgins and one special call to Mary before turning in for the night. "Goddamn hotel rooms," he said to himself. "I want my own bed in Colorado, and I want Mary sleeping beside me."

Laying his head on the soft pillow, his thoughts turned to how much he missed Jeff. Blake remembered in the fall of 1999, he, Jeff, and two friends were elk hunting near the Rocky Mountain State Park. During their first night at their hunting cabin, the men got into a few bottles of Jack Daniels. The four of them ended up target practicing with their high-powered rifles in the darkness of the quiet night. The next morning when they arrived at their designated hunting location, they saw not one elk. Jeff said, "Well, you dumb shits, you scared off all the game with your night firing. If I had not been asleep in the cabin I would have stopped y'all from being such dumb asses."

They all broke out in laughter. Blake and friends knew that only Jeff could come up with a line like that.

Something did not seem right with Gloria. She just was too damned moody. "Tomorrow is another day, keep going, Tanner, and don't give it up," he murmured aloud.

Having no fun on a six-hour flight from JFK to London Heathrow is criminal, Blake thought as he got up from his seat and walked to the toilet. The New York Mutual Life Insurance Company was paying thousands of dollars for him to fly first class; he liked the seating and service, but he was just plain tired of traveling. He did love his job, and he was damn good at it. He had been able to buy the mini-ranch with his earnings, and he had all a man could ask for. *Well, I don't have a dog,* he thought. *I keep saying I am going to buy a dog when this job is completed.*

There was much for him to do when he arrived in London. He was thankful that his friend Erhan would meet him and brief him on the situation there.

Blake glanced over at the woman sitting across from him, a damn fine-looking brunette, dressed like a New York City executive and beating out words or graphs on her notebook computer. She wore a long brown skirt with a matching jacket. She detected Blake looking at her, and she turned her head toward him and smiled.

He smiled back and turned on the video located next to his seat, pulled the screen over to him, and scanned the channels. The movies offered were weird. *Why the hell don't they have any John Wayne or Clint Eastwood?* He felt the presence of the young woman sitting across the aisle looking at him. *What the hell, I'll give her a thrill and speak to her.* "Are we having fun yet?" was about all he could come up with.

To his surprise she replied, "No, not really. How about you?"

Blake, feeling like a cocky rooster, replied, "No, not really. How about a glass of wine?"

The aisle seat next to Blake was empty, and a man sleeping next to the pretty woman occupied the seat beside her. She leaned over toward Blake and whispered, "How about if I join you?"

Without waiting for an answer, she rose from her seat and sat down next to Blake. He saw big gray eyes and a trim body. She extended her right hand. "Nicole Parker, New York City."

Looking into her gray eyes, he took her hand in his. "Blake Tanner, Castle Rock, Colorado."

"Are you going to London on business?"

"Yes, I am."

She turned more toward him and slightly tilted her head. "May I ask what you do?"

Blake could not resist using his old line that he had picked up from an Air Force fighter pilot in Bangkok. He smiled and said, "I am a sugar beet inspector."

"Mr. Tanner, I have heard many lines before, but that is the dumbest line I have ever heard." She began laughing and slapped him lightly on his arm. "Now, will you tell me what you really do?"

Now Blake was laughing. "Okay, you got me. I am a Bible salesman. How does that sound?"

They both were laughing when the flight attendant asked them what they would like to drink. They ordered chardonnay. "No French wine," said Blake.

"Why, Mr. Tanner, you are shameful," Nicole said, and she laughed again. "Now I am having fun. How about you, Blake?"

"Yeah, me too. All it takes is a little laughter and a pretty drinking companion."

"Are you this funny with your wife?"

"I am always funny, says my young girlfriend. She doesn't quite understand all my jokes."

She looked at Blake with a sparkle in her eyes that would melt any man. "Your girlfriend is a lucky woman to have a man who has a good sense of humor. So many of the men I meet have no pickup routine. They just go straight into their bullshit lines, and they are pathetic. I guess that is why I go for older men. A man's man, that is what I like. Oh, dear, I am talking to you as if we have known each other for years. Sorry."

"That is quite all right, my dear. The conversation is refreshing." He could not resist the temptation. "Now, how about us having sex?"

Nicole looked at Blake with a blank look on her face. Then he started laughing, and she joined in. "I just might take you up on that offer, you big talker, you."

Blake quickly changed the subject before he got in deeper than he should. "What do you do, Nicole?"

"Oh, I am a thousand-dollar-a-night hooker." She did not smile or stutter.

Old Tanner was speechless. *Shit, maybe she is an expensive New York City hooker,* he thought. Then he could not resist. "Really?"

The gorgeous young woman sat for a few seconds without outwardly showing any emotions. "Gotcha." She smiled and crossed her legs. "Okay, no more games. I am a journalist for the *USA Today* newspaper."

"Shit hot," Blake said. "I just love newspaper reporters. Want to hear the story about the Lone Ranger and Tonto?"

"I beg your pardon," she said with a look of confusion.

They broke out in laughter again, and they could not stop laughing. The rest of the flight was very enjoyable for the newspaper reporter from New York and the mysterious man from Colorado. They bid each other good-bye as they left the customs area. Blake and Nicole exchanged hugs and sincerely hoped to see each other on another trans-Atlantic flight.

CHAPTER 24

London

Erhan was waiting for Blake as he emerged from customs and baggage claim at Heathrow. It's not every day that a Turkish man can meet an American man at the London Heathrow Airport. "Hey, you old cowboy," said Erhan as he grabbed Blake's hand and kissed him on both cheeks. "How was your flight?"

"Not bad at all. Long but enjoyable this trip." He returned the embrace from his friend. "We have got to stop meeting this way. People will think we have a thing for each other." They both laughed.

Jack Bentley, one of the British Interpol agents, was leaning against the wall next to the Ritz-Carlton courtesy desk, looking at a *London Times* newspaper. He was a big man, not fat, just a big man. Blake did not care for him personally, but he could work with him.

"Want a ride, mates?" Jack asked Blake and Erhan as they walked by where he stood.

"No, thanks. We have a car waiting," answered Erhan.

"See you later, Jack," Blake said coolly.

The black Mercedes limo belonged to the Turkish Embassy, and standing beside the car was Erhan's old and trusted friend, Turkish Army General Anadolu. The general was always called by his first name, "General." Even his longtime friend Erhan called him "General." *He should be called general,* Blake thought. *There is not a doubt but what he is a general, and he is in charge.*

"I've archived a lot of files from the Interpol secure network," said Erhan. "We can review them at our embassy, if that is satisfactory with you."

"Great. Do you have a suspect list, Erhan?"

"We do have a list. The individuals we are after are in Southern Turkey, the Antalya area, and you know that land well. It looks like we might need to involve our Turkish Army Special Forces, along with Interpol. That should make you feel right at home, being a former Green Beret. They eat snakes just like you do." Erhan laughed.

Blake, laughing at his friend's remarks, suddenly said, "I take it they have a stronghold that we must raid to get to our targets?"

"Yes, we have been in touch with the Turkish Interpol agents, and, of course, the General is the supreme commander for all Turkish military." The General smiled and held up his right index finger. "We have found that the ring consists of drug dealers from America, Turkey, Great Britain, Spain, France, Croatia, and probably other countries in the Middle East and Africa. They are widely known to be heavily armed with modern military weapons and state-of-the-art sensing equipment."

"What about here in London? Are there any main players we could detain and question?" Blake asked. "Hope the hell we are not going on a wild goose chase by planning a raid in Turkey."

Erhan and the General shot a glance at each other with a puzzled look on their faces. "What do geese have to do with the plans?" the General asked with confusion in his voice.

Tanner tried to keep a positive and professional expression on his face before explaining about the American idiom. After he explained to the General what he meant, they all laughed.

"I must come to America and spend some time with you at your Colorado ranch," said Erhan. "There is much I would like to learn from you."

"You are welcome at my home anytime, my dear friend. We will talk and drink cold Coors." Again, he explained about the Colorado beer and how the people called it "Colorado Kool-Aid."

The Turks looked puzzled again. Blake told himself to stop while he was ahead.

Erhan spoke about the apprehension of Julie Spenser in New York City. "I just can't believe little Julie is a drug dealer. My daughter and she were such good friends. A person just never knows who is going to turn out bad."

Blake hesitated before making a comment about Julie Spenser. "I personally believe that she just got hung up with the chance to travel to exotic locations. Her direct involvement with Frank Pane and all the promises he made her were just too much for a protected daughter whose mother had just died. She loved Jeff or Frank Pane. We did discover that she had visited New York and Atlanta last year. The FBI is sending her back to London, and their authorities will deal with her."

The loud ringing tone of Blake's satellite phone interrupted the conversation. "Tanner here. How are you, Norman?"

"Blake. The little Turkish man who is in custody at our New York detention center has spilled the beans on the drug contacts he has been dealing with. It seems as though two Mexican detainees raped him last evening in his holding cell. He must have gotten a sneak preview of what is ahead of him in a Turkish prison."

"Now that is damn good news. Do you have a file on any of the people he identified?"

"We do, and four out of the five live and work out of Atlanta. They all have mafia links. Does the name James Connors mean anything to you?"

Blake took a deep breath and let out a low sigh. "Yes, I have met him. He is on the management team at International Atlanta Engineering, and he worked with my friend Jeff, and Frank and Rhonda Pane. Do you have enough evidence to arrest him?"

"We do, but not enough to put him away for good. I was hoping that you would turn the Turkish raid over to the Turks and Interpol, and come back to Atlanta. Will you help us nab Connors?"

"Damn straight I will. Erhan can represent me. The Turkish General in command is seated across from me as we speak. My only reason to be involved over here is to help apprehend the person or persons who were responsible for blackmailing Jeff and maybe killing him. I will be on my way back to Atlanta on the first plane smoking West."

"Great," said Norman. "Let me know when you are to arrive, and I will meet you at the Atlanta airport."

"Roger that." Blake disconnected the call and turned to his friends. "Did you two catch most of the conversation?"

"We did," answered the General. "You take care of your business in the States, and we will capture the enemy in Turkey."

"I'll drink to that," said Blake. "Hell, I will drink to anything." They laughed and shook hands.

Erhan spoke. "We have a special early dinner planned for you. Remember the trout that come down from the mountain streams into our fish camps?"

"I certainly do. Are you doing the special trout and vegetables cooked in clay pots in an open bread oven with freshly baked bread?"

"And a lot of cold beer," Erhan said with pride.

There is no way one can describe the taste of fresh mountain trout cooked with vegetables, and eaten out in the open, Blake thought. He thanked his friends for the feast and told them all that they were always welcome in Colorado. "We do similar types of cooking," he told them. "And we do have plenty of cold beer."

"Cheers to the cold beer," said the General. "May all the beer in the world be drunk between friends."

Blake always had flashbacks of his tours in Vietnam when the subject of cold beer came up. GI's drank more damn hot beer than the Budweiser brewery could distill. Beer would come in on pallets, and each GI was authorized two cans of beer per day. That was not a golden rule as he remembered. Jeff found out all the men in the camp who did not drink. He talked them into picking up their beer rations and giving the beer to him. When the Bud and Falls City beer ran out they would drink "33" Export (aka Tiger Piss). Blake started laughing out loud thinking about a "Tiger Piss" patch he had somewhere in his footlocker back in Castle Rock. *Some experiences a person who has been in a war cannot easily forget*, he thought. Not having cold beer was a memory that he would cherish, especially since he was a boy from Colorado, Coors country.

CHAPTER 25

January 12, 2005, Atlanta

Blake called Higgins and Mary before getting on the plane at Heathrow. He updated Donald and told him that he was near closing the case, thanks to the FBI. He also asked if Mary could meet him in Atlanta to assist with his final investigation. With Mary posing as his wife or girlfriend, it would be easier to make valuable contacts. Donald and Mary agreed to the creative proposal. Mary was especially happy to accept, as she would be with the new man in her life. Blake was equally happy. He did love Mary, and wanted to be with her all the time.

Norman Gregory was waiting at his normal spot when Blake exited the baggage claim area at the Atlanta airport. Norman grabbed Blake's garment bag. "I bet you are getting mighty tired of jet-setting back and forth between the U.S. and Europe."

"I am. Nice to see you, Norman. You and your agents are doing a damn good job investigating the international drug ring. Keep America clean. That is what I say."

"Thanks, Blake. We are pleased that you have decided to work with us instead of independently."

"My job has always been to investigate the death of Jeffery Sanders. I got in a little over my head due to my pride. I just could never sit back and let other people do all the work while I stood by and watched."

"You've done more than your share. George Holden of our New York office told me about your interrogation techniques. You are the one who broke the Turk, scared the shit out of him. Then when he was attacked in his jail cell, that forced him to sing."

"Do you have a plan for getting additional information on James Connors?" asked Blake.

"We do have our suspicions and standard FBI operating procedures we must follow. We will review and finalize our plans with our agents and you working in our think tank. After a day of putting our ideas together, we will come up with a good soundproof plan."

Blake told Norman he would be busy that evening. "I have a partner flying into the Atlanta airport from New York at seven-thirty."

Mary's plane landed right on time, and she flew out of the baggage claim area and spotted Blake immediately. "Hey, cowboy. You looking for some company this evening?"

"You bet. You know of anyone interested? Damn, you look and smell good, woman. You even feel good. I might be interested in a few days with you. Are you free? I only have ten bucks, but I can get you some instant coffee."

"Tanner, you amaze me. How do you stand moving around so much? Don't you ever miss being at home? What the hell does instant coffee have to do with us?"

"I do, and I will be home for good very soon. The sooner you and I get this case closed, the sooner I can show you my little ranch in Colorado. Would you like that? Instant coffee is an old GI thing. You know, like trade a jar of instant coffee for a short time."

Mary just looked at him with a smile; she then kissed him and hugged his neck. "Does this give you my answer?"

Blake and Mary spent a joyful evening together. They walked from their hotel and found a small restaurant that had the perfect setting. The pleasant aroma of the prime rib was delightful, and the taste of the meat was beyond description. "Damn good prime rib," Blake said as he took another bite of the tender meat and then drained the last drop of wine from his glass. "How about we order another bottle of cabernet?"

"Not for me, dear. I want to be alive and awake when we go to bed," Mary said as she placed her hand on his.

"Sorry, babe, I've got a headache."

"No deal, bud. You will not have a requirement for the head on your shoulders to ever ache." She laughed a soft and happy laugh.

The scheduled morning meeting at the Atlanta FBI office started promptly at nine sharp. All the major players were in place sitting around a conference table. The code name for the group meeting was "The Think Tank."

Norman Gregory chaired the committee, as he was the lead agent in the Atlanta Bureau. After introductions Norman announced, "The room is secured." He then turned on an overhead projector connected to a computer, which was operated by a woman computer specialist, an FBI agent. The open view on the screen was filled with federal regulations of what not to do.

The setting and atmosphere brought back memories of a similar briefing during his second tour of duty in Vietnam. The year was 1971, and he clearly remembered it was October, during the monsoon season. Blake was sitting next to Jeff listening to a stiff-necked U.S. Army intelligence major who was the briefer. He was a known prick to all the Special Forces team members. He had never seen combat, and he had never been shot at by the enemy, and unlucky for them, he had never been hit. The major began the brief with all the government red tape and bullshit. "Men, today I will brief you on how you will proceed to your target area, how to get there, and what you will do after you have found your targets."

"You going with us, Major?" asked a crusty old master sergeant.

"No, I am not. It's not my job," the major answered as he turned his back toward the A Team and continued to brief, looking at the screen.

The master sergeant would not give up on harassing the intelligence major. "If it is not your job to go with us, then why the hell are you briefing us on what we already know how to do?"

After what seemed like several minutes, the major turned toward the team members. "Who is in charge of this team?"

A tall, broad-shouldered captain raised his hand and spoke with a slow Southern accent. "I am in charge of this team, and we have just concluded this briefing. You can go back to your air-conditioned hotel room and drink hot chocolate with marshmallows floating on top. We have a job to do." The captain stood up and walked out the door of the briefing room. Following him were all the members of his A Team.

The sound of Norman Gregory's voice caught Blake's attention. He did not mean to show disrespect toward Norman, but he hoped the hell he got into the details and quickly finished with the government crap.

"I have introduced you to Mr. Tanner. He will be working undercover on this case as a subject matter expert and as a special investigator on contract with the FBI. Working with him to assist us is Miss Mary Stewart, who is another private citizen volunteer. She will pose as Mr. Tanner's longtime girlfriend. Now, on with the briefing." Norman could not help but look at Blake and smile.

The first picture on the screen was of James Connors. "This suspect is the money man behind most of the Atlanta drug trafficking. We will keep him under close surveillance by our agents, and Mr. Tanner will make contact with him. You have met Connors. Is that correct, Blake?"

Blake acknowledged that he had met Connors at the office of International Atlanta Engineering. "He does not fit the profile of a drug moneyman, but who the hell can tell nowadays?"

Norman continued. "Investigation into the murders of Frank and Rhonda Pane in their mansion in West Atlanta is ongoing. Our clues indicate that the Mexican mafia was involved, but we have no firm evidence as of this date. We have undercover agents operating and gathering evidence in Atlanta and Mexico. We do know that the pair was involved in extortion, money laundering, and drug trafficking in Europe and the Middle East. Let us act with what evidence we have as of today, and then we will review and update our plans as we gather additional evidence. Have I made myself clear?"

Well, that narrows it down to only a few suspects, Blake thought. *This James Connors has me baffled; he just doesn't seem like the type of person to be involved with drugs, or murder.*

"Are we having fun yet?" Blake said to Norman as they departed the briefing room.

"If it stops being fun, then it's time to retire," answered Norman with a simulated hand salute, and he blurted out, "Semper fi."

CHAPTER 26

Cold rain beat against the hotel room windows; the wind was blowing like a mini hurricane, and the weather was just plain shitty. It was cold for a January day in Atlanta, too damn cold for outside surveillance, Blake thought as he stood by the balcony window peering out into the west Atlanta skyline.

Impatiently Blake wished the torrential rain and wind would stop. The storm brought back memories of weather and the extreme heat and humidity that always seemed to plague him when he was in Vietnam. *Damn rash and black fungus. It's a wonder our damn feet didn't fall off.* He knew his memories would never go away; he would just deal with his memories the best way he could.

The sound of the hotel house phone startled him. The front desk informed him that he had a registered envelope.

He opened the official-looking large brown envelope with his pocketknife. "Official FBI Documents" was plastered all over the envelope with U.S. Government red tape. The contents inside were from Norman Gregory. There was a hand-scribed note on the outside of a smaller brown envelope.

Blake,

You will find the pictures quite interesting! Please read the notes carefully. These documents should assist you with your plans. Call if you need us. You know that we will have an agent following you at all times. Do not shoot him!

Respectfully, Norman

Blake sat down at the desk near the window. He then began going through the pictures and the notes printed on each photo. "Shit fire," he said aloud.

"What is it, darling?" Mary asked from the bathroom where she was putting on her makeup.

"This is good, hard, and sound evidence. We got Connors by the balls, and we will put them in a vise real soon. Would you like to have dinner with the thieving bastard, say tomorrow evening?" Blake picked up the room phone and dialed the number to International Atlanta Engineering.

"What's that, darling? What vise and balls are you talking about?"

He had to put the telephone down as he was laughing so hard at Mary's innocent remarks.

Mary did not see the photographs, nor did she read the notes that were in the envelope. Blake wanted her to form her own opinions of James Connors and not have any biased feelings about him when they met him and his wife for dinner.

Everything is in order, Blake thought as he placed his short-barreled .357 Magnum in the black leather shoulder holster and then changed tapes in his mini-recorder. *Sure as hell hope this little recorder doesn't squeak. Next time the FBI will wire me up, and then it is for real.*

At a stoplight near the restaurant, Blake asked Mary if she was nervous. He could tell by her body movement that she was a bit worried, but she was calm. "I love you, Blake," Mary said unexpectedly. "Do you love me?"

"Of course I love you. Why wouldn't I?"

"Just checking. If we get killed I want to be sure that it is for love and not just for the long arm of criminal justice."

"We will not get killed, don't worry, darlin', I will take good care of you. Besides, you owe me an apple pie, remember?"

Mary, looking over at the man sitting next to her, playfully blurted out, "You crazy shit, Blake. Can't you be serious for just once?"

"Have I told you how beautiful you are this evening? You are always beautiful. Now, on to our evening of fighting crime and seeking adventure. Are you ready?" Blake placed his hand on hers, and smiled an encouraging and loving smile. He then rubbed the back of his hand on her leg, causing her to jump a little in surprise and in the pleasure she had of his hand gently rubbing her leg.

Mary knew that she would be safe with Blake Tanner; he would protect her and love her forever.

Darkness had fallen when they walked in the front door of the Blue Lagoon Restaurant. A young Spanish-looking man met them. "Do you have reservations, sir?" he asked politely.

"Yes, the name is Tanner for eight o'clock."

"Oh, yes sir, Mr. Tanner, table for four. Would you prefer to be seated now?"

"Our guests' names are Mr. and Mrs. Connors. If you would show them to our table when they arrive, we would appreciate it."

Despite the large crowd in the dining room, people turned their heads and stared at Blake and Mary as they walked toward their table. Mary's red hair was flowing down the back of her black jacket, and her gray slacks fit snug to her body, revealing a body that was all natural. She was a sophisticated-looking woman with a beauty that glowed. Blake was dressed in a dark blue suit with a button-down shirt and a necktie that was choking him.

"How do you like this setting?" Blake said.

"I love it, but I am now getting a little nervous. What do I do? I forgot."

"Just follow my leads. You will be just fine. I see them coming through the front door. Mary, please don't grab my leg while they are with us."

Mary could not help but laugh. Blake's remark made her feel fully comfortable now.

An instant later James and Mrs. Connors arrived and followed the young Spanish greeter to their table. James extended his hand to Blake. "It is nice to see you again, Mr. Tanner. This is my wife, Donna."

"Good to see you again, Mr. Connors. Nice to meet you, Mrs. Connors. I would like for you to meet my longtime friend, Mary Stewart."

Blake took the lead and began the conversation by suggesting the menu and the selection of wine. Donna Connors was a pretty woman, not beautiful, but a very nice-looking Southern belle. "Have you been traveling, Mr. Connors?" Blake asked, hoping that he would bring up London or Istanbul.

"No, I have been staying close to home for the past month. We are very busy with new contracts here in the Atlanta area. By the way, how is the memorial for Jeff coming along?"

"We are almost finished. A few more weeks and my role will be over with."

Mary listened carefully to Blake's clever questions. She sensed that Blake was talking about closing the cell door on James Connors. *He is darn good*, Mary thought.

As the evening gradually progressed and they were finishing their dinner, Blake did not have a clue that would tie Connors with any drug dealings or murders.

For some unknown reason Blake thought he saw a nervous twitch in James Connors' left eye. What could he possibly say to get hidden information out of him? *Come on, Tanner, you are better than this,* he thought. All of a sudden, a light turned on in his head, and he had the perfect scenario.

"I found some pictures of Jeff and you taken in London and Istanbul. The pictures in Istanbul looked like a dinner party. Of course, I only recognized Jeff and you. There was a young Turkish man standing next to you. I will make copies if you want."

That certainly got James Connors' complete attention. His hand and his left eye began to twitch, he glanced at his watch, and he quickly said, "No, no, I probably have the pictures at my office. Donna, we must be going. Remember your phone call from your mother at ten this evening?"

Donna had a puzzled look come across her face. She nodded her head like a puppet, or like she had been formally instructed to do.

James Connors said the good-bye and thank you part of the evening very quickly.

"Got you, you bastard," Blake said under his breath where only Mary could hear him. "Did you see the change in him when I brought up the young Turkish man? The FBI have him locked up in New York City, and he identified Connors as the money man for the Atlanta drug trafficking."

Mary smiled at the excitement in Blake's voice. "You got him, baby. He will be on the defensive now. Is that good?"

"You bet that is good. Norman will be happy to hear that we have a button to push that makes James Connors squirm."

Even in the dim light of the taxi, Blake could see Mary smiling. As he held her hand, he thought, *What an absolute treasure I have in this woman. She is everything a man could ever hope for, or want.* Smiling at each other, holding hands during the taxi ride to their hotel in silence excited them both.

She paused inside the door of their hotel room, put her arms around him, kissed him, and pressed her body against his. "I love you so much, Blake. Please take me to bed."

"Your wish is my command, my dear."

During breakfast, Blake was in deep thought. He did have a few unsolved cases in his career. You cannot solve them all, he knew, and any investigator would willingly admit defeat at one time or the other. Except for the death of Jeff and the murders of Frank and Rhonda Pane, this case stuck with him. He repeatedly vowed not to give up until he solved the case.

"Blake? Blake? Are you okay?" Mary said softly.

"Sure, yes, I am just fine. You know me, always thinking about what I will do next. Sorry for neglecting you. You know that the number one person on my mind is you."

"I do. Thanks for loving me," Mary said with a vibrant glow on her face.

CHAPTER 27

FBI Headquarters, Atlanta

The same players who attended the first briefing used the FBI-secured conference room for the second briefing. Norman Gregory stood next to the female agent who would provide the briefing slides from her computer.

With coffee in hand, Blake took a seat at the middle section around the oval-shaped conference table. He had briefed Norman and provided his input for the briefing beforehand. Tanner also provided Norman with some personal thoughts that would be of interest to the group.

The same typical government introduction filled the screen before the actual briefing could begin. Norman presented an overview of what evidence they had found so far. Next, he explained what necessary processes would be taken during the next updated plan of action. "The next portion of the investigation will be presented by Mr. Tanner." Pointing to Blake with a friendly nod, he said, "It's all yours, killer."

There was no doubt in anyone's mind that Blake Tanner had given briefings before. He was comfortable in front of an audience, he was to the point, and he held the complete attention of all the agents. "What I am presenting to you has been approved by your boss. Thanks, Norman. We believe that our suspect, James Connors, has ties with the mafia in London and Istanbul. Your fellow agents have a young Turkish engineer locked up in New York

City. He has been charged with international drug trafficking. He also has been singing like a birdie to protect his ass. Wrong choice of words—he is gay—to protect *himself*." The room filled with laughter. "He has informed the FBI interrogators that James Connors is the money man for the international movement of drugs from London and Istanbul, to right here in Atlanta. We have personal evidence on Mr. Connors that could cause him to make a fatal blunder in our favor. He is not aware that the Turk is in custody, nor does he have an idea that you, the FBI, have identified him. Our plans are to use the Turk as bait, bring him to Atlanta under an armed escort, and turn him loose on Connors."

After the briefing, Blake and Norman discussed the upcoming events that would take place, and the crucial role each one would play during the plan. Blake spoke with a concerned look of disgust on his face. "You know, Norman, I am getting no closer to finding out if Jeff Sanders killed himself or if he was murdered. The answer appears to be impossible."

"It is possible that after we nail James Connors, we will have additional evidence. Possibly, it could link him to the ones who were in on the blackmailing with the Pane couple. We do have evidence that Mr. Sanders was being blackmailed by Frank and Rhonda Pane, but we have not implicated anyone else."

"You're right. I'm just getting damn tired baby-sitting all these bad guys. We should just hang them like they did back in the Old West. It would sure save a lot of taxpayers' dollars, that's for damn sure." *That is the Tanner way*, Blake thought.

"I heard that, but we both know that cannot be done. A few more weeks and we should have this case wrapped up, and with luck we will know the way in which your friend really died."

The shower pelted hot water on Blake's neck and back. When it came to taking hot showers, he took full advantage of each opportunity. There had been many times in his life that he went for days, even months, without being able to shower or brush his teeth. Those were the memories he wanted to remember. He was still alive. That is what he remembered.

"Want some company and someone to wash your back, cowboy?" Mary stood outside the shower door with nothing on but a smile.

"Get your pretty butt in here, girl. Damn, you are a fine figure of a woman." They embraced each other as the hot water poured over their bodies. They made love as if it was to last them forever, and kissed passionately as their bodies moved against each other in rhythm. Clinging to each other, their love for one another exploded into a wonderful climax.

"Now that was a shower." Blake held Mary tight to his chest.

"I do love you so," Mary said as she dried off his back.

"I know, and I love you. You are my woman, and don't you ever forget it."

"Yes sir, and no sir. I will never forget."

It had been drizzling all morning, which was normal for this time of the year in Atlanta. The FBI informed Blake that the young Turk had been moved to Atlanta from the New York City detention center. They cut a deal with him and told him that he would serve his prison sentence in New York State instead of in the dreaded Turkish prison. The FBI informed the Turk that only if he cooperated and went along with the plan to implicate James Connors would the deal be honored. If not, he would be lost in the deep, black Turkish history.

Connors was a low life. He just had power and money. The bastard even went to church on Sunday. If the Turk could scare him into making a foolish mistake, then the FBI would seize him. The big question was how the FBI would get him to reveal a relationship between the Turk and James Connors. The missing link must be the gay Turk. Maybe old Connors was gay. *Who knows?*

Having this much fun with work is crazy, Blake thought, throwing a gum wrapper in the garbage can. *One day I'm drinking coffee at my house, and the next day I am on a case to find out if my best friend killed himself. Here I am in Atlanta, helping the FBI catch a former colleague of Jeff's for running drugs. Now, does that make sense or what?*

Mary was out shopping and enjoying some much-needed rest. She dearly loved to shop, and she knew what the best bargain was for the money. Blake jumped when the room phone rang. It was Norman Gregory, and he wanted Blake to come to his office. Norman told Blake that they had new updates concerning the case.

He left Mary a note and told her where he would be if she needed him. "How about dinner at The Outback?" he wrote. "P.S. I love you."

Norman was waiting in his office for Blake. "Come on in. Want some coffee?"

"No, I'm full of coffee. How about some scotch?"

"That would be great, but you know, a federal office."

"Yeah, and that is bullshit. All those senators and congressional representatives have booze sitting out in the open. I watch a lot of 'Law and Order' on television." Of course, Blake laughed at his own joke, but he liked the TV program.

Norman pulled out a gray folder from his desk drawer. "Have a look. Tell me what you think."

There were more pictures of James Connors, but this time they included the young Turk. Two Mexican men dressed in business suits looked like money was no object by the way they were dressed. They were sitting with Connors and the Turk.

Blake stared and blinked. "The Mexican mafia, I take it?"

"Yes, and these are the first known photographs we have seen of them all together. Our intelligence experts informed me that the pictures were shot and developed in Atlanta, a place called El Chino restaurant. Ever hear of it?"

"Not only have I heard of it, I have been there. Jeff Sanders had a meeting there with two Mexican men just a few days before his death. Now we are getting somewhere."

"Do you want to go with me to the restaurant?" Norman asked. "They do not know me, and maybe they will remember you. Did you make any contacts there?"

"I did. The bartender is a former paratrooper with the 173rd Airborne, a Vietnam vet also. I believe he is clean, but I won't bet my jump boots on it."

"You think he will talk to a former jarhead?"

"Probably not. Just don't jump up and down on the bar and show everyone your Marine anchor. Don't embarrass me, will you, Norman?"

When Norman stopped laughing he said, "After we gather some additional Intel information we can make our plans to have a drink at the El Chino. You still game?"

"You bet. Just let me know when."

"Blake, you might want to talk with Mrs. Sanders. She may have some additional information that could shed more light on her husband's death." Norman rose from his desk and extended his right hand to Blake. "You never know about these suicides, especially when a pretty wife is the beneficiary of a large life insurance policy."

Blake's satellite phone rang, and he reached in his coat pocket and pulled out the black-faced phone. He looked at the caller ID on the screen; it was his oldest daughter, Kristy.

"Hi, Dad, where are you? And how are you?"

"Hey, darlin', I'm in Atlanta, and I am doing just fine. How are you? Is everything okay?"

"All is fine here. We want to know when you are coming back home."

"Damn soon, I hope. How is Karla? And how are my sons-in-law doing?"

"We all are well. Dad, Karla and I bought you a present today, hoping that what we bought you will bring you home sooner. You will find two little black Labrador puppies in a basket when you come home. They are brother and sister, and they are so cute. Hope you are not mad?"

His voice cracked. "Thanks. You girls are wonderful. I am quite excited to see them. Will you care for them until I come home? It will probably be next week sometime."

"You bet. They are in our family room, and Rob is playing with them. I told him not to get attached to them, as they were my dad's puppies."

"Thanks again. What shall I name them?"

"Oh, you will come up with names for them."

"I got to run, darlin', talk to you later, and I love you and your sister. Tell the boys to treat you girls right or I will whip their asses."

Blake was beside himself knowing that he now had a dog—make that two dogs to take care of.

CHAPTER 28

On a chilly Sunday morning on January 15, Blake Tanner rang the doorbell at Gloria Sanders' home in the plush northwestern suburbs of Atlanta. She insisted that he come over early and they would have breakfast together. He sure hoped that she could provide him with some kind of clue, or that maybe she had remembered a detail about Jeff's death that she may have forgotten.

The large front door opened, and Gloria stood there dressed in what Blake thought was a light blue Hawaiian low-cut top and skirt. "Hi, Blake. Please come in." She put her arms around him and kissed him on the cheek. "It is a little early for scotch, but I have some Bloody Marys mixed up."

"Sounds great," he said and hugged her back. He kissed her cheek and held her a few seconds. "You sure are looking good. How are you getting along, living all by yourself in this big house?"

She closed the door and walked toward the kitchen. As Blake followed her she asked, "Where the hell have you been lately?"

"All over the universe. Well, it feels like it, anyway. Back and forth to London and Istanbul, then New York City, and now I am working out of your city, good old Atlanta."

"Have you found a woman yet? I bet they are lined up to catch you."

"I don't know why they would want to line up for me. I'm just a nasty-mouthed retired GI."

"Yeah, you are, but you're a damn good one, Blake Tanner. Annie would have wanted you to move on with your life. I know she would."

Blake hesitated and then told Gloria about Mary Stewart.

"Good for you, Blake. I wish you and Mary the best of luck, and I do expect an invitation to the wedding."

The two old friends talked about their families and remembered the good times they had together when Annie and Jeff were alive. "Damn shame they both had to leave us at such an early age. They both died horrible deaths," Blake said sadly. "Gloria, have you thought of anything else that might help me or the police with the investigation of Jeff's death?"

"I have given considerable thought to Jeff's death, especially after Frank and Rhonda were murdered. The Atlanta police have closed Jeff's case and called it a suicide. Did you know that?"

"I did, but the FBI has reopened the case. I am working with them, but we don't have many leads. I was hoping that you might come up with something, anything that you may have forgotten to tell the investigators."

Gloria raised her eyes and gazed into the eyes of her longtime friend. "I found a note in one of Jeff's golf shoes last week. As I was cleaning out his sports closet, the note fell out. I locked it up and told no one. I was waiting for you. There is no other person I trust."

Blake sat down on one of the kitchen bar stools. "Can I read the note?"

"Of course. Let me go get it. Pour us a couple of BMs, will you?"

While Gloria was away, Blake poured the drinks and looked around the kitchen. The room was empty, not of furnishings, but of Jeff's spirit. He could smell the breakfast casserole in the oven, and he caught a scent of Gloria's cologne. *What a damned mixed-up situation*, he thought. *Jeff, old friend, if you hear me, help me out. I'm stuck in a rut and can't seem to get out.*

Gloria returned and handed Blake a small pink Post-it, folded in half.

"Before you read the contents, prepare yourself for a shock. It liked to have knocked me for a loop," Gloria said softly as she walked toward the kitchen stove as the timer went off.

Here we go again, Blake thought. He unfolded the note and looked over the few words that were written in beautiful cursive—a woman, no doubt, by the penmanship. As Blake read the short note, lights began to go on in his mind. "Son of a bitch," he said aloud.

Jeffery,
Meet me this evening at the AAH lounge, 8:30 sharp. RP.

"What do you make of this, Gloria?"

"I take it to be at the Atlanta Airport Hilton, and RP could be Rhonda Pane." Gloria then walked up to where Blake was sitting at the kitchen bar. "I always thought Rhonda had the hots for my Jeff."

"But why would she and her husband want to blackmail you and Jeff? This will take some thinking about. Our friendly FBI agents will help us. They have all sorts of methods to evaluate handwriting and the type of paper used. It might not have been Rhonda who wrote the note."

Gloria took a seat beside Blake. While looking into her half empty glass of Bloody Mary mix she began to cry. "Sorry, I just get these crying jags and cannot stop. I am scared. This big old house is so lonely without Jeff. The kids are busy with family functions, and besides, they have their own lives to live."

Blake put his hand on hers and tried to console her. "It will all work out. Try not to worry. You must be strong for your kids and grandkids. I will ask the FBI to place you under their protection program until we get this case solved. You will be okay."

She thanked Blake for his longstanding friendship and for letting her cry on his shoulder. Her sadness and sorrow would go away in time. Blake knew she would never forget her loving husband.

Somewhere deep down, Blake sensed that Gloria was not being completely truthful with him. There was darkness and a puzzling mystery about the relationship between Gloria and Jeff; he just could not put his finger on his suspicions.

The morning had started with rain, and then the sun began to peep through the clouds, bringing a sigh of relief to Blake. He liked the sounds of gentle rain, but when he was in bed trying to sleep was his favorite time for rain.

He had too many obstacles fighting each other in his mind, like the unforgettable years of war, the death of his best friend, and the visit with Gloria this morning.

Norman Gregory stood at the coffee bar when Blake entered the FBI special agent's office. "How about a cup of coffee?" asked Norman as he grabbed a doughnut from the open box. "It is time to have a drink at the El Chino. Are you free this afternoon—say, around happy hour time?"

"Happy hour is my favorite time of the day. Hell, yes," muttered Blake. "We should go casual and be ready for some war stories."

"It has been a long time since I went out drinking with a snake eater." Norman smiled.

Blake laughed at the former marine's remark. "It's been a long time since I have been out drinking with a jarhead."

"We checked out the bartender at the El Chino, Ray Bennet. He is a good guy," Norman said to Blake as they walked toward the secured briefing room.

The FBI had analyzed the handwriting on the note that Gloria found. Norman gave an official copy of the report to Blake. It was determined that the handwriting was not that of a woman. A man had written the note, and he may have changed his natural writing habits.

Special Agent Norman Gregory parked his unmarked gray Dodge Intrepid in the El Chino Restaurant and Bar on the western edge of Atlanta. The restaurant had been a favorite watering hole for locals since 1973. Located in a blue-collar neighborhood of the city, Western Atlanta was known for numerous veterans of Foreign War and American Legion chapters. "If you don't like America, then keep your ass out" was the general feeling of the residents.

Blake arrived a few minutes before Norman. He sat toward the middle of the bar talking with a big, gray-headed man standing behind the bar washing glasses.

"Howdy, partner, how about a drink?" Blake said as he shook Norman's hand. "Haven't seen you for a while. Been out of town?" *Good acting, Tanner*, he thought.

"Yeah, you know, traveling is a way of life for a software engineer. What the hell have you been doing?"

"You know, the usual for an old retired fart. Ray, this is my good friend, Norman. Norman, Ray. You have to watch him, Ray. He is a former jarhead, and you know how rowdy they get after a few drinks."

"Yeah, I remember. What will you have, friend?"

"Crown on the rocks, thanks."

The bartender brought Norman his drink and placed another Johnnie Walker Black on the rocks in front of Blake. "These are on the house. God bless America, and welcome home, brothers."

"Cheers. Thanks, Ray," the two said.

"You notice anyone who looks out of place in here?" asked Norman.

Both men had observed the entire bar and dining area upon their entrance to the restaurant. Being highly trained in such matters, they were always looking for an out-of-place person. "There are quite a few Mexicans in here," Norman drawled.

"Duh, yes. It is a Mexican restaurant, you know," Blake said with a slight nudge to Norman's arm. "I recognize the voice of the man sitting at the table directly behind us. He was sitting at the same table the last time I was here. It could just be he is a local, or he may have another life that we are interested in?"

From where he was sitting, Norman was able to glance at the table where the man Blake described was sitting. There were three men, all Mexican. They were dressed in expensive-looking suits, and one wore a black leather jacket. "The one that you recognize. Is he the one wearing the black leather jacket?"

Blake was able to turn slightly on his bar stool and sneak a look at the man. "Yep, that's the one."

Blake and Norman had a few more drinks and pumped Ray, the bartender, for more information. “Would you happen to know any of those three men sitting behind us?” Blake asked.

Ray looked over at the table, and then he focused his eyes on Blake and Norman. “Yes, they are businessmen, and they are frequent customers. The two men in suits are executives for Mexcon Engineering Company. The other one in the black leather jacket is Ramos Portales. I believe he is with their sales department. Hey, remember that business card I gave you, the one you wanted because your friend met with a Mexican man? Well, the one in the middle is him, Hector Franco.”

“Very interesting. Thanks, Ray. We appreciate the information,” Blake said in a low voice so as not to be overheard.

“Let’s get out of here. I want to put a tail on those three.” Norman called his office using his cell phone when he and Blake arrived at Norman’s car. He gave specific instructions to the agent he was talking with. “Let’s head back to my office. We will pull up some files on thcsc hombrcs.”

“Bingo,” Norman blurted out as he put his finger on the mug shot of Ramos Portales. “Our Señor Portales has a record.” He read the files aloud so Blake could hear. “Minor drugs, suspected DUI, and an outstanding traffic warrant. That is enough to bring him in, but he would be released within hours. It is better to just place him under tight surveillance, and see what he is up to.”

Moving from the government-issued chair he was sitting in, Blake walked to the window behind Norman’s desk. He was deep in thought about the involvement of the Mexican men and Jeff. Why would Jeff be dealing with these characters? *Just doesn’t make any sense,* he thought. He sure had his job cut out for him, and the difficult challenges that lay ahead of him were unknown.

Murder is not amusing, Blake thought. He still had the gut feeling that Jeff had been murdered, and he felt he was getting close to finding out the truth.

CHAPTER 29

Mary flew back to New York, as she needed to return to work and her normal life. The valuable assistance she had provided to the FBI and to Blake's investigation received recognition. Besides her first-class travel, the FBI presented her with a check for two thousand dollars. Along with receiving the money, which would go toward her daughter's college expenses, she was with the man she loved and sincerely hoped to marry someday.

"I might have found something here," the FBI handwriting specialist said with excitement. "We completely analyzed the handwriting and the Post-it that was used. The handwriting is positively that of a man, probably Hispanic, and highly educated, either by a credited university or just street educated."

"Why do you say that?" asked Blake.

"By comparison of handwriting samples," the specialist answered quickly. "We have specimens from all sources and all sexes. Our analysis indicates that the man is slender, and traces of hair follicles found indicate he is dark-headed, probably with long hair. He also uses styling gel on his hair, and he is right-handed. We found traces of cocaine residue from under his fingernails. Special Agent Gregory asked us to perform analysis on the handwriting of the late Rhonda Pane. The handwriting is definitely not hers."

Norman thanked the specialist and turned to Blake. "Now, my friend, we are getting somewhere. We can update our strategy and our plans. There have been updates on the young Turk that we turned loose as bait. Of course, he does not know that. He has made contact with James Connors. They met yesterday for lunch. Our agents got pictures and good audios of their conversation."

The loud sound of thunder woke Blake up when he had just drifted off to sleep. He glanced at the clock sitting on the night-stand next to his bed. Four damn thirty in the morning. He then realized that his sleep was over. It was a good time for thinking, in the early morning. The steady downpour of the rain outside his hotel room calmed him. *I sure as hell hope that with all of this water, it helps the rhubarb grow,* and he smiled knowing that most people would not know what he was talking about, or even what rhubarb was. His thoughts drifted back to when he was a boy and his mother would make rhubarb pie and cobbler. His dad loved sweetened rhubarb. Great memories. Those were the good old days.

Tanner had just stepped out of the shower when the hotel room phone rang. Before he could say "hello," Norman Gregory blurted out, "Grab your cock and then put on your socks. We got a live one."

"Is this some kind of a friggin' marine joke?"

"No, it is for real, Blake. We have arrested James Connors and the Turkish kid. They got in a fight at the Airport Hilton, and the kid shot Connors. He will live, but the kid tried to kill him. We believe that Connors is scared and ready to talk. I'll pick you up in front of your hotel in thirty minutes."

"I'll be waiting," *Off we go again on another goose chase*, he thought.

With his hand over the top of a Styrofoam cup filled with hot black coffee, Tanner slid into the front seat of the unmarked FBI Dodge Intrepid. "All right, Mister Hot Shot FBI Man, I am ready to listen. What the hell is going on?"

Norman could not help but laugh at Blake's funny way and down-home humor. "How the hell did you ever make it as a chief warrant officer? Better than that, how did you remain a GS-14 during your civilian career?"

"Because I stayed away from college officer pricks like you. Talk to me, Norman. By the way, you are a GS-14, big damn wheel."

"About four o'clock this morning, the Hilton manager called the facility security guard and asked him to check into the sounds of reported gunfire from the third floor of the hotel. When the security guard arrived he found the room door ajar, and James Connors was lying on the bed with a gunshot wound to his left shoulder. He found the Turkish kid sitting in a chair with a short-barreled .38 Smith and Wesson revolver in his hand. The police were called, and in turn, they called our Operations Desk when they realized that Connors and the kid were on our watch list."

"I woke up at four o'clock this morning. Damn thunder liked to have knocked me out of bed, about the same time as the shooting incident supposedly occurred. Interesting. It is time for me to retire."

"You want to be with us when we interrogate these two, don't you?"

"You bet. Give me a rubber hose, a twenty-four-volt battery, and some wire, and I'll get them to talk. Yes, I would like to be present. Thanks, Norman."

"Your way is probably the best, but we know you can assist us. Both of them are deathly afraid of you, and didn't you tell the Turkish kid that you would put him in a cell with three burly man rapists, and you would stick a cattle prod up his ass?"

"I would not say a thing like that. It is against the law to endanger suspected murderers and drug dealers." Blake laughed, but he did feel that he should have his way to perform interrogations the old-fashioned way.

The young Turkish engineer was sitting at the interrogation desk when Norman and Blake entered. His facial expression when he saw Blake was as if he were about to be executed. He commenced to squirm in his chair, and he would not make eye contact with either Blake or Norman.

Blake walked to the corner of the room where he had perfect eye contact with the suspect. Norman began on the Turk in a very reversed method than he usually took. "We have your fingerprints on the weapon you were holding, we have samples of your DNA, and we have three witnesses who can identify you as the shooter who tried to kill James Connors. More than that, we have additional evidence that will link you to the organized crime of drug trafficking and blackmail. You might get only ninety-nine years in prison, without parole, or maybe we will just deport you back to Turkey. What do you have to say about that?"

The sweat poured down the Turk's face, he began swallowing dry-mouth saliva, and by his dramatic actions, he was definitely ready to talk.

Norman walked away and nodded for Blake to take over.

Blake continued hammering the Turk, using similar techniques that Norman had been using. He raised his voice a little louder, and he leaned over in front of the suspect, speaking in a low voice. "Now, you sick-minded son of a bitch, why did you try and kill James Connors? Was he your lover? Had he been cheating on you?"

"No, no, no," he shouted. "I only defended myself. He tried to shoot me, and I fought with him, and took the gun away from him. When he continued to threaten me, I just pulled the trigger. Believe me, I never shot anyone before. I just wanted to protect myself."

"He was not your lover then?"

"No, he wanted money from me. He threatened to kill me if I did not pay him three million dollars."

"Do you have three million dollars?"

"Yes, I was paid for delivering drugs to a contact in New York City."

"Where is the money now?"

"It is secure in a locker at the JFK airport. I was arrested by your American authorities before I could hide the money in my suitcase and then board the plane to Istanbul."

"What is the name of the person you delivered the drugs to?"

The Turk hesitated and looked down at his hands, which were folded in front of him on the table. "Can I have some water, please?"

"Sure you can have some water, after you give me the name of the person you made the delivery to."

"No, I cannot tell you. They will kill me if I tell you."

"Yeah, you are right. Norman, you want to let this guilty drug dealer out of jail? He can go live with his drug buddies up in New York City."

Norman could tell that Blake was not serious, but it sure got the immediate attention of the young Turk. He walked toward the interrogation table and sat now across from the suspect.

"No, please. You must protect me. They will kill me," the Turk cried.

Blake sat down in the chair across from the Turk, next to Norman. He crossed his arms and snarled, "Well, there you go. Either way you get killed. Tell us what we want to know, and we will protect you. If not, you will be on the street before the sun goes down on your cute little ass."

It did not take long for the Turk to start chirping like a bird. He moaned and blurted out, "I do not know the name of the man, and he made sure that I was aware of the situation before I departed Istanbul. He was from Mexico, and he spoke very poor English. He told me that I was not to leave the airport terminal building under any circumstance. I was to leave on a Turkish Airline flight at six-thirty, the same evening your authorities detained me."

"Did you ever see this man again?"

"Mr. Connors met with him before I arrived at his hotel room. They did not see me, as I was getting out of a taxicab, and it was dark. It was the man from the New York JFK airport."

Blake turned his head toward Norman. "Do you have any more questions?"

"Not now. Probably later." He and Blake walked out of the interrogation room.

"We made progress, brother," Blake told Norman.

"Yes, we did," answered Norman. "James Connors should be released from the hospital later today. We will see what he has to say. There are always two sides to every story."

This is getting to be like a damn game of hide-and-seek, everyone hiding, and no place to go, thought Blake. He tried not to think about the fate of Gloria if she were involved with any of these people. The worst part was not knowing which one, if any, of these people who were detained was involved with Jeff's death.

Blake called Higgins in New York and updated him. He told Donald that they were making headway on the case.

"Good work, Mr. Tanner. I look forward to your phone call when you have wrapped things up. Do you need anything from me?"

"No, no, sir. I am doing just fine."

Mary was happy to hear Blake's voice. "I miss you so much. When are you coming up to see me?"

"Soon, baby, soon. Another week and we should have all our work completed. Have to run. I love you. Talk to you soon."

Blake made his weekly telephone call to his daughters in Denver. They wanted him to come home, stop running around all over the world, just enjoy life, relax, and have some fun for a change. He had told them about Mary, and they were supportive and understanding about his feelings for her. *Just do what you want to do, Dad* was their reaction. Of course, he would do as he wanted to do anyway, so they might as well agree with him. It was good to know that they wished only for him to be happy. He asked about his new little puppies, and if they were growing.

Thc phonc call came in from Gloria while Blake was having his four-thirty drink of scotch in his hotel room. She was crying, and her shrill voice was that of a scared and shaken woman. "Blake, someone has followed me home. They are sitting in a car parked in front of the house. I'm scared. Please help me?"

"Calm down, dear. They are probably FBI agents. Take another peek outside and tell me what make of car they are driving. Don't let them see you."

"It looks like a BMW or Mercedes, four-door, I think. I just can't tell for sure."

"Turn your house security system on, and I will contact the police and FBI. I am on my way to you right now. Just stay calm. Gloria, do you have a pistol in the house?"

"Yes, I keep a .38 revolver in my bedside nightstand."

"Get it, and sit in your chair that is in the corner of the family room. I'll see you in a few minutes. For God's sake, don't shoot me."

Blake called Norman, who in turn called the local police to expedite a patrol car to Gloria's residence.

When Blake and Norman arrived, two police squad cars had pinned in a black BMW, and they had two men leaning against the trunk of the car. They both were spread-eagled, and their hands were handcuffed behind their backs.

Norman flashed his badge and identified himself. He introduced Blake as a special investigator. "What do we have here, Sergeant?"

"Dispatch informed us that the FBI was involved, and we were to treat any suspects we confronted as hostile. These two are as bad as they come. mafia hit men from Mexico. They both are on our Most Wanted List," the sergeant told Norman and Blake.

While Norman and the police were preparing the criminals for transportation to the police station, Blake went to Gloria's front door. He rang the doorbell and called her name loud enough for her to hear his voice. Gloria looked through the security glass and identified Blake.

"Just a minute. Let me turn off the security system."

She was so happy to see Blake that she just flew into his arms. "Did you catch them? Are they under arrest?"

"Yes, the police had them in custody when we arrived. Are you okay?"

"Why me? Oh, I am so scared. Don't leave me alone. Please don't leave me," she cried as she clung to Blake.

Blake knew that he could not stay and be alone with her. He might drop his guard and let her take advantage of him, which would be okay with him. His main concern was why would the Mexican mafia be targeting Gloria? Did she have anything to do with the murders of Frank and Rhonda Pane? Did she know more about Jeff's death than she was letting on? He realized that he had more questions than answers. The FBI would certainly investigate this incident. *Damn, is Gloria involved with drug trafficking, mafia, and murder? No, she couldn't be, not her*, he thought.

Gloria decided it would be best if she went to her daughter's house for a few days. Her decision brought instant relief to Blake; he was relieved to be out of a sticky situation. The police sergeant said that they would escort Gloria to her daughter's home in nearby southwest Atlanta.

"James Connors will be ready for us to interrogate tomorrow," said Norman. "Do you want to be involved, Blake?"

"I wouldn't miss the chance to find out what he knows. I'll be there."

At exactly nine forty-five in the morning, James Connors was escorted to the interrogation room by two armed police officers. His shoulder was heavily bandaged, and his arm was in a sling. He declined to have an attorney present; he told the officers that he had nothing to hide.

Norman started in on Connors with a friendly type of approach. After a few minutes, he felt that he must change tactics and try a different method of questioning. "Mr. Connors, we have enough evidence on you to send you up the river for many years. If you cooperate, we may be able to get your sentence reduced. I want to know your involvement with Engin Mersch. Why were you two meeting at the Airport Hilton? And why did you try to kill him?"

James Connors moved around a bit in his chair, shifted his position as to look away from Norman. "I have no idea what you are talking about. That Turk tried to rob me, and then he tried to kill me. I never saw him before in my life."

"You're lying to me. We have pictures and audios of you two meeting within the last few weeks. If you continue to bullshit me, I will turn you over to Interpol Headquarters, in Turkey. Would you like to be detained by the Turkish police?"

Connors began to perspire; sweat beads gathered on his forehead. He shifted around more in his chair. "No, please, don't deport me. I will cooperate with you. Just don't send me to Turkey. They will kill me."

Norman turned over the interrogation to Blake. Connors was extremely nervous when Blake leaned over the desk in front of him. Blake began by just staring at Connors. The presence of Blake standing over him, just glaring at him, caused him to panic.

"Okay, okay, what do you want from me?" he cried out.

"First of all, I hate your guts, and I think you are a lying, cheating, no-good son of a bitch. You should be, and you probably will be, charged with murder, blackmail, extortion, and drug trafficking. In the state of Georgia, that means the death penalty. If you cooperate, and I highly advise you to do so, your life may be spared by a federal judge. I sure as hell hope so. Life in a maximum-security prison will be a great life for a southern gentleman like you. Drugs, all the sex you want, or all the unwanted sex you want from your prison mates. Damn, Connors, you will have fun. Bubba will have fun with you, too."

"I would not survive in prison. Someone would kill me. I want to make a deal, but not with you. I want to talk with the FBI agent, Gregory. I also want my lawyer present before we go any further."

"Good, damn good," Blake said with anger. "I just might have you killed anyway." Tanner walked away from Connors with so much hatred toward him that he could actually waste him and not feel guilty in the least.

Connors cooperated with the demanding questions that Norman asked him. He provided names, addresses, telephone numbers, and dates during his tape-recorded and videotaped interrogation. Norman told Connors and his lawyer that he would ask the district attorney to file for life in prison and not the death penalty.

"Wait a minute. I did not kill anyone. You can't accuse me of murder as I killed no one," Connors cried out. "The Mexican mafia killed Frank and Rhonda, not me. I am not a murderer."

"You were an accessory to murder. You knew about it. You will be charged," Norman announced to Connors and his attorney.

The attorney for James Connors snarled, "You have no evidence to charge my client with murder."

"You know better than that. We have your client's confession on tape. He admitted he knew about the murders." Norman waited for their reaction.

Connors spoke quietly with his attorney, who announced, "My client has no more to add. I ask that he be released immediately on bail until a hearing is arranged."

"Sure, he will be released to the county jail, where he will be held for murder one. A judge will arrange for a hearing date. Until that time, we have the right to interrogate him at any time we feel it is necessary. Anything else you need to know?"

That statement sure pissed off the attorney. He got up and stormed out of the room. "You will be hearing from me, and very soon."

"We will be waiting for you. Have a nice day," Norman said with slight smile.

Blake and Norman headed for the briefing room to review the tape recording, videotapes, and written transcripts of the interrogation.

Something about Connors had Norman and Blake puzzled. If he had been the money man for years, how many other people were involved with his operation, and how many countries did he deal with?

"Special Agent Gregory, this is beyond belief. You just have to view the tape of the interrogation with Connors," Jack Thomas, one of the FBI agents who had videotaped the interrogations, said.

As Norman and Blake watched the tape of Connors, they noticed his body language. The agent running the video froze a pane. "Look, the names and addresses he gave you change from the next set of questions you asked him." He forwarded the tape a few panes and froze the picture again. "Now, watch him when you ask him for the names of the Mexican contacts."

"Damn, you're right, Jack. What's your take on this, Blake?"

"Bastard is lying through his teeth," Blake replied. "We need to keep surveillance on him twenty-four-seven."

CHAPTER 30

January 20, Atlanta

When Blake looked back, it was all like an incredible dream. What started out to be an investigation into Jeff's suicide had turned out to be an international circle jerk, with the murders, the blackmailing, the attempted extortion of Erhan, the money laundering, drug trafficking, attempted murder, and the Mexican mafia. A few months ago he was enjoying his life in Colorado, the next day he was in New York, and then three days later, he was in London. The best thing that came out of it all was his meeting Mary Stewart. Well, the money was good, that's for sure, and his Turkish friend Erhan was a once-in-a-lifetime friend. *Friends are easy to find, but they are harder to keep.*

The phone call came in while Blake and Norman Gregory were going over transcripts and recordings of the interrogations of James Connors and the Turkish engineer. They had spent the last two days going over evidence and clues that might implicate Connors, the Turk, and the two Mexican men linked to the Mexican mafia. DNA that had been extracted from the murder scene of Frank and Rhonda had been matched. The fiber, hair, and the handwriting on the note found in Jeffery Sanders' golf shoe were matched to Ramos Portales.

The FBI in Atlanta was detaining Ramos Portales and the two Mexican mafia men caught by the Atlanta police in front of Gloria Sanders' house. Due to them not being American citizens and because they had entered the States illegally, they could not be openly questioned until authorized by the Mexican International Police.

Blake was silent for a moment while he listened to Norman read the DNA report aloud. "We sure need to talk with the Mexicans," Blake declared. "Can you put some pressure on the Mexican police?"

"Don't worry," Norman answered. "We have enough evidence on the Mexican International Police to have them executed. I will have the federal judge assigned to the case prepare an arrest warrant with a little pressure from the higher courts. We should be able to detain them."

Blake shook his head and went into deep thought. Once again, something was not making sense, but damned if he could figure out what it was. Why were the Mexican mafia meeting with Jeff? This crap must stop. It was getting to the point that suspects had been apprehended, but who was the guilty bastard, or bastards?

Special Agent Gregory of the Atlanta FBI formally met with Federal Judge Andrew B. Cline early Monday morning at the federal building. Judge Cline issued an arrest warrant for the Mexican suspects who were being detained at the International Police Station annex. A "Bulletin Fugitive Alert and Wanted Notice" supported the justification for the warrants. An **ALL POINTS BULLETIN (ABP)** was transmitted to all law enforcement agencies in the United States and to Interpol headquarters. The involvement of geographical coverage would provide additional justification for the arrest warrants.

Norman contacted Blake on his satellite phone. "We got confessions from the Mexicans, all three of them. Other words, the full 'holy grail' of evidence was collected. Can you drop by my office? You can review the confession reports."

"I'm on my way. Put the coffeepot on."

Tanner looked at Norman when he entered the special agent's office. "You got the bastards, did ya?"

"We got them. The problem we are looking at is they probably will be deported back to Mexico. If that happens, they will go free with all the corruption that goes on in their police agencies."

"That's not good news at all. Let them escape and then we can shoot the bastards," Blake said with a smile. "I'm really not excited about this situation, but I can deal with it."

Norman handed Blake three folders. Each folder had data on the top indicating the name of the suspect and an evidence file number. "You are aware, Blake, all of the information is classified."

"Yes, and thanks for your professional and personal dedication to the case. You've done more than what was required of you, and it is appreciated."

Blake opened the folder of the first mafia hit man. The alleged crimes of his confession were highlighted in yellow. He went down the list and then opened the folder of the second man. The men's confessions were virtually the same, give or take a few words and some minor details. Blake then read the confession reports in detail, and he stopped when they both confessed to the murders of Frank and Rhonda Pane. Both men's confession of the murders and their different reasons for the killings were identical.

OFFICIAL FBI REPORT

Frank and Rhonda Pane stole five million dollars of drug trafficking money from the Mexican mafia. They both told us that they would have the five million dollars upon their return from Istanbul, Turkey, which would be within a few weeks. They did not have the money, so we blew them away.

Blake turned to page two of the investigative report. He noticed that Gloria Sanders' name had been highlighted by Norman during his review of the report:

We found the names Jeffery and Gloria Sanders on several documents in the safe at the Pane residence. It looked like they were involved with the missing five million dollars. After we were arrested, we knew that the Panes were using the Sanders' identity, and Mr. and Mrs. Sanders were not involved.

"This is really interesting," Blake said, with a look of concern. "Looks to me like you file murder charges against them. I can't believe that suspects confessing to a double murder would make a statement that would clear unknown people."

"We have already filed murder one. We do not have enough evidence against Ramos Portales to detain him. When you read the report, you will see that the only thing he did was carefully place the note in Jeffery Sanders' golf shoe. The initials R.P. were not Rhonda Pane's, but Ramos Portales. The dumb ass used his own initials. You will find it very interesting to find out who hired him to hide that note. Why James Connors would accuse him is beyond me."

After Blake read the interrogation report on Ramos Portales, he threw the folder down on the corner of Norman's desk. "I thought so. Connors, that little bastard, knows a hell of a lot more than he has told us. He is afraid of Portales. That is why he lied to us about him. Ole Señor Portales would make his life miserable."

"You're correct. We have more work to do on Mr. Connors." Norman picked up his telephone and gave strict instructions to his lead agent concerning the surveillance of Ramos Portales.

The man waiting in the decorative lobby at the Atlanta airport Hilton looked just like a Mexican comic book cop. Maybe it was the long trench coat or the sunglasses he wore at eight o'clock in the evening or the Snivley Witlatch thin mustache above his upper lip. Blake walked directly up to the man. "I'm Tanner. You the one who called me?"

"*Si*, I am Lieutenant Garcia, Mexican International Police. I have some information pertaining to a James Connors that might be of interest to you."

"I'm listening. You want a drink? The bar is just around the corner."

"No, I am on duty. I will be quick, as I am returning to Mexico City in two hours. This Señor Connors is on the hit list by the Mexican mafia. If your local police release him, we believe they will kill him. The hit man is here in Atlanta, but I cannot touch him. I have no official authority, and I cannot prove he is standing by to murder the Connors man."

"Will you give me his name? I can do something about arresting him. Why do you have concerns about Connors being murdered?"

"He is scheduled to make contact with a member of the Mexico City mafia this week. He is to deliver ten million dollars in exchange for a drug shipment going to an international dealer in Istanbul. If they kill him, then the Mexico City mafia family will receive no money, and the drugs will lose their street value. You see, there are two large mafia families in Mexico City. Both are after the money that this Connors man will pay for the shipment. As you say in America, 'First come, first serve,' or something like that. Oh, the hit man's name is Ramos Portales. You know, he has just been released by your police."

"Damn, thanks, Lieutenant. I appreciate the information. Can I do anything for you? Assist you in any way?"

"*Si*, I have one favor to ask from you. Put Ramos Portales away in your American prison. Do not send him back to Mexico. The local Mexican police will turn him loose as soon as he arrives in Mexico. I know it is not possible, but if Señor Connors goes to prison, then our economy will lose millions of dollars each year. Drug money keeps our country's economy going."

"I can oblige you with your request for Portales, or maybe he will end up dead. But as for Connors, he is going to prison for a long time. With your information, we have enough evidence on him to put him away. If we can arrest him during the transfer of money and drugs, we can nail the coffin shut.

"*Adios,* Lieutenant. Thanks again. Maybe next time we will have that drink." Blake turned around and walked toward the bar.

He walked up the front entrance stairs of the Atlanta Federal Building; he went through security and rode the elevator to the third floor where Norman Gregory's office was located. *These government buildings all look the same*, he thought as he grabbed a cup of coffee, and then he knocked on Norman's closed office door.

Norman motioned for him to come on in. He was talking on the telephone, and he pointed at the brown leather chair, which was in front of his desk.

When Norman hung up the phone he was fuming. "Goddamn government red tape. We were ordered to release the mafia men we arrested at the Sanders' house to the Mexican police. The bastards are probably in Mexico by now, drinking tequila and laughing at us. They are murderers, son of a bitch. I'll be go to hell and kiss my ass."

"Damn, bud, is that any way for an FBI special agent to talk? Sounds more like marine talk to me," Blake said, and then he busted out laughing.

Norman laughed, but he was still in a rage. "Can you believe that our law permits Mexican mafia gang members who are on the Most Wanted List to come into our country, kill two no-good criminal citizens, admit to their crime, and then some panty-assed federal judge lets them go back to Mexico?"

Blake knew that his friend was right, but they both knew there was nothing they could do about it. He stood up and drawled, "Let's go get drunk," and doing his best John Wayne imitation said, "We will circle the horses and mount the women, uh-huh, uh-huh."

Norman cracked up. "That's the worst John Wayne imitation I have ever heard. I will take you up on the drinking part. Let us get out of here and go to the El Chico."

"I needed to get away from the office. This investigation has more snags in it than any case I have worked for the last ten years," Norman said as he grabbed a handful of peanuts from the bowl sitting on the bar.

Blake told him about his meeting with the Mexican International Police lieutenant. That really made Norman's day. "All we have left is Connors and Portales."

Norman finished the last drop of his Crown. "We really need to put our heads together to solve this one. It is possible that one of them has information about your friend's death. Hell, they might even have killed him."

"Tomorrow is another day. Just forget it for an evening, what do you say?" Blake then ordered them another round. "So, Norman, you were in the first Gulf War?"

"Yes, we kicked ass and took names. The combat did not last long, but war is war. Isn't that what combat veterans always say?"

"Damn straight. Whether it is one year or one minute, war is not fun. You ever miss the corps?"

"Sometimes, yes, I do miss the camaraderie, but most all of our agents are military veterans. We have the same ideas about fighting crime as we did fighting our enemies in war. How about you? Do you miss the Army?"

Blake smiled. "No. Being a civilian in the CID was about the same as being on active duty in the Army. I liked the role of being a civilian employee versus being on active duty. It was easier to disagree with the top brass."

Norman ordered another round of drinks. "I can't imagine you ever disagreeing with the top brass." He then started laughing. "Nope, not old Tanner. He is a yes man."

"Yeah, right. If I had been a yes man, I would have been a colonel, or even a general. Buy that, and I will sell you a bridge going across the Grand Canyon."

"What do you say we get out of here?" asked Norman, with a little slur in his voice.

"I'm with you, brother. My old heart is not into this bar scene." Tanner stood up, looking at Ray the bartender. "See you around, Ray. Don't try and spend those bills the jarhead left in your tip jar. They're military script he stole from a hooker."

Ray laughed and just threw his hands in the air.

CHAPTER 31

At seven-thirty a.m., Blake was having breakfast alone in the hotel dining room. The scrambled eggs, bacon, hash brown potatoes, and biscuits would give him a good start for the day. The waiter filled his coffee cup with hot black breakfast blend and topped off his water glass. He thought about his ranch house back in Castle Rock. Thcrc was nothing like a Colorado morning to make a person feel good. His mind filled with thoughts of Mary, and him having their morning coffee in the spacious, sunny kitchen, or on the covered front porch. He did love that woman; she was as sweet as they came. Damn fine-looking, too, and what a great lover she was. *Damn*, Tanner, he thought. *Call her and tell her so, you big dummy. Don't just sit here and talk to yourself.* He did call her, and now his day was complete after a lengthy conversation. A little telephone sex was always good for the soul.

The front desk manager walked quickly up to Blake's table. "Sorry to interrupt your breakfast, sir, but I have a package for you." She handed Blake a long brown envelope.

"Thanks." He opened the envelope and unfolded the stationery inside. The words were cut-out colored letters of the alphabet. The message read, "*Back off and go back to Colorado. We know where your family lives.*"

"Bastards," Blake said aloud. "Now they are threatening my family." His thoughts were deep about the safety of his daughters and their husbands in Denver. He would find out who these sick people were, where they lived, and beat the crap out of them. He even thought about just blowing them away. You don't mess with the Tanner family.

He stopped by the front desk and asked the manager who had delivered the envelope, and if she could describe the person.

"Yes, sir. It was a teenage Spanish-looking boy. He might have been Mexican. That is all I can tell you. He just handed me the envelope, and then he ran out the front door."

Since Blake and the FBI had been unable to forcibly detain the Mexican mafia men, the evidence only led to James Connors and Ramos Portales. Tanner decided to tell Norman, and he might tell him that he was going after the murderer or murderers who he believed killed Jeff. He had to find the people who had just threatened the lives of his Colorado family. When he found them, then he would possibly have the people responsible for killing Jeff. No more face-to-face meetings, no more waiting for the red tape of the federal system. Bounty hunting is legal in America, and that is just what Blake Tanner intended to do. He was licensed in Colorado, and the state of Georgia recognized his license.

Norman and the FBI could not stop Blake from his manhunt. "Just don't obstruct our investigation," Norman said. "I wish you would not go it alone, but maybe it is the best method. You stay in touch with me. I will always be a phone call away. Good luck, you old warhorse." The two friends shook hands, and Blake walked out of Norman's office.

Tanner called Higgins in New York and provided him with an update on the progress of his investigation.

Blake rented a car at the Atlanta airport, drove back to his hotel, and loaded his gear into the trunk of the white Buick sedan. He filled the knapsack with the items he had purchased at an Army surplus store, and walked out into the Georgia rain.

On January 25, Blake Tanner began his new role as bounty hunter. He made a call from his satellite phone to Erhan in Istanbul. He informed his friend of the progress and the disappointments that had taken place with the investigation. "You should be able to carry on a normal life, my dear friend. The next time you hear my voice will, hopefully, be from my ranch in Colorado."

Bounty hunters were illegal in Mexico, Blake believed. *If the bastards can enter our country and kill Americans, then go back to Mexico and brag about the weak Americans, then I can go into their country and eliminate them from society.* He knew that the two mafia kingpins released from custody by a federal judge knew more about Jeff's death than what they admitted. Going into Mexico would be extremely dangerous, and he would only go if his plans failed in Atlanta.

Tanner paid a visit to Connors, who was being detained at the maximum-security area at the Atlanta county jail. Connors did not want to see Blake, but Norman Gregory had instructed the authorities that James Connors was to speak with Blake whenever he requested. Connors did have the right to have an attorney present during any visitation.

"You don't need your attorney," Blake told Connors. "I can probably be more help to you than your attorney. Tell me about your association with your so-called friend Jeffery Sanders, and I may let you live."

Connors' eyes bugged out, and he commenced to sweat. "What do you mean? Let me live?"

"Just what I said. Tell me what you know about the blackmailing and death of my friend Jeff Sanders, and I may let you live. If you don't talk, then you will not be alive to eat breakfast tomorrow morning. You hear me?"

"No tape recorders or taking notes. Do I have your word on that?"

"Yes, you have my word," answered Tanner. "What can you tell me about Jeff's death?"

Connors hesitated, and then he coughed, leaned forward over the table, and took a drink of water from the bottle sitting in front of him. "Jeff got on to our drug trafficking network. He threatened to go to the authorities if we did not turn ourselves in to the FBI."

Blake glared at Connors, then snarled, "We? Who is we?"

Connors answered sharply, "Frank and Rhonda Pane."

"Okay, go on," Blake ordered.

Through his fear and panic, Connors explained. "Frank told Jeff that he would have his wife and family killed if he pursued the issue. Jeff backed down, as he did not want any harm to come to his family. Frank then told Jeff that he was to keep quiet and close his eyes to what we were doing. Frank also told Jeff that we wanted fifty thousand dollars from him. We would fix a drug deal on him that would put him in prison, or the drug dealers would have a price on his head. That is all I know about Jeffery, except I did like him, and I know nothing about his death. I thought it was a suicide."

"If you have lied to me, so help me, I will kill you myself," Blake yelled, pointing his finger at the suspect.

After a minute or so of silence, Connors looked up at Blake. "You should talk with Ramos Portales, if you can find him. He is a slime bag, junkie, and a cheap thief, but I do not think he is capable of murder. He will do most anything for a price. I heard through the mafia rumor mill that he has a big desire to live in Spain. They say he likes the beaches, and he especially likes the Spanish women."

"Are you lying to me, Connors?"

"No," Connors replied. "I am telling you what I know to save my ass. I do not care what happens to anyone else, and you have to believe me. Please believe me."

"Remember what I told you, Connors. If I catch you in a lie, you are a dead man, understand?"

At a stoplight on a busy intersection in the outskirts of Atlanta, Blake suddenly felt lonely. He could almost see Mary sitting beside him in the passenger seat. He thought that he got a whiff of her perfume; he even thought he could place his hand on her leg. *Damn, Tanner, it is time for you to hang up your traveling boots and go home.* He had more thoughts about Mary, and how it would be to wake up every morning with her lying beside him. Yep, after this case was closed, he would be finished with trying to catch the bad guys and girls.

Calculating his contract wages in his head, he figured he had over one hundred thousand dollars coming to him from New York Mutual. He thought about him and Mary taking a long cruise to the Caribbean and any location west of California. His travels had been mostly in Europe, Africa, and the Middle East. With the exception of his tours in Vietnam, he had not spent much time anywhere else.

The front desk manager handed Blake an email that had arrived addressed to him through the hotel's Internet. It was from Mary, telling him she loved him and for him to be careful. *What a nice end to a long day*, he thought as he thanked the desk manager and headed toward the elevators.

It was the second day of staking out the Flamingo Apartments. Blake had picked out the perfect location very carefully. He would not be noticed parked across from the tree-lined area near the apartment buildings. It would be his last day to wait for Ramos Portales to appear, as the FBI had informed him that Portales would be returning to Mexico tomorrow. He noticed a male figure emerge from the front door of the building. It was Portales. The Mexican wore his trademark black leather jacket and pointed toed cowboy boots with the steel caps on the toes. Tanner's plan was to follow the suspect and find out just what his activities were during the day. A yellow taxicab drove up and stopped in front of the apartment building. Portales jumped in the backseat, and the taxi sped away.

Impatient, Blake was tired of waiting and doing stakeout duties. He followed the taxi at a safe distance. The morning traffic was a bitch, as was normal in any large city this time of the day. He was caught at a stoplight and the taxi moved forward in the traffic. *What the hell*, Blake thought; he hit the gas pedal and ran the red light, just as all the other commuters do on a daily basis. He had the taxi in sight, or he hoped it was the same one.

He is going to the El Chino restaurant, he thought. He probably will have breakfast burritos with his amigos. The two Mexican men Portales had been seen with before had been deported. *Interesting*, he thought. Since Portales knew who he was, Tanner could not do a thing but wait, or he could attempt a disguise. No, Portales would recognize him, and then the game would be finished for him.

It was past ten o'clock when Portales walked out the front door of the El Chino. Following him was a Mexican man dressed in a dark business suit and sunglasses. He had long hair slicked back, and then he put on a dark raincoat. The two men walked to the parking lot and climbed into a black Lincoln Town Car. Tanner was on their tail as they sped away, driving west. Blake was close enough to read the license plate number on the Town Car. Using his satellite phone, he called Norman's office and asked him if he would put a make on the license plate number.

"The car is registered to a Jose Gonzales at 2104 West Central Street, Atlanta. No phone number and no outstanding warrants."

"Thanks, bud. I'll brief you later today."

Blake knew he was on a roller-coaster ride of danger and excitement. Staying at a safe distance, he saw the car turn into a driveway and stop toward the rear of the house, in front of a double-door garage. Blake stopped across the street and saw the two men getting out of the car just as the trunk popped open. The driver, who must be Gonzales, lifted a large blue duffle bag from the trunk, and then they walked to the back door and into the house.

Probably drugs, Blake thought. He ran a plan through his mind that he felt would work, providing more drug dealers did not occupy the house. This was a job for the police and FBI, but Tanner knew that time was running out on Portales. He would flee to Mexico and very soon.

Tanner adjusted his shoulder holster and unsnapped the hammer tie down to his .357. He placed the sawed-off shotgun under his trench coat, dropped three pairs of plastic handcuffs and a can of pepper spray in his jacket pocket, and walked around to the backside of the house. He knew what he must do, and he must do it very quietly and quickly. Gently he turned the doorknob to the back door. Shit, it was unlocked. Just as he had done so many times on raids in the remote jungles of Vietnam, he was like a ghost when he entered through the door and found himself in the kitchen. There were male voices coming from the front of the house, and it sounded like there were three of them. They were speaking Spanish. Tanner understood what they were saying, and as he suspected, they were dealing in drugs. Blake was fully aware that drug dealers would do anything to protect their drugs and money. No heart for a drug dealer. They would kill their mothers to save their stash.

With the shotgun in his left hand and his .357 in his right hand, he stepped into the room and confronted three men. He caught them by complete surprise. In perfect Spanish Blake yelled, "Hands where I can see them. Make one sudden move and I will scatter your brains all over your yellow wall. Get on the damn floor. On your bellies, hands behind you, and now move." Blake handcuffed the three men, and he was not gentle. He said to Portales, "I am going to send you back to your homeland. You won't be happy as I am going to cut your balls off and glue them to your ear. In addition, you two other bastards, you will burn right where you lie. You have one chance, and one chance only, to answer my questions. Any doubt as to what I have said?"

The men were in no position to disagree with the bounty hunter; they could hear the deadly hatred in his voice. They just shook their heads and said, "Yes, we understand."

"Tell me what you know about the death of Jeffery Sanders."

Sweat poured off the three men. Their shirts were soaked with body fluids. There was not a word from any of them; no one wanted to be the first to squeal. "This is not going to work, boys," Tanner said, still speaking in Spanish. He walked over to where the third man was lying. He placed the shotgun to the man's ear. "You are first to get your brains blown out. I don't need you anyway. So long, asshole."

The man begged for his life. "I do not know the name Jeffery Sanders or whatever name you said. I am a dealer, not a killer. Please, I have a family, and I have many children."

"Well, Señor Gonzales, you will be the one that I will cut up in little pieces. Oh, I failed to show you boys my knife." He pulled out a ten-inch survival knife that he kept in his belt above his right back pants pocket. "How's this for a knife?"

Ramos Portales turned his head to the side so he could see Blake. "These are my brothers-in-law. They know nothing about Mr. Sanders," he moaned. "I only knew him from a few meetings I had with him. I was the go-between man for Mr. and Mrs. Pane, and Mr. Sanders. I picked money up from Sanders and delivered it to the Pane couple. They hired me to place a note in your friend's golf shoe while he was at the country club. That is all I know about him. Have you contacted his girlfriend?"

That last statement caught Blake's attention like a flashing red light. "What girlfriend? What in the hell are you talking about?"

Attempting to swallow dry saliva and twisting in his position on the floor, he finally replied, "He had a Spanish girlfriend whom he would meet at the Airport Hilton. I saw them together on many occasions. Mr. Sanders would arrive at the hotel before she did. He always kept the same schedule when they met."

"Describe her to me." Tanner demanded.

Ramos was squirming and his mouth was dry. "She was beautiful, so very beautiful. Very tall, long hair, and she wore expensive clothing and jewelry. I know that she would fly into Atlanta, but from where, I do not know."

"Are you sure she was Spanish, or was she Mexican?"

"Spanish. She was definitely Spanish."

Tanner left the three men where they lay; he told them that he would burn the house down if they moved before the police arrived.

Damn, maybe the woman was the Spanish doctor from Barcelona, Blake thought. Why in the hell hadn't the police found out about her? The clues were all located in the Hilton's register records. He thought back. *Jeff died on September 21, 2004. The hotel will have records going back to that time.*

The manager of the Airport Hilton was cooperative. Blake found the entries for September 21, 2004. He could not believe that the police had not investigated deeper into Jeff's death. Jeff had registered at three-thirty in the afternoon of September 21st. He had noted on the registration that two adults would occupy the room.

"Do you have additional records that can be archived for this registration?" Blake asked the manager.

"Yes, we do. May I ask what specifically you are looking for? It will be easy to find if I know the subject."

"Do you require identification of a second guest if they arrive after the initial check-in?"

"We do. We ask for a valid state driver's license on all American citizens and a valid passport on guests from out of the country." The manager found the entry and printed it out for Blake.

"Well, I'll be go to hell," he said out loud. He was looking at an official copy of the passport of Dr. Casilda Baccara, Barcelona, Spain.

Blake asked the manager, "Would you have the time she checked out?"

"We have the time, as we had her passport. She never came back to pick it up until she departed. If you look on the lower corner of the copy of the passport, you will see the date and time we gave her passport back to her."

The stamp read, *September 21, 2004, 9:00 P.M.*

"May I have this document?"

The manager quickly answered, "Of course, sir. An entry on the records indicates Mister Sanders had another female visitor on September 21st." He then printed out the document and handed it to Blake. "These documents were not available on September 21st. Our system was down for maintenance, and the documents were saved in our backup system. The police never came back to get copies of the registration records."

When Blake read the entry, cold chills went up the back of his neck. "Son of a bitch. Julie Spenser," he said aloud. "Excuse me, I didn't mean to speak so you could hear me." There were no records indicating when she departed the hotel premises. He put the document in his jacket pocket along with the other documents. What in the hell were the police doing during their investigation? He thought that they must have had a good reason for missing clues that were so important.

Driving back to his hotel, Blake concluded that he needed help from the FBI. He had evidence, but he still did not have the answers he wanted. A phone call to Norman Gregory found him still in his office. They agreed to meet early the next morning and Blake would update Norman on his exciting last two days.

The evening call delighted Higgins. He told Tanner, "I know you are tired and worn out. This case has certainly brought you more grief than what you bargained for. Thanks, Mr. Tanner, you have done an outstanding job. Makes me wish I could get out of the office and go with you. Sounds exciting."

"Exciting!" exclaimed Blake, with a smile. "Yes. Having fun, no. I will go back to Colorado when this is finished. I may steal your right-hand assistant when I go."

"She would be thoroughly missed, but she deserves the best. Mary will make a fine wife for that special man." Donald let out a little laugh. "Maybe you will be the lucky one. Talk to you later."

"Funny you would say that. Yes, I will talk to you later." Blake hung up the phone and headed for the bathroom and a long hot shower.

CHAPTER 32

Federal Building, Atlanta

Blake dropped a bombshell on Norman. "Damn, Blake, you have been collecting some hard-shelled evidence. Our police investigators should have uncovered the information that you discovered."

"Yeah, they sure blew it. That's for damn sure. Who the hell was the officer in charge of the investigation?"

"We have the records. We will archive the data, and I will personally take it to the police commissioner."

Norman printed out the report that Blake had provided him. "This will take assistance from our Interpol friends. You want to read over your report and make sure it is correct? And then after you sign and date it, I will file the report officially."

Tanner knew that there was missing evidence, mainly due to the blunders of the police investigators. He and Norman could not find a statement from one of the guests who was staying at the hotel the evening of Jeff's death. The distinct sound of a .38 special firing should have alerted most of the guests.

"It's a losing battle," Norman said with disgust. "You remember the drill. No one wants to get involved, especially when it's murder."

Blake read his printed report in detail.

OFFICIAL FBI DOCUMENT

Jeffery Sanders died at 10:48 PM, on September 21, 2004. A police report filed the same date at 11:46 PM indicated the victim committed suicide by a self-inflicted gunshot from a .38 caliber bullet to his left temple. NOTE: Jeffery Sanders was right-handed. Two female guests were at his hotel room on the evening of his death. The first was Dr. Casilda Baccara of Barcelona, Spain. She departed from the hotel at 9:00 PM, same date. The second female guest was Julie Spenser of London, UK. There are no records showing when she departed from the hotel premises. Airline passenger records show she boarded a British Airways plane departing for London Heathrow at 11:55 PM, same date. Julie Spenser is a prime suspect in the death of Jeffery Sanders. Dr. Casilda Baccara is wanted for questioning about why she flew from Barcelona, Spain, to Atlanta, then returned to Spain the same day. In concurrence with the Atlanta FBI, Special Agent in Charge, we request immediate apprehension of both suspects by Interpol agents. Extradition warrants will be issued for their return to Atlanta, Georgia, USA.

//Signed// Blake Tanner,
Special Investigator

"Now what do we do?" asked Blake.

"This case has been a circle jerk from the beginning. All law enforcement agencies have screwed up, including my office. I am requesting that Jeff's body be exhumed, and a second autopsy be conducted by a federal laboratory. Do you agree?"

"Damn straight I agree, and good move, Norman. Should we let the British and Spanish authorities take care of the women? I could jump on a plane and go get them. Julie Spenser has been released by the UK authorities. They found no evidence of her committing a crime in Great Britain."

Norman thought for a few seconds. "By law we should not get involved, but my instinct tells me you should head to Europe as soon as possible. If you act quickly enough, and before the foreign press finds out and prints a headline story, you could, let us say, apprehend them and bring them back here. We could question them before they could find attorneys. It's up to you, partner."

"Let me run this by my banker, Higgins. If he approves then I will charter a private jet and pick them both up and be back to Atlanta on the fourth day."

Donald told Blake to go for it. "Get this nightmare over with, and let us all get back to our normal life."

Blake was able to give Mary a quick call and let her know that he was okay, and he was about ready to complete the investigation. He told her that there were no new details for her this evening, and he would see her in a few days. He did not want to disclose his plans for fear of Mary worrying about him.

Charting a business jet was an easy task, expensive, but relatively simple. Blake specified to the manager of the charter service that he wanted pilots who had military experience. The manager explained to Blake that all of their pilots must be experienced military pilots before they were hired.

CHAPTER 33

February 3, 2005, High over the Atlantic Ocean

The luxury Gulfstream G550 streaked across the dark Atlantic Ocean at thirty-eight thousand feet. Blake was reviewing his reports while sitting in one of the twelve white leather seats. The first stop for the charter jet would be Lufton, England, just outside of London. The plans were for Blake to kidnap Julie Spenser from her father's apartment, which they shared. She would be easy to handle, and she would be scared shitless.

Blake had given in-depth instructions to the pilots of the Gulfstream about his return to the aircraft. "When you see me drive up, get clearance, and get the hell out of British airspace." The captain of the charter had flown AC-130 gunships in the first Gulf War, and he had been a contract pilot for the CIA for a few years. His copilot was a former Navy P-3 pilot, and he fully understood what their mission was. No questions asked. They were flying for the money and, of course, the excitement.

It was just after midnight when Blake entered the bedroom of Julie Spenser. She looked so peaceful lying in her bed asleep. She looked damn good, too, Blake thought. He placed the handkerchief, which was soaked with a few drops of chloroform, over her mouth and nose. Her body was light as he wrapped her bed blanket around her and carried her right out the front entrance to the apartment. The black sedan was waiting for them near the front door of the apartment. Thanks to Blake's good friend Erhan and a trusted Turkish friend who was driving his own private car, they sped toward the airport north of London with Julie fast asleep. Blake thought, *I hope the hell she did not kill Jeff. She just does not seem like the type. When she wakes up, she will be ready to talk.*

Captain Walker lined up the Gulfstream, and the sleek jet was in the air and climbing rapidly within minutes after Blake arrived with Julie. During the flight to Barcelona Julie woke up. She looked around and was frightened, and she showed a fear that you could only see in a person who does not know what is going to happen to them next.

"Mr. Tanner," she said. "What are you doing with me? Where are we going?" She felt the handcuffs on her left wrist, and when she tried to move her hand and arm, she discovered the handcuffs were securely locked to her seat. Then she put her head in her lap and began to cry.

Blake sat in the seat next to her. "I am taking you back to the United States to stand trial for the murder of Jeffery Sanders."

She reacted in a manner that Blake was not expecting. "I did not kill Jeffery. I could not kill anyone or anything. You see, we were lovers, and I have lied to you all along about Frank Pane portraying him. I did that to protect Jeffery. I loved him so much. I found out he had died after I returned to London on September 22nd. I had just left him. We had made plans to run away to the Cayman Islands. Then your authorities caught me with drugs that were in my suitcase. Drug dealers in London planted the drugs there. I was coming to pay tribute to Jeffery. I wanted to visit his grave. I loved him."

"You know, Julie, I might even believe you if you can answer a few more questions. Do you know a Dr. Casilda Baccara of Barcelona?"

"Yes, I know her. She was Jeffery's doctor. She had traveled to Atlanta bringing medicine for Jeffery. The plan was for me to meet her there, but my plane departing from London had been delayed due to technical problems. After I arrived at the hotel, Casilda had departed for the airport to catch her plane back to Barcelona. I only had a short time to be alone with Jeffery before I had to catch my plane back to London. He was feeling very good, and he had the medication with him that Casilda had brought him. We made love, and he gave me documents for a bank account in Georgetown, Grand Caymans, and plane tickets for my trip to meet him there the end of September. I gave him a British Midlands certified check for one hundred thousand British pounds made out in his name. The money was mine willed to me from my grandmother who died last year. She left me over one million pounds in cash. When I left Jeffery, he was still alive. You must believe me. I loved him. Can you not tell?"

"Yes, I can tell, and you must be telling me the truth. All the facts I have add up. If I am wrong, all that I can do is to humbly apologize to you, as I loved Jeffery also. He was my best friend."

Julie put her free arm on Blake's shoulder, "Please trust me. If you are taking me to Barcelona, then Casilda can tell you what we both were doing in Atlanta the night Jeffery died. Have you talked with the bitch? You know, Jeffery's wife, Gloria? She was ruining his life. He just wanted to get away from her."

The jet landed in Barcelona just at daybreak on the third day since Blake had departed from Atlanta.

Casilda was most cooperative, just like she had always been. Blake listened to her side of the story, and it coincided with that of Julie's.

"It looks to me like I have done you both a grave injustice. I do apologize, and in the name of Jeffery, I hope you both will forgive me."

With sincerity in their voices, the two women who loved Jeffery, but in different ways, told Blake that he was forgiven and for him not to worry. They both firmly understood the loyalty and love he had for his friend.

"I have always wanted to visit Spain. Now that I am here I hope Casilda permits me to stay for a while. I have no clothing, money, or passport, but maybe we can work around that."

"My father knows many people in the Spanish government, and he even has some good English friends. Besides, Mr. Tanner will take care of you, won't you, Mr. Tanner?" Casilda said with a laugh.

Blake called Norman and Donald and told them what he had discovered. "I am in the air now and expect to land in Atlanta at four-thirty this afternoon. Can you meet me, Norman?"

Leaning back in the plush seat of the fast-moving jet, Blake thought that he had it all figured out. The murderer had been in front of his eyes the entire time.

CHAPTER 34

February 6, 2005, Atlanta, Georgia

The body of Jeffery Sanders was exhumed on February 2, 2005 as ordered by the Office of Medical Investigations, Atlanta, Georgia, Federal Judge Amos Johnson. He directed a second autopsy be performed on the body, and that a final toxicology report be issued to the Federal Bureau of Investigations Area Office, Atlanta.

The official report read in brief, *Death caused by a toxic chemical that was injected into the body by a puncture behind the left ear. The time of death was 10:48 P.M., September 21, 2004. Damage to the nervous system and brain contributed to the death of the deceased. Prior autopsy and toxicology reports failed to detect the chemicals caused by contracting Agent Orange. Cancer was detected in the liver and brain area of the victim. The bullet that entered the left temple of the deceased was not the cause of death. The deceased was dead approximately sixteen minutes before the bullet struck the victim's brain.*

Gloria Sanders opened the large front door to her expensive home in the Atlanta suburbs. Her eyes lit up when she saw Blake standing there. "Well, what a pleasant surprise. Come in, Blake." Then she noticed the police cars and the four uniformed police officers, two men in business suits, and a woman dressed casually standing to the left of Blake. "What is it? What is wrong?" Gloria said with fear in her voice.

"Gloria, we are here to arrest you for the murder of your husband, Jeffery Sanders."

The police sergeant stepped up and quickly handcuffed Gloria; he then read her her rights.

Blake told Gloria, "You made a huge mistake when you deposited the one hundred thousand pound British cashier's check that Julie Spenser gave to Jeff."

Placing both of her hands to her head, she began to sob. "Oh no, I didn't mean to hurt him. I just wanted to give him enough insulin to make him go to sleep." She went on, telling how she put the gun to Jeff's head and with her hand on his, pulled the trigger that blew his brains out. She pleaded guilty to the murder of her husband before the police could even get her into the police car.

Her voice drawn with emotion, she cried, "He was cheating on me, Blake. You must believe me."

Blake stared at her with a gaze filled with daggers. "No, I don't believe you. You were poisoning him all along with a toxin in his food and the scotch he loved to drink. The cancer caused from Agent Orange was already killing Jeff. The weed killer used in Vietnam was kicking his ass, and you just took his life before he was ready to go. You also were lovers with James Connors and Frank Pane. Is that the truth? You lost it all, your husband, your family and friends, and the five-million-dollar insurance policy."

Gloria hung her head in shame. Icy blue eyes stared down at her feet, unblinking. There was an awful silence, broken only by her heavy breathing. She was crying again. "Please, please let me be free. I was no longer in love with Jeffery. Not the normal way, at least. I did not mean to take his life, please. I just wanted the money. All I wanted was the money."

"You took the life of my good friend. You were a beautiful woman hiding a murderous secret. The **Forgotten Honor** that Jeff and I thought we had lost has been fully restored. May God forgive you."

EPILOGUE

One Year Later

The soft sound of the wind blowing through the evergreen and aspen trees at the foot of the Colorado Rockies was sweet music to Blake Tanner. He had been on the move since he was eighteen years old, and now he was at peace with the world and himself. There was nowhere in the world he would rather be than sitting in the large pine rocker beside his beautiful wife, Mary. Life had been good to Blake and Mary since their marriage ten months ago. Mary's daughter Holly loved Blake, and she was happy for her mother. Blake's daughters, along with their husbands, adored Mary. They were happy their dad had found a woman who was good to him and loved him as their mother did.

Blake promised Mary that he would never leave the ranch without her; she would always be by his side. Life was good on their comfortable mini-ranch nestled just east of the Colorado Rockies.

"Will you look at that crazy cowboy? He is riding the palomino like he has springs in his ass," said Blake, laughing so hard it hurt his side. The two little Lab puppies, Samson and Delilah, were barking and running around the horse, nipping at its high-trotting feet.

"What do you expect from a Turk?" Mary answered while laughing along with Blake.

"Whoa, you damn horse," said Erhan as he finally got the horse to stop in front of the porch where Blake and Mary were sitting. "Who do you have to know to get a beer around here?" he said in his best American accent as he dismounted.

"My good friend, you are not a very good cowboy, but you are one hell of a Turkish soldier," Blake told his longtime friend. "Sit your ass down, and let's talk about blond-headed and blue-eyed women." He looked over at his wife, Mary, and she just smiled at him, knowing he was joking with Erhan.

A voice from the kitchen loudly said, "I heard you, Erhan. You Turkish lovers are all the same, big talk and no action."

"Is that why you married me, my dear wife?" Erhan said as he stood up to greet his blond wife as she walked out on the porch carrying a tray full of longneck bottles of Coors.

Erhan and Sonia had met at an international antiques show in New York last summer. It was love at first sight, and they got married in Las Vegas with Blake and Mary standing up with them. They had homes in Istanbul, the Turkish coast, the French Riviera, and New York. Of course, any chance they had, they visited their good friends in Colorado. In turn, Blake and Mary could visit them at any of their homes, and at any time.

Blake stood and held his longneck bottle of Coors high above his head. "I salute my lovely wife, my great friends, all of our families, and my good friend Jeff Sanders, and may we all live in peace. I love you, brother."

AUTHOR'S BIOGRAPHY

GERALD "JERRY" SNODGRASS was born in Butler, Missouri, in 1938. He was raised and went to school in Indianola, Iowa. He entered the military after graduating from high school in 1957, and successfully fulfilled his dreams of serving in the military and traveling to exotic locations. He married Elizabeth Fleming in the 1960s, and they produced a daughter and a son in the 1960s. The family traveled extensively during his career in the military and federal government, living in Spain, England three times, Naples, Italy, Athens, Greece, and Wiesbaden, Germany before Jerry retired, and they settled down in Killeen, Texas, in 2002. Jerry is an adventurous retired Vietnam veteran and is a life member of the Veterans of Foreign Wars and American Legion. His passion for thrilling adventure and the Old West inspired him to write his first novel, ***Frontier Justice.*** He provides the same thrilling adventure with ***Forgotten Honor***, an international fiction/suspense and romance novel that takes place in many of the same locations that Jerry worked and lived in.

LaVergne, TN USA
17 September 2010
197503LV00001B/93/P